THE SWEETEST RISK

"Whatever our souls are made of, his and mine are the same."

— EMILY BRONTË

First paperback edition March 2025

Cover design by Alt 19 Creative

www.authorlesliemcelroy.com

Paperback: 979-8-9926505-0-1
ebook: 979-8-9926505-1-8

*This one is for all my readers who have been told to douse the fire
inside of them.
Ignite it.
Take that chance.
Do what makes you happy.
Prove all of them wrong.*

AUTHOR NOTE & CONTENT WARNING

Dear amazing reader, I appreciate that you wanted to take a chance on Tristan and Brooke's love story. For the majority of the book, I have written it to be lighthearted and full of comedic and chemistry-fueled banter. However, the story also contains adult language and explicit sexual scenes. If you prefer to keep their love story closed-door, please mind the spicy chapters listed below. XO, Leslie

Spicy Chapters:
    Chapter 3
    Chapter 12
    Chapter 18
    Chapter 19
    Chapter 20
    Chapter 21
    Chapter 22
    Chapter 26
    Chapter 27
    Chapter 29

THE SWEETEST RISK

A NOVEL

LESLIE MCELROY

1

—————

Brooke

I hate everything about Tristan Lawson.

Ever since I met him ten years ago, I have hated him. The sucky thing about all of this is, I can't ever escape him. It's a cruel joke from the universe that he is my brother's best friend.

He's also on the same hockey team as my big brother. And it's because of Tristan Lawson that I have my one rule: never date a hockey player.

He is pompous, arrogant and the biggest playboy I've ever known. I have no idea why my brother, Bradley, ever became friends with him. I mean, maybe it made sense when they were stupid college kids, but now we are almost thirty and Tristan is still up to his antics. At least Bradley found himself a good woman who brings out the best in him.

Bradley and Tristan are the most talented players for the Dallas Storm hockey team and they are basically the ying to each other's yang. There is no disputing that. Unfortunately, I see more of Tristan than I really want to. He has become so close to my family over the years that he is basically my parents' second son.

I need to stay civil tonight, though. I am here to celebrate Bradley and Jennifer's engagement. Not get into a duel with hockey's hottest player (according to GQ magazine). Not that I've willingly paid attention to any of that. But when my parents insist on celebrating that accomplishment and my coworker and work bestie, Tess, is obsessed with all hockey players, there is no way to avoid it. Oh and he's also the damn poster child for the Dallas Storm, so any billboard you see around the metroplex has his face plastered on it.

Jen has a signature drink for tonight that is honestly pretty decent. It's some sort of strawberry gin and tonic and I am on my second glass for the evening. I am trying to prepare myself for the entrance of my sworn enemy. It also doesn't help that I had to come alone to this event, since I just broke up with my boyfriend of two years, Nick.

"Hey Brooke! You're here!" My brother bear hugs me from the back and I spill my drink all over my light pink dress. Perfect.

"Bradley! You just made your sister spill all over her dress! Warn a girl before you hug her like that! I'm so sorry, Brooke!" Jen grabs a bunch of mini black napkins from the dispenser on the bar. She starts to pat down my dress and I become increasingly aware of the fact that the drink spilled all down my cleavage.

"It's okay, Jen, really. I'm just gonna run to the restroom and try to fix this. I'll be right back."

Thankfully, when I reach the restroom, no one is in there. I grab some paper towels and run them under the sink. It's just my luck. Just give Tristan more ammunition to make fun of me. I use the hand dryer to try and salvage my dress in any way that I can. When I look back in the mirror, I give myself a pep-talk: "Remember that tonight is about Brad and Jen. Don't let Tristan get the best of you. You look hot, sans the whole cocktail spill on your dress and all." I breathe out. "You can do this! You are a grown woman. No need for childish games."

I comb through my caramel highlighted hair and rub a little under my eyes. My hazel eyes are popping tonight, probably because I wore more eyeliner than usual. Maybe when I walk out that door, I'll meet my Prince Charming. Positive vibes. Positive energy.

I swing open the door and who do I see at the damn bar? The worst person in the world. Already surrounded by busty blondes who miraculously wear a size 0. And here I am in my size 8 dress, with thicker thighs and B-cup sized boobs. I exhale again and walk toward where I was previously sitting. I gesture to the bartender for another drink. My fingers tap the bar and that's when I hear a laugh that sends chills all up and down my spine.

"Hey my man, can I get a couple of Jen's special drinks and one of whatever the hell is Bradley's drink?"

Maybe he won't notice me. I'm not wearing my trusty knotted pink headband after all.

"Well, well...if it isn't my favorite person in the world?"

Damn.

I finish my drink quickly, so much so that it fizzles down my throat and I choke a little bit. The three drinks make their way onto the bar. Tristan flashes a smile toward the bartender and places a very generous tip in the jar. "Thanks." He hands the drinks back behind him to two women graciously awaiting his attention. He swivels around and grabs his own drink. I swear the universe hates me because of course Tristan is looking like a thirst trap. He is wearing a white button-down with his sleeves rolled up, showcasing his sleeve of tattoos underneath. His gray dress pants are hugging his muscular legs and ass and his wavy hair is slicked back into a perfect bouffant. Some of his dark brown hair is peeking out from behind his ears and he has not yet entered the playoff beard phase. I cannot stand that phase. Everyone's beard gets a little too long and they look more like cavemen than hockey players. Another reason I can't stand hockey, or sports for that matter—all the silly superstitions.

I blink my eyes fast and look away before Tristan notices I am practically ogling him. His Rolex watch glistens against the sunset light as he raises his drink to his smirking lips.

"How are you, Cupcake?"

Ugh, I loathe that nickname. I made one bad batch of cupcakes ten years ago and I will never live it down. I know that he is teasing me every time he says it and he says it ALL. THE. TIME.

So, I decided to come up with an equally annoying nickname long ago. Because he thinks he is the hottest thing to walk this earth, which trust me—he isn't. *Remember to be civil, Brooke.*

"Oh just dandy, Hot Shot. And yourself?"

"Dandy as well." He looks around. "Where's that desperate puppy dog you call a boyfriend? What is his name again, Nate?"

"Nick," I retort. He is going to find out eventually and I'd rather be the one who lets the cat out of the bag: "He's not here."

"Working late?"

I rub my finger around the glass. "I wouldn't know. We broke up."

"Let me guess, he broke up with you because he finally realized what a pain in the ass you are?" He leans against the bar and cocks his head to the side, waiting for my response.

Dick. "Actually, asshole, I broke up with him. Just didn't work out. Not that it's any of your business."

"Huh." Tristan surveys my body. "So what, you are now out on the prowl for your next victim? That dress probably isn't going to help your chances, Cupcake. Especially since it looks like you spilled your drink all over yourself. You have always been a bit messy, haven't you?"

"I could say the same thing about you." I turn to the ladies that are anxiously awaiting Tristan's attention: "Be careful, ladies." I grab my new drink that the bartender graciously poured me without me even asking. He must have sensed the sinister vibe that is always between Tristan Lawson and myself. "He just got a call from his doctor—" I glance down at his groin. "--it's not good news. I think they make creams for that. See you around, Hot Shot."

2

Tristan

I watch as Brooke walks away. Of course she came to the party wearing a pink dress. A dress that hugs every damn curve on her body. I gulp down the rest of my drink and actively direct my gaze on the two women who are gabbing about something, trying to push up against me and run their hands up and down my arms. At this point, I am used to this attention and for a long time in my career, it has been one of the best perks of this job. Having beautiful women fawn over me and scream when I walk by them is not a surprise anymore.

From Day One, Brooke has always hated me for reasons I will never understand. It's always been just as well, since she is off limits—she is Bradley's younger sister and he made that pretty clear the night I met Brooke. It has been my favorite pastime to go to battle with her every time I see her. I love making her face get flushed when I get a rise out of her and the small line that is developing between her eyebrows from the years of being furious with me. I had to get used to her disdain of me since I knew Bradley wasn't going anywhere and I consider him to be a brother.

For some reason, I never saw Brooke as a sister. Just like the off limits rule, I actively placed Brooke in this sort of limbo category–seeing her as a sister seemed wrong, but seeing her as an option to be with, is also a line I can't cross. I will never cross. All I know for certain is that woman drives me insane.

"Is what she said true, Tristan?" One of the girls finally gets my attention.

"No, that's just Bradley's little sister being a pest like always."

Glasses start clinking and we all turn toward Bradley and Jen. It's crazy to think that a couple years ago, these two met at this very spot. I've never seen instant love like what I saw that night. Don't get me wrong, it gets nauseating at times. I don't think I've ever witnessed them fight with each other. Maybe Brooke and I fight enough for all of us.

I'm not going to lie: ever since Bradley has been with Jen, I can't stop thinking about how much I want what they have. I want someone I go home to. I want someone consistently in the stands. I want to look up at the box where all the wives and girlfriends watch the games and cheer us on and just know that I have someone solid. I'm over all the one-night-stands or girlfriends that last for maybe a couple of months because they can't handle my grueling schedule of being a professional athlete. Or unfortunately, some of these women only want to be with me so they can tag me on their Instagram stories or posts. Even the girls standing next to me now are trying to take a picture of me behind them and I am just anticipating all the likes and comments. It's fun to flirt but I am also looking for someone who challenges me. Someone who can give back what I dish out.

"We just want to thank everyone for coming to our engagement party. Every single person in this room has been nothing but supportive of our relationship from the start and we couldn't be more excited to take this next step in our lives. So, enjoy your Jen & Tonics and Brad-fashioneds." There is a laugh from everyone in the crowd. Funnily enough, I know that those names were Bradley's idea. "Cheers!" I raise my glass up and down the entire contents of the glass.

I scan the rooftop. I spot a bright pink dress and my body is craving the duel that was about to ensue for her telling these girls that I have some sort of god-awful venereal disease. I will see them at the games later this week since they are part of the ice girls. "You ladies have a good night."

Before they have a chance to respond, I walk toward my nemesis who looks like a damn Barbie doll. She is talking with her parents. The Becketts are always so welcoming to me. I never feel unwanted in their house. They have acted as my surrogate parents, since my parents still live in Canada and can't travel too much. My parents are very supportive of my career, they just also still work full-time and can't always make it down to games. Same goes for my sisters, Nora and Andi. I miss my family like crazy, but I make an effort to spend a good amount of time back home during the off-season. I know that they are all going to make it down in a couple weeks, for the recognition ceremony of me breaking the record of most goals for the Storm.

I almost reach Brooke when the team douchebag, Dean Hastings, steps in front of my path. Because Bradley was Mr. Kumbaya and wanted peace with everyone on the team, he invited all of our teammates, including the only teammate I've ever despised in my entire career. I thought *I* slept around. Hastings is much worse. And the way he talks about the women he sleeps with is disgusting. Yeah, I hook up with women, but I don't talk about them like he does. Like they are his damn conquests and they should worship the ground he walks on. The thing is—he's a damn good hockey player. The Storm is lucky to have him. He's just cocky as all hell and lets everyone know it.

The thing about Hastings is that he is vetting for the captain's spot that is inevitably open next year. One of our teammates, Brett Adamski, who has been playing for over twenty years, is retiring after this season. He has been a great leader and I am sad to see him go. I just want that captain's spot so bad. I know that I can lead this team to another Stanley Cup and I am at the point in my career where I am entering a veteran position. I can teach these young guys who are coming in straight out of college, or even out of high school, a great deal about not only the game but about what it takes to be a leader. I am also not above defending my teammates out on the ice. I have gotten in plenty of fights and spent more time in the sin bin than I care to admit.

"Hey Lawson." Hastings already looks like he has been drinking a bit. "Are you fucking insane, man? You just left those two fine puck bunnies at the bar. What the hell is wrong with you?"

"Well I could ask you the same thing, Hastings, but I fear that we will be here until morning." My eyes shift over to Brooke for a millisecond. She throws her head back at what I am assuming is a dad joke from Mr. Beckett. I take in the rare sight of Brooke uninhibitedly laughing. Her smile lights up her whole face and her dimples make their appearance.

"Oh damn, who is that?"

My eyes dart back over to Dean who is staring at Brooke like she is a fucking meal. His eyes are hungry and he turns his body completely in her direction. Locking in his prey.

I clear my throat and keep my voice as steady as possible. Why is my body reacting this way? It's the same feeling as when I want to slam someone into the sideboards. Pure adrenaline courses through me and my fists are clenched like I am ready to punch this asshole. Like I need a reason.

"That's Bradley's little sister." My jaw tightens. I know what is going on in Hastings' mind and it is infuriating me for some reason.

His eyes are dangerously raking over her body and I hate it.

"Damn, his little sister is fucking hot. What's her name?"

I have to calm my breathing down. *Relax, she's not your sister.*

You have no say in who Brooke dates or sleeps with. She can be with anyone she wants to be with. Even if you don't approve. When have I ever approved of who Brooke is dating?

"Brooke." I say through clenched teeth. And then I remember a little fun fact about Brooke that gives me some sort of relief. "But I wouldn't get any ideas, Hastings." *Yeah, back the fuck off.*

"Why not, Lawson? Are you into her or something?"

I can feel my face get really hot and my stomach flips. "What? Dude no. That girl is a nightmare." I rub the back of my neck. "It's just she has this one rule."

"Yeah, and what's that?" His eyes haven't strayed away from Brooke's direction.

"She doesn't date hockey players."

"Who said anything about dating, Lawson?"

My blood is boiling. Even though I can't stand Brooke, the thought of anyone taking advantage of her or only using her for one thing, makes me sick. No matter how much I hate her, she is still Bradley's sister. I've known her for a decade and have seen her during heartbreak, and it isn't pretty. If I know anything about Brooke, she is not one for sleeping around. She has made that clear when she has called me out for being a fuck boy and how disgusted she is with me.

Instead of sauntering over to Brooke, Dean heads toward the bar where I left the two women. My body relaxes for the first time since Dean walked over to me. I can't help but think at that moment: *thank God for Brooke's rule.*

3

Brooke

The next day, I bake almost the entire day. Baking is my passion and I hope that I can open my own bakery one day; it also acts as my therapy and outlet for when I am pissed off. That is the reason for the excess baking today. I can't get my brother's stupid best friend out of my mind. It is annoying how almost every encounter that I have with him merits this type of reaction. He infiltrates my mind with his comments and actions, and he isn't so bad to look at either. That is probably the most annoying part about him. Everyone, including my entire family, thinks he is irresistible. Not me.

I decide to make an assortment of pastries including lemon blueberry scones, mixed berry muffins, strawberry poptarts, and my favorite chocolate cupcakes. I have *The Great British Baking Show* on in the background. It's one of my many comfort shows. It would be a dream to go on the show, but I also don't know how I would do under pressure. It's a lot easier to bake when you do it on your terms, with familiar recipes, and without a time limit or knowing that the best bakers in the world are judging you.

I am the happiest when I am baking. I know it is my dream. I just need to keep working hard to make it happen.

After indulging in one too many cupcakes and one too many glasses of wine, I fall asleep on my couch.

I'm in the Storm arena and it is completely empty except for me and this very muscular man with tattoos all along his arms, who is pressing me against the sideboards of the penalty box, grinding his body against mine. I am in nothing but a green hockey jersey, legs spread open wide and wrapped around his chiseled torso. This man mutters my name but I can't make out who it is. His voice sounds oddly familiar, but I can't make out his face. All I know is that I am tangled up with this man and my body is electrified by every kiss and lick against my collarbone and nibble on my ear. Even though this is such a public place, I don't care at all. I am completely turned on and enraptured by this man propping me up against the boards. I give into him with every caress over every inch of my body with his rough, strong hands.

Our breaths become in sync as I move up against this dreamy man and he matches my movement with his body. My fingers dig into his shoulder blades and pull on his dark hair and as my toes curl under and my heels dig into his lower back. He lets out a groan and mutters a word that shakes me to my core and startles me awake: "Cupcake."

My eyes pop open. I have never been so disoriented in my life. What the hell was that? Why was I even dreaming about Tristan freaking Lawson? Especially in a dream where everything felt so vivid, so scintillating–it felt like I was really there with Tristan, in his damn jersey, completely at his mercy.

I reach for the remote, turn off the TV, grab my large water tumbler and head to my room to get properly ready for bed. I hazily peek at the time on my phone. It's already after 10:30 p.m. Shit, I hate falling asleep on the couch. I have to tell Tess about this dream ASAP. She is the only one who I trust enough to confess this to without judgment. Actually, she would be all for this dream coming true for me. Hell she would even want in on this dream since she is obsessed with hockey players. Tristan would be right up her alley.

I yawn, scroll through my latest messages and start transcribing my entire dream out for Tess to read and no doubt analyze. I can't wait to hear her interpretation of this twisted scenario where I am having sex with my enemy.

I throw my phone onto my bed and walk into my bathroom. I vigorously brush my teeth as if I am trying to scrub away the events that took place in my dream. I want to scrub away the surge of want and lust that I felt for Dream Tristan. Once I am done flossing, swishing mouthwash and washing my face, I head back into my room and plop into my bed. I aimlessly search for my charging cord in the darkness. I find it and plug my phone in and click on the messaging icon, assuming that Tess responded. Hoping that she responded. I already have my phone on Do Not Disturb so I didn't see or hear the message come in.

My heart plummets when I see the message appear on my phone.

"Well that's quite the dream, Cupcake. The sin bin, huh? Interesting choice."

Oh my God. At first I think Tess is messing with me and using my oh-so-endearing nickname as a joke. Then my eyes finally are pulled into focus and instead of seeing Tess Lewis I see the name of the last person in the world that I would ever want to see the message I sent: Tristan Lawson. Shit.

I see three dots load and then another message pops up.

"How was I?"

This is my own personal hell. My ears get extremely hot at the thought of how it felt with Tristan's hands all over my body, holding me up with ease against those sideboards. How I would imagine his tongue would feel against my skin. I am so thankful he is not here right now to notice the shift in my complexion and staggered breathing or how incredibly flustered I am. As payback, I want to get into his head a little bit since he is so clearly in mine for some reason.

"I've had better."

I am about to click the side of my phone and forget about this horrendous turn of events when I see another text come in.

"Doubt it."

I STUMBLE my way into my classroom the next morning, with a large container full of a variety of baked goods that I made yesterday. Tess comes in behind me with copies we need for the day. I am thankful every day that the universe set me up with Tess as a co-teacher. We became best friends instantly and any strangers looking in on our relationship assume that we have been friends all of our lives.

"Good morning, B!" She bumps my hip with hers, given that both of our hands are full. She clocks the large plastic container full of goodies, drops the copies and swipes the container from my hands. Already knowing the dynamic between me and Tristan, she says, "Good lord, what did Tristan do this time? Not that I am complaining. I am reaping all the benefits from this dysfunctional relationship."

"Oh you know, just being Tristan. He is the same pompous, egotistical, supercilious, cocky asshole that he's always been."

"Wow, you are feisty today. I love it!"

"I knew he was going to be at Bradley and Jen's party, it's just...I don't know, my body has this strong reaction whenever I am near him. And he is just so full of himself."

"Yeah, got that from your list of adjectives. Ooooh, maybe the kids can help come up with more words for arrogant. You know, to keep up with your running list. It would be a good vocab lesson for them." Tess stuffs her mouth with a scone and winks. "Kidding," she muffles, crumbs falling out of her mouth. We have about five minutes before the kids start walking in. It's now or never.

"I have to show you something, but you have to promise me that you'll never tell anyone."

Tess claps excitedly. "I love a good intrigue!"

I open my phone to my text messages and give her the device, simultaneously eager for and dreading her reaction. Knowing Tess, she is going to eat this up and make it seem more than what it is: a stupid dream.

Tess' jaw drops and then she breaks out into a full-fledged smile.

"You did *not* text Tristan Lawson your very detailed account of a very spicy dream you had of him last night!"

I slap my hand to my face. "I did."

"I have so many questions. But first, how did that happen? Did you intentionally text him?"

My voice goes up what seems like a thousand octaves. "No! I fell asleep on the couch and woke up super groggy and disoriented..."

"Ha, I would be a little disoriented too if I was doing anything resembling what you were doing with him in the sin bin." Her eyebrows wiggle and she smirks as she drinks from her oversized tumbler of coffee.

"Tess, focus please. Anyway, I just saw the T & L and assumed that I was texting you." I cover my face again. "Ugh this is the worst thing that could ever happen. Tristan is going to hold it over my head until the end of time." I hold my hand out to get my phone back from my best friend but she looks back down at the screen, still with a silly smile on her face.

"Is he flirting with you?"

I guffaw. "Absolutely not." I grab my phone, turn it on silent and place it down on my desk.

"I don't know, B." She says accusingly, "Even though you two allegedly hate each other, I have always felt there is something underneath the surface of pure loathing."

"There is no allegedly. And there's nothing underneath other than more hatred. It was just a stupid dream, Tess. It wasn't real." My stomach is aching. I blame hunger, so I take another bite of a scone. Tess is observing my every move like a detective trying to piece all the clues together to solve the case. "What?"

"And why can't this become a reality again? Remind me."

"Well, first, I despise the man, and he feels the same about me, so it would never work. Plus, he falls under my one and only dating rule." Our students start to trickle in. Perfect timing because I want to change the subject and focus on work. "So like I said, Tristan and I will never be a reality."

4

Brooke

10 Years Ago

"Brooke, you are making a mess! Your brother and his guest are going to be home any minute and I don't want it to look like a bag of flour exploded in my kitchen."

I take out the batch of cupcakes from the oven and replace it with a fresh one. Closing the oven door, I say, "I am almost done, Mom! I am trying to make cupcakes from scratch and it's taking me a little longer than expected! Besides, I'm sure whatever girl Bradley has decided to bring home for Thanksgiving won't care that the kitchen is dirty...she's probably too busy fawning over him to notice." I stir the batter vigorously, annoyed that I am feeling rushed.

"I don't really fawn over Bradley. He's not my type."

I slow my stirring and look over at the hottest guy I've ever seen in my life. He is wearing a backwards hat and a black full-zip hoodie and dark sweats. He has the most perfect hazel eyes and knee-weakening smile. His wavy, dark brown hair peeks out of the sides of his hat and he has the smallest amount of stubble on his jawline. My body feels tingly all over. I mean, I've had crushes on guys before where I get cute, innocent little butterflies–but these butterflies are not so innocent and are flapping wildly in my stomach. My mouth becomes dry and I feel like the breath has been knocked out of me. He is about as tall as my brother, yet seems so much larger.

"You must be Tristan! Bradley has told me so much about you!" My mom's voice snaps me out of my trance. I put down the bowl and wash my hands in the sink. I must be scrubbing really hard because Bradley comes up to me and asks, "Hey little sis, are you okay? You're super flushed and you haven't even said hi to your big bro!"

I grab a hand towel and take a deep breath before turning to my brother. He gives me a huge bear hug and then decides to do the thing I hate from us growing up. In front of his friend from college. Correction: hot friend from college. He puts me in a headlock and messes up my hair.

"Ugh Bradley, why are you the absolute worst?" I push him away and slowly make my way around the island to greet this hunk of a man standing a mere two feet from me.

"Hi! Um, I'm Brooke. Bradley's little sister."

His large hand grabs mine and he says, smiling, "Nice to meet you, Brooke. I'm Tristan."

Okay, those butterflies are traveling all over my body. My name coming out of his mouth is pure magic.

"You have a little..." His finger wipes the bridge of my nose and my eyes flutter at the sudden touch. "...flour."

I instinctively wipe my nose after he returns his hand to his jacket pocket. Perfect Brooke.

"Woah, B, are you opening your own bakery or something?"

"That is the dream. One day. These are the first cupcakes that I have made from scratch. No help from Betty Crocker. All Brooke Beckett. Do you want to try one and tell me what you think?"

"Duh. How about you, Tristan, do you want to try one?"

"Sure." Tristan moves a little closer to the island as I hand him a chocolate cupcake.

"I even made the frosting from scratch," I say, beaming at my efforts.

Bradley takes a bite and my smile fades when his face looks like he just ate a vomit flavored Bertie Botts Every Flavor Bean. "Ugh, Brooke. What the hell? This is the most disgusting cupcake I've ever had. It tastes like salt."

"What? No way! You are just being a dick." My ears become really hot. Why is he trying to embarrass me in front of his hot friend? I take what is left of the cupcake out of Bradley's hand.

"Taste for yourself."

"Fine, I will." I take a bite and my heart sinks, but I'm too proud to spit it out. *Shit...*

I look over the recipe and reread the ingredient lists with the measurements. My eyes dart to the measuring spoon labeled tablespoon that I have laying on the counter. I was supposed to do 1 teaspoon, not 1 tablespoon. My eyes must've tricked me. I was so excited to get my first batch into the oven that I didn't taste my batter at all. Probably rule #1 in baking. Always test out your batter. I so would be eliminated from *The Great British Baking Show.*

"Oh my God. I am mortified! I'm so sorry, Bradley." I turn to Tristan, prepared to snipe the disgusting cupcake out of his hand, but it is nowhere to be found. His mouth is full of the cupcake and he starts licking the frosting, which thankfully did not have any salt in it except for the salted butter, off his fingers. I am transfixed on those fingers and my mouth becomes dry again, but I am sure some of that dryness is from the ungodly amount of salt that just went into my body. How is Tristan not throwing it up right now?

"Bro? Did you just eat all of that?" Bradley asks still with a disgusted tone.

After he is done licking the last bit of frosting from his index finger, Tristan licks his lips and says, "It wasn't too bad. I bet you will get better the more you practice. Just like with anything. Practice makes perfect." He playfully raises his eyebrow and smirks at me.

He is so sweet for even taking more than one bite of my cupcake, let alone finishing the whole thing, frosting and all. Maybe he thinks I'm cute too. My heart feels like it is going to leap out of my chest. To focus on something other than my raging hormones right now, I throw the bowl that has the remaining batter into the sink and turn the water on full blast. "So what movie did you want to watch tonight?"

"I was thinking about the new G.I. Joe movie?"

Oh great, just what I need: to be in the same room with one of the hottest guys I've ever met while watching Channing Tatum fight bad guys in all his muscular glory. Cool cool cool. As if I wasn't flustered enough. But I have to save face and pretend I am totally fine with it. "Sure. Just, um, let me clean up and throw away the rest of these disgusting cupcakes. Again, sorry."

After I clean up the kitchen and return it to my mother's immaculate standards, I head toward the hall bathroom. When I go in and look in the mirror, I see this horrific mess looking back at me. Oh good lord, I cannot believe I met Tristan like this. Flour is all over my face and a little in my hair. I wet a washcloth and wipe away any flour that I see. I quickly put some more deodorant on and brush my teeth. I put on a single swipe of mascara and lipgloss and tousle my hair a bit.

My oversized Cheap Trick t-shirt hangs off my shoulder and exposes my bralette. Not too bad, Brooke. Maybe you have a shot with this guy. He did eat your disgusting cupcake after all. And he did look at you with that dangerous smirk of his.

I hear some murmuring outside in the hall so I lean my ear against the door. It's Bradley and Tristan. My stomach flips when I hear Tristan's laugh. Is it crazy that I am already falling for someone and we barely even met?

"Dude, seriously, I think my sister has a little crush on you." *Shit, is it that obvious? I loathe that Bradley has to be connected with this guy and he isn't just some random person I met at school or something.*

"How do you figure that?" Tristan says. He sounds serious.

"Because I know my sister. She's always worn her heart on her sleeve. You wouldn't try anything with her, right?" *Dammit Bradley, can you not cock block me right now?*

There is a pause. "No way, man. I mean, no offense, but she's not nearly hot enough for me. You know how I like them. Blonde and busty. Your sister is neither of those things. Plus, she's your little sister. I would never. Bro code all the way man."

I hear a distant "Oh good" from my brother and suddenly that excitement I was feeling fifteen seconds ago is replaced with absolute dread and disgust. Did I really imagine him flirting with me in the kitchen? Was he just being nice because I'm Bradley's silly, unattractive younger sister? I can't believe I am so stupid for feeling these feelings so fast. Every single hockey player that I have met has been a complete douche. Tristan is just the icing on top. They all have one type and that's not me. Sure, they may be the easiest pool of guys to choose from because they hang out with my brother and we go watch Bradley play so inevitably I am going to run into his teammates. But all of them are the same. I sigh and wipe away a rogue tear that escaped my eye. *No one deserves your tears, Brooke. Especially not a guy you just met.*

I go out to the living room and plop on the love seat, completely avoiding any eye contact with Tristan or Bradley. I cross my arms. "Okay, are we going to start this stupid movie or what?"

"Geez what's the matter with you? Are you on your period or something?" Bradley throws some popcorn at me.

My eyes grow wide. I grab a pillow and throw it at Bradley, "What the hell, Bradley!?"

"What? It's a legit question. You were baking chocolate cupcakes and now you seem all pissed off. Just checking."

Tristan is pursing his lips to keep from laughing. Guys are jerks. And Tristan Lawson is certainly not the exception.

"Just start the movie," I say through my teeth. I grab another pillow and drape my hair over it. The only good thing about this whole night is I get to watch Channing Tatum on our TV for a couple of hours and completely ignore the asshole who I am not "hot" enough for.

5

Tristan

Tonight the Storm celebrated me and Bradley for both breaking the record for most goals scored within a single season, and it's not even the end of the season yet. We are labeled "Dallas' Dynamic Duo" and this night just validates everything we've worked for since college.

"How long are your parents and sisters going to be in town?" Bradley asks me.

"A couple more days. They fly back to Canada on Monday." I slide on my shoes and begin tying them.

"I'd like to see them. Are they going to meet us outside?"

"Yeah." I am actually excited to see my family. It has been a bit since they have come down to Dallas to watch a game. I try to go back as often as possible during the off-season, but it's definitely not enough. My goal this year is to try and get up there more often. I don't have a wife or family yet. Nothing is really here for me other than my job and I guess The Becketts, who have really become my surrogate family. They have always welcomed me with open arms. Well, everyone except Brooke.

"So is my family, and Jen of course. It'll be cool for our parents and siblings to finally meet."

Oh good. Brooke will be there. I haven't talked to her since she accidentally texted me last week. That was one of the best texts I've gotten in a while. I cannot wait to give her crap about detailing what I apparently did to her in a very steamy sex dream. There is a little tug in my gut at the thought of seeing her face get flushed and annoyed at me. I pull my clean shirt down and throw on my newest hat from my brand, Lawson, turning it backwards.

"Hey bro, that design turned out great. I like that it's clean and simple with just your initials."

"Thanks man. Yeah, we have another one that is just going to have Lawson sewn across the front. I think they want to make the thread green. I get to see a prototype in a few days." I was strongly encouraged to create my own brand since I am basically the face of the Storm and they knew it would be beneficial to me financially. But I insisted that if I were to create this brand, fifty percent of the proceeds would go to charities that help fund cancer research. My grandmother died of breast cancer and I want to do everything I can to make a difference and help find a cure.

We both stand up and grab our duffles and make our way out of the arena, where as expected our families are waiting. My mom, whose blonde hair is starting to turn whiter every time I see her, holds out her arms and has a huge smile on her face. "There he is! Congratulations sweetie. I am so proud of you." I lean down and embrace my mom, who has always been my biggest supporter. She would drive me to every practice, every game, every tournament. I owe her everything.

I feel a large hand pat my shoulder. My dad says, "I am proud of you, too, son. Okay, Jo, you are suffocating the boy. Plus I want a bear hug." My mom finally eases up on her hug and I turn toward my dad. "Seriously, I am so proud of you, Tristan. All your hard work has really paid off and you seem like you still love what you are doing out there on the ice."

"Thanks, Pop. I really do love it. It means a lot that you all made the trip."

"We wouldn't have missed it."

Then I see my sisters, Andi and Nora, who people always assume are twins because of how much they look alike. The only difference is that Andi has dark hair like me and my dad, and Nora has blonde hair like my mom. But otherwise, their faces, – down to the shade of their icy blue eyes – are exactly the same. I am the only one of the Lawson children to inherit my mom's hazel eyes. Save for the eyes, I am a dead ringer for my dad, who also played hockey when he was younger. He never went pro but he passed down his love for the sport onto me. The nice thing about my dad is that he never pressured me to pursue hockey or even want to make it a career. He is not haunted by his past and in turn, never made me follow in his footsteps because he wants to live out some sort of lost dream. I always had the choice to play or not to play. My dad was perfectly happy with his life as a regular old dad who provided financially for his family, while my mom stayed at home with us and took care of basically everything else in our lives.

Busy shamelessly ogling every single one of my teammates that walked out of the arena, my sisters didn't notice me approaching them. "What the hell are you both doing?"

They finally notice my presence and both give me a hug at the same time, practically knocking me off my feet.

"Ahhh! I am so excited to see you, big brother!" Nora says.

"Me too!" Andi says. They both loosen their grip on my neck. "Oh and to answer your question, checking out your teammates. They are all extremely hot."

"Ew. Don't talk about my teammates like that." I grimace.

"Why? I am single and ready to mingle," Andi protests. Then Andi looks over my shoulder at Bradley, who is practically making out with Jen. Those two are nauseatingly cute. "It's a damn shame your bestie has a fiancée. I would be all over that." I see my little sister's eyes devour my best friend.

"Talk to Nora about what you want to do with men. Do you think I want to hear those things? I am your brother, Andi."

"Oh and you are such a saint, right? You've never seen someone and wanted to pursue them? I know you, Tristan. You are no saint. Far from it, if I recall."

"Who is that behind Bradley?" Nora nods towards the Becketts, and then I see her. My arch nemesis, who apparently decided to venture out of her introverted cave to come to one of our games. I almost didn't recognize her since she is wearing Bradley's jersey. The only thing that acts as a classic Brooke identifier is the knotted pink headband she always wears.

Brooke catches sight of us looking over at her and we lock eyes for a second. Her face suddenly matches her headband. She flutters her eyes and looks back at her parents, trying to actively engage in their conversation.

Without looking away from Brooke, I answer, "That's Bradley's little sister, Brooke."

"Wait. *That's* Brooke?" Nora points toward Bradley's feisty little sister. "The same Brooke you evidently hate? She's hot. I'm surprised that you hate her, Tristan."

"No, it makes sense. Brooke's not even close to Tristan's type," Andi pipes in.

Before I can delve into the comment "evidently hate," Andi and Nora make their way over to where Brooke is standing. Jesus Christ. Once they lock in on something, they are impossible to stop. I run after them, but before I can intervene, they are shaking hands with Daphne, Bill and Brooke.

Dammit.

"It's so nice to meet you, Brooke. Tristan has said nothing but great things about you!" Andi exclaims.

"He talks about you all the time," Nora adds. I feel myself starting to turn the color of Brooke's headband. *Jesus, get a grip.* If I did ever talk about Brooke, it was to comment at what a pain in my ass she is.

Nothing else.

Brooke crosses her arms as I approach. "Oh really? Well I promise you that I am not as bad as he makes me out to be."

"He told us that you drive him crazy. I can see why. You are stunning."

Brooke shoots me a wide-eyed look and her lips part slightly. And a weight the size of Texas drops in my stomach.

I nervously laugh, but before I can explain anything, Brooke plainly says, "I guarantee you that's not why I drive him crazy." Her face is still flushed and I don't know if it is because of what my sisters just said or because of the sex dream she had of us. I am eager to find out. There is a heated gaze between us now. One we never had before. This weirdly doesn't feel like hate.

Andi and Nora purse their lips and back away simultaneously. They really are like twins. "Okay, well we will be over here talking with Bradley and his lovely and lucky fiancée," Andi says.

Once they are out of earshot, I say, "I am sorry about my sisters. They have it out to embarrass me any time they have a chance."

"They are my kind of girls," Brooke says with a smirk. The color has not left her cheeks. Maybe it is out of habit, but I desperately want that color to deepen.

"So, that was a pretty spicy dream you had last week, Cupcake."

I can already tell I am getting a rise out of her and making her skin crawl in a good way. She is flustered Brooke, and I love flustered Brooke.

"That text wasn't meant for you, Hot Shot. Forget about it. It was just a dream. There must've been a fluke in the cosmos or Neptune must be in retrograde or whatever for me to ever have a dream about you in that way."

I step closer to her and lessen the gap between us. "But you did."

Her eyes are ablaze with something other than annoyance. I can barely make out the shade of green because her pupils are dilated. Is she thinking about the dream right now? It sure seems like it.

She notices my hat, clears her throat and tries to detract. "Are you wearing your own brand? Seriously, Hot Shot, who does that? Aren't you a little full of yourself?"

"Well, it's pretty standard for people to have their own brand, especially when you are the face of the franchise like I am. It's been in the works for a while now, Cupcake. Where have you been?"

"Avoiding you." Crossing her arms again, she walks away from me. "Mom and Dad, I'm heading to the car."

They acknowledge her with a nod and continue their conversation with my parents, who at some point started talking with the Becketts. I watch as Brooke walks away, her long dark caramel hair swaying back and forth along Bradley's number and their last name. My stomach clenches again for some unknown reason. Actually, there is a reason. A little piece of me wants my number to be on the back of her jersey.

For the rest of the night, I wonder why I want it so bad. I don't want to see Brooke in that light, where I am aching to see her wear my jersey. I know what that will mean. There is so much weight to that possibility that I need to bury it deep inside. Should be easy enough. When it comes to Brooke, I am an expert at keeping things under lock and key. Except I never throw that precious key away, and I am not sure if I maybe want to use it.

6

Tristan

"To Tristan!" My father raises his mimosa. "We are so proud of you, son. For you and Bradley to break the record for the number of goals scored in a single game is quite the accomplishment and we are so lucky we were able to travel down from Canada to see you celebrated."

My family all clink their glasses together. Everyone had a mimosa except me. I don't like to drink all that much during the season, especially the morning after a game. There may be a handful of times where I will party with my teammates or if it's a special event. Not this morning. This morning I need to stick with water.

"Thanks for coming out, you guys. It means a lot to me that you would travel so far to celebrate with me." My parents were insistent that we go out to brunch this morning since it was too late to do a celebratory dinner last night. I took them to Oddfellows in the Bishop Arts district. It's one of my favorite breakfast spots in Dallas and I know they serve beignets, which are both my sisters' favorites.

"So, honey." My mom turns to my dad. "When do you want to head to the airport tomorrow?"

Their conversation started to trail off as I dug back into my food. Andi and Nora were sitting directly across from me. I can tell in their faces that they wanted to talk about last night. I can read both of them like a fricken book. They wanted to talk about Brooke.

"So..." Andi starts, smirking while playing with her food with her fork.

Here we go.

"So what, Andi?" I muster up the most annoyed tone I can, even though I am already halfway there.

"What's going on with you and Brooke?" Andi asks, her eyebrows wagging.

"Nothing is going on between me and Brooke." My jaw clenches at that reality and I hate it that my body responds that way. It reveals too much about what is going on in my head.

Nora chimes in, "She's gorgeous, by the way. Her caramel hair. Her hazel eyes. I love her style, too. She looks like she came straight from Barbie Land with the pink headband." She takes a bite of her beignet and looks accusingly at me.

"I haven't really noticed." I shrug and take a drink of my water. Of course I noticed. I've always noticed.

"Oh, please, Tristan. You have goo-goo eyes anytime you look in her direction or if we even say her name. Your face lights up in a way that I've never seen before. Out of ALL the women you've been with..."

"I haven't been with that many women." My stomach twists that my sisters have been keeping track. I guess I am their older brother and they have been my shadows from the moment they could walk, always following me around the house. Getting in my business.

"Uh, yes you have," Andi and Nora say in unison.

I don't like talking about my relationships with my sisters. I feel pressure to set an example for how they should be treated by their partner, and I feel like I've failed them because of my lack of long-term relationships. I've never truly had a girlfriend. I always use the excuse of my grueling hockey schedule, but even I knew that is a bullshit excuse. People across the league are married and have kids and they make it work. It's not that I don't want to make it work. Trust me, I do.

"Whatever. And I do *not* have goo-goo eyes around Brooke." I reach over and steal some of Nora's beignet. Avoiding eye contact at all costs. If I can read them like a book, they can read me, too. "You both have it all wrong. Brooke and I hate each other."

Nora raises her eyebrows and takes another bite of her beignet. "I don't know, big brother. You can cut the tension between you two with a knife."

I raise my glass to my lips. "Maybe because we want to kill each other."

"Or you want to rip each other's clothes off," Andi says mid-chew.

I do a spit-take with my water. That catches our parent's attention, who were still busy talking about their travel plans. It feels like the whole restaurant is looking our way. I lower the bill of my cap to deter anyone from recognizing me.

"Are you all right over there, honey?" My mom's signature worried look crosses her face. I give her a thumbs-up as I clear my throat for what seems like the thousandth time. Thankfully my parents' attention returns to each other as I take the cloth napkin and clean the mess I made. People at other tables also return to their own conversations. Andi and Nora are snickering across the table, looking satisfied with themselves. Some things never change.

"You both are toddlers." I wave the server down, desperately needing to change the subject. "Hey, can we have the check? All on one tab. Thanks."

She smiles, nods and heads toward the register.

I reach in my pocket to get my wallet. I glance over at the two goofballs that are my little sisters. They are just smiling at me and shaking their heads. "What? Stop looking at me like that."

"We will, once you admit to us that you are so in love with Brooke Beckett," Andi says before taking another drink of her mimosa.

"Well, I guess I'll have to get used to you looking like fools all the time, because that will never happen."

The server returns and hands me a black check-holder. I raise my hand up to my dad before he can protest, stick my card in the slot and hurriedly hand it back to the server, who by the look on her face, has clocked who I am. She not-so-subtly rakes her eyes along my body. I mean, my face is on multiple billboards in the metroplex. I can't exactly hide who I am in this city. Even if people don't watch hockey, they recognize me regardless.

"Never say never, Tristan. Life has a way of surprising you," Nora adds.

Life isn't going to go my way on this one. There are too many obstacles, one being Brooke's dating rule and the other being her older brother. I only tell my sisters about one of those obstacles, because the other one shouldn't matter or have any stock in why I can't be with Brooke. "She is Bradley's little sister. She's off-limits anyway."

7

Tristan

"**G**ood practice today, guys!" Brett yells in the locker room. "A few more weeks until the playoffs. Let's stay focused."

I pull my practice jersey off my back and throw it against the wooden panel of my locker.

Bradley is sitting on the bench in front of his locker, which so happens to be next to mine. He pulls off his skates and places them on the ground. "So dude, I haven't seen you take a girl home in a while. Are you feeling all right?" Bradley puts his hand to my forehead, checking to see if I have a fever.

I swat his hand away and growl, "Bro, I'm fine. Just been focusing on the game, man. Didn't you just hear Adamski? Playoffs are right around the corner. My head has to be in it fully." I really don't want to talk about this with him right now.

"I've known you for almost a decade, man. You've never taken a break from women. If you have the opportunity to take a girl home, you always seize it."

Even though what Bradley is saying is the truth, it still stings that my reputation with women has gotten so to a level so egregious that my best friend is calling me out on it.

I shrug off his comment. "I guess there haven't been any opportunities then."

"Um, were you not there at my engagement party? I saw those two blondes at the bar with you. I would say those are two opportunities right there."

"Well, I decided not to take it. Just because an opportunity presents itself doesn't mean you have to take it, bro. They were too desperate for attention. I am not about that anymore."

"Are you telling me that my best friend for almost a decade, Tristan Peter Lawson..."

"That is not my middle name," I interject.

Bradley ignores me. "...has turned into a romantic and wants to actually pursue a woman?"

"So what if I do, man? I don't think it's a bad thing. Maybe I want what you and Jen have. Have you ever thought of that?" I still avoid looking at him. I am scared that he will see right through me and read my mind: the only person I've ever thought of being with long-term shares the same last name as him.

"Wow. I didn't realize that's what you wanted. I hope that you find her soon, because let me tell you, finding your person is the best fucking feeling in the world."

"What are we talking about?" Oakley, our main goalie, chimes in. He still has all of his gear on and his head looks too small for his body.

"Nothing," I say almost too quickly. My voice cracks in the process.

"Why did your voice go up like two octaves?" Oakley sits down next to me and pats my back.

"Because we are talking about finding Lawson his person."

Bradley volunteers the information without hesitation. Goddamn him.

"I'd really not like to involve the entire locker room in this conversation."

"Is Tristan Peter Lawson having issues with women?!"

"Oh my God, that is not my middle name. I hate you Bradley for even starting that fucking rumor. My middle name is John, okay? Can we just clear that up right here and now?" Bradley gives me a shit-eating grin as he continues to take off his equipment. I continue, "And no, I am not having issues with women."

"He's having issues finding the *right* woman. Plus he hasn't gotten laid in a while," Bradley adds nonchalantly, as if we are in a support group or something.

I press my hands to my face and raise my voice. "Dude, will you shut up?"

"I'm just trying to help."

"How? By telling everyone my business? And business that is not even true, I might add."

"So, you are sleeping with random women and you don't want to find love?" Bradley looks me dead in the eye and bats his eyelashes innocently.

He's lucky that I love him like a brother, because if it was anyone else infiltrating themselves in my business, this would be a very different story. I pop up from the bench. "I am ending this conversation. I am going to take a shower." I stride toward the showers. I need to get away from the guys before I punch a hole in the damn wall.

After I wash up and put on clean clothes, Hastings approaches me. Great.

"So, Bradley's sister. What's her name again?"

"Brooke. Why?" I glance around for Bradley, hoping he'll come over and kick Hastings' ass for asking about his little sister.

"Well, I was thinking. I bet I could break that little rule of hers. The one where she doesn't date hockey players."

I snort. "I'd like to see you try, Hastings. I've known Brooke for a long time and that's a hard and fast rule that she never breaks." I grab my hat from the hook on my locker and put it on. "Trust me." There is a heavy weight in my stomach, and I don't know if it's because of Dean's interest or because I hate the fact that she has that rule. Either way it shouldn't matter. She's not my sister. But if it was one of my sisters, I would do everything in my power to keep them away from a guy like Hastings.

"Do you want to make this a friendly bet? Maybe you can get something out of it, Lawson," Hastings says with a devious smile. I don't like where this is going.

I tie my shoes. "What the hell are you talking about, man?"

Dean says smugly, "If I get Brooke to be my girlfriend by the end of the season, you have to step aside for the captain's spot and endorse me. Captain's spots are decided mainly by the team, right?"

It is obvious that he knows nothing about me or Brooke. "Right." I say cautiously. Why does he even want to pursue Brooke? "But why even bring Brooke into this? You know that Beckett will kick the shit out of you for even thinking about dating his little sister, right?"

"I am not afraid of Beckett. I get punched out on the ice all the time." *Yeah, because you're a dirty player and a prick of a human.* "And as for Brooke, because I love a challenge and I know that I will get her to date me. Plus, she's hot and I always get what I want." He pauses and I can feel him staring at me. "And something tells me that you care about her more than you let on, given how much you are fuming right now."

He's getting under my skin and I am fucking over it. I scoff as I stand up and throw my duffle bag strap over my shoulder. "You are that confident you can get a girl that has no interest in you and never will. Did you not hear me? She will never break that rule." Because *I* am confident in that fact and because I also want to see how badly Brooke is going to turn this asshole down, I say, "All right, Hastings, you have a deal. If you can get Brooke to date you by the end of the regular season, I will endorse you for captain. I'm a man of my word.

But, if you fail, then you will step out of the running completely, even as an option for an alternate, and you will endorse me."

"Deal." We don't even shake hands. We just stare each other down like we're in one of those old Western films, ready to draw our pistols and duel at any moment. Ever since Hastings joined the Storm, we've always had a contentious relationship. We are both good at our respective positions and we know it.

Someone clears their throat behind me. "Um, is everything okay, or do I need to step in as a lineman right now and break up whatever the hell is going on between you two?" Bradley's voice startles me, probably because I already feel guilty that Brooke is in the middle of this war.

"No need to step in, Beckett. We're all done here." Hastings smirks, picks up his own bag, and strides out of the locker room. "See you tomorrow."

I shake my head but I can't shake the pissed-off look on my face.

"Woah. Seriously, bro, what were you two talking about? Was he also trying to give you advice on your love life? Is that why you have a crazy look in your eye?"

"Nothing. Just Hastings trying to stir up trouble and get under my skin."

"Well, I hope you can put that aside for next week. I have a huge favor to ask of you and I know that you will be my boy and help a brother out!" Bradley gives me two thumbs-up and a cheesy-ass smile.

I sigh. "Why do I even put up with you? Okay, what do you need?"

"So...Jen kind of scheduled a cake tasting for next Monday, but I totally forgot that I promised Brooke I would speak at her school's career day."

"Okay, what does this have to do with me getting along with Hastings?"

"Maybe because I roped him in to do it with me."

"Why didn't you ask me to go with you in the first place?"

"Well, I figured that the elementary school wouldn't want

bloodshed after you and Brooke are in the same vicinity. I assumed you wouldn't want to go, so that's why I didn't ask you."

Even though he has a point, he also knows the next point that I am going to say. "You know I love working with kids. As much as I hate your sister and Hastings, I will put those feelings aside for the kids. But you owe me later." I point to him and he nods feverishly.

"Thank you so much, bro! I will let Brooke know so that she isn't surprised when you do show up. See you tomorrow. Are you ready for the game?"

"Always ready." Talking to an auditorium of elementary school kids is easy. I do press conferences all the time. It's talking in front of Brooke that I am feeling nervous about because she has always been my toughest critic.

8

Tristan

I step back into the locker room after the first period and I can't get the thought of the damn bet that I made with Hastings last night out of my head. It is risky, and I clearly wasn't thinking when I made the deal with that asshole. I reach out to grab my hockey stick as Bradley takes one final glance at his phone before placing it in his locker. "Oh, damn."

"What?"

"I guess my sister did come tonight with my parents. I wonder what prompted this change of heart in coming to my games more. Maybe now that she isn't with Nick, she has more free time?"

I shake my head and begin walking to the entrance of the locker room. "Yeah, maybe." Bradley mentioning Brooke's ex-boyfriend makes my stomach flip in the most uncomfortable way.

GOSH, seeing Brooke out in the stands really throws me off at first. Brooke rarely comes to our games and I feel like the past couple of weeks, she has been to more home games than ever before. I don't hate it, but now I feel some extra pressure to show off a little. I know that Brooke could care less how I perform. There's no way she could know about the bet, but I have this intrusive thought that she might be here to watch fucking Hastings. That thought fuels me this whole game: my anger for the fact that Hastings is weaseling his way into her life. I need to be the next captain for this team. I can unite the team more than he can, plus I know that I am better than him.

It is the middle of the third period and we are up two to one against Colorado. I am fucking exhausted; I've probably been on the ice for longer than our standard minute. Jageilski got a good shot but it was blocked by their goalie. We are advancing and about to score when out of the corner of my eye, I glimpse one of our opponents grab Bradley by his jersey and throw him down onto the ice. *Oh fuck no.*

I skate over to assess the situation, since that was clearly a foul. But another Colorado player, Paul Nichols – who has been my main nemesis even before Hastings came along – gets in my way. Out of frustration, I push off of him slightly. That's when he grasps my jersey by my collarbone and shoves me. I am about to shake it off, but he keeps shoving me across my entire chest, throwing me off-balance. In my peripheral I see him take off his gloves. *Okay, are we doing this?* I am not above kicking someone's ass on the ice. This might be a good time to take some swings against my opponent rather than take swings against Hastings. I take my black gloves off too and start punching. Nichols will not let go of my jersey, so I grab his jersey and keep swinging. His fist hits my jaw, which gives me the perfect excuse to lay into him. I keep punching him until I feel hands pull my jersey from the back. "Lawson, that's enough." Hastings. This asshole needs to get out of my way. I keep punching. Whistles are blowing from the linemen, and one of them wedges in between me and Nichols.

I have to stop.

Nichols finally lets go of my jersey, but Hastings still hasn't. I'm already pissed off that I am about to be assessed a penalty. Hastings is only contributing to my anger. "Let go of my jersey, Hastings. It's over," I command as sternly as possible.

"You always want to be the hero and show off," he says. "Did your girlfriend Beckett need your help?" I know that he is talking about Bradley, but for some reason Brooke's face pops into my head.

"God, you're an asshole, you know that? Just mind your fucking business. And you know nothing about me and Beckett. The way that we operate on the ice. You just joined this team. Fucking know your place."

"Well, last time I checked, we are on the same level, Lawson. We are both up for the captain's position. And once I lock it down with Brooke, say goodbye to that prospect."

That's it. I grab Hastings by his jersey and throw him down onto the ice. Whistles start to blow all around and the crowd goes wild. Hastings gets up and barrels into me hard and knocks me against the sideboards. He starts swinging at my face and he hits my cheekbone, and I know immediately I am going to bleed. I push off as hard as I can swing back at him. His helmet comes off and I throw a right hook, making contact with his eye. Hastings rips my helmet off and punches me back. A lineman desperately attempts to stop the fight. This is very unorthodox. It's rare that teammates fight with each other. I wonder what my punishment will be for instigating this fight.

Still, I am not letting down until Hastings does. I am not losing this fight. Just like I am not losing this fucking bet. Finally, Hastings listens to the lineman and lets up. That's when I relax my hands and let go of his jersey.

"What the hell is wrong with you guys? 92. I'm going to have to assess a ten-minute penalty for both you and 15, and a game misconduct penalty and suspension from one game for 92 for both fights." Fuck. I know Coach is going to be pissed at me, but I will take his wrath any day. The worst part of all of this is hearing Brooke's name come out of Hastings' mouth. It infuriates me more than I'd like to admit.

We both sit next to each other in the penalty box. I look over my shoulder and try to find Brooke in the sea of green and white. She isn't where I last saw her. She probably left after Bradley got in a fight and didn't see my fight – well fights – at all. I know how much she hates seeing Bradley get hurt.

"What the hell is your problem, Lawson?" The lines in between Hasting's eyebrows deepen. I'm sure mine look the same.

"You're my fucking problem. You listen to me."

Hastings gives me an incredulous look, almost like he thinks what is about to come out of my mouth is a joke. It's not.

"She's fucking off-limits," I tell him. "This bet is fucking over."

"Not for me, Lawson. I thought you were a man of your word. And I thought you didn't care about her at all." He gives a maniacal and calculated smile. "This is going to be even more fun. Watching you squirm, knowing that you will never have her or the captain's spot. Does Bradley know about your crush on his little sister? I'm sure he would love that."

The urge to punch him in the face again surges through my body. The only thing stopping me from doing so is my integrity, and the fact that I don't want Brooke to get the wrong idea of me. She's already written a negative narrative about me in her head. I am determined to prove her wrong. I wipe my cheek and see the blood on my fingertips. I hope I don't have to get stitches.

Once the ten minutes are up, the athletic trainer motions for me to follow him to the locker room to get assessed. As I walk back to the locker room, two thoughts cross my mind: *one, Bradley can never find out about the bet and two, neither can Brooke.*

9

Brooke

"Why am I here right now?" I say under my breath as I make my way up the steps to his front door. *Because you want to make sure he is okay. And no matter how much you hate him, he is your brother's best friend. You've known him for ten years. And he fricken got in a fight with Dean and made a complete ass of himself in front of everyone. And he got laid out by the opponent before that and had to go to the locker room to get checked out after he went to the penalty box.*

Tristan answers the door in just a towel. *Seriously, who does that?* Tristan Lawson, that's who.

"Seriously, Hot Shot? Who answers their door in just a towel? Who were you expecting? One of your many ice girls or puck bunnies you keep on standby?"

He smirks a little. "I wasn't expecting anyone–especially not *you*, Cupcake." He looks super confused as to why I am standing there. *Join the club, buddy.* "Brooke, what are you doing here?"

What? He *never* calls me Brooke. And my God, look at his face. There is a cut right on his cheekbone and another one across his eyebrow. I instinctively want to reach out and fix what is injured. But I restrain myself.

"I don't know..." I say. "I just... wanted to make sure you were okay." *Am I really going to admit this next thing to him?* "I tried to go down and see you in the locker room, but security stopped me because I'm not family. Can I come in?"

Tristan hesitantly steps aside and I make my way through his doorway.

I don't know what I expected Tristan's place to look like. A bachelor pad? Laundry strewn everywhere. Dishes piled up in the sink. Trash bins overflowing. But I see none of that. In fact, it smells so crisp and clean. Controlled. I guess we are more alike than I thought. This is exactly how my apartment looks. The only exception is there is a stark lack of color in his house. Everything is grays and blacks. Probably to match his personality. My apartment looks like a rainbow exploded in it.

I am greeted excitedly by a couple of big dogs. I hold out my hands for them to lick and say hello. Their tails are wagging so they seem friendly enough, which is ironic since I know who their dad is. And he has been anything but friendly to me for the majority of the time that I've known him.

I slowly walk through the foyer that has a massive chandelier hanging from the tall ceiling. And look around. This is the nicest house I've ever seen. It has a modern farmhouse feel to it, which hello Chip and Joanna Gaines. I am obsessed with them. I try to go to Waco every chance I get so I can visit the Silos. Tristan's house looks like he got the majority of his decor from their catalog.

I walk into the kitchen and run my fingers across the island as Tristan stations himself on the other side of the massive counter that is separating us. I finally shift my gaze from the countertop to Tristan and get a good look at his body. My heart leaps for a second. *Calm down, you've seen plenty of men naked. Well not plenty, but enough. Ugh, stop staring, Brooke.*

"Can I get you anything to drink? Water? Poison?" Tristan raises an eyebrow and smirks in the process.

"Ha ha. Water is fine." Tristan walks over to his kitchen cabinets and takes out a glass. When he reaches up, I see not only how ridiculously muscular he really is, but also the bruises that cover his torso. My goodness, he was not this muscular when we first met. Then again, he wasn't playing in the NHL. He also has a lot more tattoos than I remember. I guess over the years, I've noticed a little, but I made it a point to not give Tristan any more of my attention than the obligatory hello and goodbye when he would come by my parent's house.

My face must be contorted in a wince because Tristan says, "Is something wrong, Cupcake? You look like you're in pain."

"I can say the same about you." Then some force outside of my own control takes over. I walk toward Tristan and reach out my hand, gently touching one of his bruises. "Is this from earlier?"

"Yeah. That piece of shit got me good. That's just the nature of the game." Tristan hands me the glass and I have to actively peel my eyes off him and grasp onto the glass. "Also, fans love a good fight."

Geez, I don't understand why. I mean did Tristan look incredibly hot while throwing punches...of course, I would *never* tell him that. I couldn't help but flinch whenever anyone ran into him. And it bothered me that Tristan was the only one I was paying attention to. I was there to watch and support my brother. But, when I saw Tristan on the jumbotron, my eyes would automatically follow him wherever he went on the ice. It's like he inadvertently cast a spell through the screen and I was not immune to it.

"A lot of good that gear does you. You still get hurt anyway." I slowly caress the bruise. *My goodness, what is coming over me?*

"Trust me, I could look a lot worse." I wince at the thought. I've hated seeing Bradley in this state all these years. Anytime he would come home from a game with cuts and bruises, I would cringe. These men must be masochists for enduring that amount of pain. I finally take a sip of the water. For some reason my mouth is turning dry every second I am near this man. And I hate him even more for that.

"Do you have a first aid kit here?"

"Um, yeah. Why?"

I reach up and barely touch Tristan's face. "Your cut on your left eyebrow is starting to bleed again. Did your trainer do a concussion check on you? Because you know that concussions are serious, right?"

Tristan chuckles and reveals a smile that I've never seen. A genuine smile. His chuckle makes my body stupidly vibrate with excitement. "Yes, Cupcake. We have only the best athletic trainers on staff. I checked out fine." After taking a sip of his own water, he says, "Why are you looking at me all goofy like that?"

I bite my bottom lip. "You laughed. You should always do that."

"You should always make me." He steps closer and now the air is completely knocked out of me.

Okay, we are entering unfamiliar territory here. We are no longer bantering about how much we loathe each other. We are talking about how we make each other laugh and I am touching his perfect fricken body out of pure worry. While he is in nothing but a towel.

I clear my throat. "So, that first aid kit?"

"Hold on, I'll be back. Apparently you have a problem with people being in towels, so I will go change into my clothes and get that kit." He runs up his stairs to where I assume his bedroom is. A small part of me wants to know what his bedroom looks like. My cheeks get hot as that thought enters my mind.

As Tristan is changing, and to distract myself from thoughts of his bedroom, I take this opportunity to peruse his home. I walk into the living room and notice a large bookshelf. I did not take Tristan as a reader, but he is surprising me at every turn. Just like he surprised me by looking up at where I was sitting in that damn arena after he got into that fight with Dean. I could sense that he was looking directly at me. I even have evidence from the jumbotron to back me up. For some reason, I had this strange feeling that with every punch he swung at Dean, he was trying to prove that he cared for me. As if each punch was its own pick-up line for me.

I know that's ridiculous. Because he hates me. But one thing I know is that players don't punch their own teammates for entertainment. Tristan had a reason that wasn't directly linked to hockey.

The real question is why.

Picture frames filled with Tristan's sisters and his parents grace his bookshelves. He almost looks normal and not like my arch nemesis. Every smile in those pictures provides glimpses of who Tristan maybe truly is. He is a son. A brother. A best friend. At least to my brother, he is. Then I come across the best picture of all. I pick it up off the bookshelf to study it closer. A photo of Tristan with two elderly people, who I am assuming are his grandparents, with the Stanley Cup. He looks so happy and I can see the pride in his grandparents' eyes as they pose next to him. Now, that's a smile I've never seen come across his face.

"Best moment of my life right there," Tristan states from right behind me. I jump a little. I can feel his breath near my ear. Heat radiates off Tristan's enormous body and it sends chills up my spine. And not in a bad way. In a way that makes my core heat up and butterflies enter my vacant stomach.

"Your grandparents look so proud of you. I remember that night. Bradley was so happy. That's the night he met Jen." I vividly remember that night two years ago. We were celebrating their Stanley Cup win at a rooftop bar off Greenville Avenue. My brother saw Jen across the room and it was as if stars in the sky came down and took up permanent residence in Bradley's eyes. They've never dimmed. I also remember that Tristan was surrounded by a swarm of women, ruthlessly throwing themselves at him, hands all over, caressing his chest, playing with his hair, whispering in his ear things that made him smile deviously. A knot of jealousy tightens in my stomach as that memory infiltrates my mind.

I shake my head a little, setting the photo back on the bookshelf. *Back to reality.* I turn around and hold my hand out, waiting for the first aid kit. "Kit?"

Tristan places the small white-and-red box in my palm. His thumb lingers a little too long against the side of my hand. And just when I think he will move his hand, he keeps it there longer. "What were you thinking about, Cupcake? Your cheeks are red."

Stupid pale skin. Always betraying my inner thoughts. Why wasn't I blessed with olive skin like Tess? And then I take him in. My God, can this man wear light gray sweatpants and an old Boston University shirt that clings to his sculpted chest. His sleeves of tattoos are the only ones exposed, unfortunately. His damp hair is starting to set in slight waves and even though he has a short, almost scruff-like, beard, his jawline looks more chiseled than ever. It is fucking annoying how he can look like this without any effort at all.

I clear my throat again and gesture to his couch. "C'mon, let's go sit down." I pry myself out of the intense gravitational pull that Tristan apparently has on my body and walk toward his charcoal couch that probably costs more than my annual salary.

"I'm seriously fine, Cup–" Tristan starts.

"Can you not fight with me for once, Lawson? Come sit on the couch so I can help you!"

Tristan lets out a small laugh and plops down next to me. A little too close, in my opinion. I scoot slightly as I open the first-aid kit. I take out some gauze, q-tips, and antibacterial ointment. As I softly press against Tristan's open wound on his eyebrow, he flinches slightly but says nothing. For once, Tristan Lawson is vulnerable in front of me. No fighting. No quips. No mischievous smirks directed at me after he says something that pisses me off. His guard is down. He put down his firearms for a second. We are at a ceasefire. And I am going to take full advantage of it.

As I apply more ointment, I say, "Tristan."

"Yes, Cupcake?"

That damn nickname. I roll my eyes, shake my head and continue, "Why did you fight Dean?"

Tristan doesn't answer straight away. I shift my eyes from his cut and look into his hazel eyes, searching for some way to his inner thoughts. Maybe they are a portal into the inscrutable mind of Tristan Lawson. Maybe I can finally crack the code. "Because Dean is an asshole." His jaw clenches and he doesn't look directly at me.

He's holding back. "That's it? There is no other reason? From what I know about sports, you usually don't punch out your fellow teammate."

"He is dangerously close to getting something that I desperately want." He looks intensely at me, with fire in his eyes.

My stomach flips and my heart starts to race. "And what's that?"

Tristan plays with a piece of my hair. He leans a little closer. My breath hitches when I realize that Tristan fricken Lawson is the closest he's ever been to my face and...wait, is he about to kiss me? My fingers get tingly and my hands start to shake. My body aches from the possibility of having his lips on mine. Having his fingers grab my hair and not just twirl it around.

A knock at his door breaks the magnetic pull between us. I lean back and I swear I hear Tristan let out a small growl, as if he is frustrated that whatever was about to transpire between us got interrupted. I know I feel the same way.

The knock becomes incessant and finally Tristan gets up from the couch and makes his way to the door. I frantically place the ointment and extra gauze back into the kit. I place some hair behind my ears and try to will the goosebumps covering my entire body away.

Tristan unlocks the door and opens it and there standing in the middle of his doorway is none other than an ice girl, in just a hockey jersey. No scratch that—in one of Tristan's jerseys. Her eyes look hungry as she gazes up and down Tristan's immaculate body. That son of a bitch *was* waiting for someone. He fucking lied to me.

Tristan scratches the back of his head and says, "Uh, Alison, I kind of have company right now."

"No, no he doesn't." I snap the first aid kit shut and get up from the couch. My face is hot again, but this time out of pure embarrassment. I look nothing like this girl. Her platinum blonde hair and stark blue eyes are almost blinding, and she is perfectly spray-tanned. She is devastatingly beautiful and definitely Tristan's type. Which I am clearly not.

"Brooke..."

"It's fine, Hot Shot. You were waiting for her anyway, right?" I sear my stare into his eyes and his eyebrows furrow as if he is insulted at that accusation. He almost looks mad at me for leaving! Why the fuck would I stay?

I address the ice girl: "I was only cleaning him up for you. Alice, was it? He's all yours."

I brush past her and quickly make a safe distance between me and my enemy. I am glad Alison did show up so it could snap me the hell out of whatever trance I was in. Stupid me for thinking that Tristan Lawson has changed his colors. Nope, he is still the sullen gray man I've always known him to be.

10

Brooke

"Hey, B, what time do we need to leave for the auditorium? Your brother is coming, right?" Tess is helping one of our kids tie his tiny shoes.

"In about a couple of minutes. As far as I know, yes. I think he is supposed to bring Dean, too." I am trying to clean up the manipulatives off the tables and back into the bins. My Apple Watch has been going off a bunch of times this morning. When I glance at who is trying to call me or text me, I see that it's Bradley, but I am a little busy wrangling five- and six-year-olds.

"Miss Beckett?" Our little red-headed cutie, Hudson, tugs on my skirt.

I open the classroom door and prop it open with the door stopper. "Yes, Hudson, what is it sweetie?"

Hudson points to something behind me. I turn.

No. This cannot be happening.

What the hell is Tristan doing here?

Before he can advance any further, I press against his chest and keep him out in the hallway while Tess leads our class toward the auditorium for the career day presentation.

"What are you doing here?" I say through my teeth.

"Nice to see you too, Cupcake. Bradley called me and said that he's in a bind. Jen needed something done for the wedding. Some tasting or other. He said he would let you know."

I wasn't about to admit that I never got a chance to answer my brother's phone calls or even the several text messages I left unread. "Well he didn't." I grab my coffee tumbler and start walking toward the auditorium. "Thanks for coming, I guess."

I try so hard not to notice how hot Tristan looks today. Ever since my stupid sex dream and seeing him in a towel, I can't stop thinking about his washboard abs. And his perfect V leading down to...*Nope! Stop that thinking, Brooke.* But still, he looked extra hot today. He is wearing a backwards Storm hat and a black Storm t-shirt that barely fits his torso and his arms are bulging out of his short sleeves. His legs are like tree trunks in his basketball shorts. How can someone's legs be that muscular?

He puts his hands in his pockets and clears his throat. "Also, I wanted to talk to you about the other night. I wasn't exp..."

"It's fine. No need to explain. It was a mistake to come by anyway. You're a big boy. You could've taken care of yourself." We reach the auditorium. I swing open the door and gesture for him to walk in. "Just don't start a fight in front of the kids. Can you handle that, Hot Shot?"

Tristan walks over to the last empty seat next to Dean on the stage. There are about a dozen people who have shown up for the Career Day panel. Excitement fills the room as kids and adults alike fawn over the two pro athletes who decided to grace us with their presence. I see my principal walk some press into the auditorium. This is probably good for Tristan and Dean's public relations, considering the fight they got into the other night. Maybe that's also why Bradley was so eager for Tristan to take his place. Other than the wedding stuff, Tristan needs to make nice with Dean.

Tess saved me a spot next to our little kiddos and I huff as I sit down. I'm annoyed, both at the fact that my brother bailed, and also at the fact that I am ridiculously turned on by one of the men sitting on that damn stage.

"This is going to be interesting," Tess leans over and whispers.

"Yup," I say curtly.

"I really don't understand why you even have that rule. Do you want my opinion?"

"If I say no, are you going to give it to me anyway?" I pretend that I am writing something on my clipboard, even though I am just making the same small line over and over again. I'm going to make a hole through this paper.

"Of course. And only because you need to hear it. I think you need to get rid of this super outdated, and dare I say it, stupid rule. I think it would be fun to have a little rebound," she lowers her voice even more, "S-E-X. And since you loathe Tristan, I think that Dean would be the perfect person for that. I am sure he is going to be way more exciting in bed than Nick. He was so boring."

Everything that Tess is saying is unfortunately true. I was with Nick for two years and I really thought that he was the person for me. He was stable with his job at an accounting firm. I thought stability was what I wanted, but I also realized that he was okay with putting our relationship on auto-pilot. I was just there. Yeah, he made me laugh with his silly dad jokes and the sex with him was fine. That was just it–it was fine. I convinced myself that it would get more explosive and exciting over time, but it didn't. The worst thing was that I thought he was going to propose to me at a fancy dinner a couple of months ago, but he just wanted to take me out because of a big account that he acquired.

Why settle for someone who doesn't make your heart burst out of your chest?

That's why I walked out of that restaurant and never looked back. And now I am sitting here, single, while my best friend tells me that I need to go out with one of the hottest hockey players in the NHL.

Our principal opens up the floor to questions. One of our students raises their hands and our assistant principal comes over with the other microphone. We hand the mic down to him.

"Um, hi, my name is Hudson and my question is for Tristan Lawson and Dean Hastings."

The principal excitedly runs over to where Tristan and Dean are sitting and hands the microphone over to Tristan. I stare at his massive, veiny hand holding onto the base of the microphone. I hate that I am noticing the little things about Tristan's body now. It's like going over to his home the other night opened a portal into an alternate universe where I don't hate his guts.

Tristan says, "What's up, little man?" Shivers run up my spine. It's like I have been replaced by the old me from ten years ago, the girl who was enamored by Tristan rather than repulsed by him. To distract myself, I look over at Hudson and try to keep my focus there.

"What's your favorite dessert?"

Aww, that's such an innocent question. I totally thought he was going to ask something about what it is like being a hockey player. This is why I love teaching young kids. They bring back the innocence that life inevitably forces out of you. Experience and knowledge takes its place.

"That's a great question, Hudson. Well, my favorite dessert would have to be..." Tristan's voice trails off as he purses his lips together, seemingly thinking about his response. "Cupcakes."

I lock eyes with Tristan. He has my attention now, and he knows it. He smirks and continues, "Chocolate cupcakes, to be specific." He peeps his tongue out slightly as he breaks into a full-on smile. Those are the exact cupcakes he tasted the night we met. I don't know if he is being serious or just fucking with my head. I don't know what's worse. Either way, my heart begins to beat really fast and it seems that the heater suddenly turned on in the auditorium.

Tristan hands the microphone over to Dean, while still maintaining eye contact with me. All sound is drowned out because of my focus on Tristan. I don't even register what Dean's response is.

Tess must notice the intensity of our stare because she nudges me out of my trance and says, "What is going on? You are super red right now, is everything okay? And why is Tristan staring at you like you are a piece of meat?"

I scowl. "He is not!" Even though he totally is. I've known Tristan long enough to know how he looks at women he wants to go home with. The real question is: why is he staring at *me* like that? Maybe I'm confusing a lust stare with a killer stare. That's it! He wants to kill me. That's the narrative and I'm sticking to it. "And I can't stop looking at Dean. That's why I am red," I lie.

"Like I told you before, girl. Your rule is outdated and just plain dumb."

I hate that she might be right.

After about an hour of Q&A, the career day presentation is over and it's time for lunch. I am lining up the students when I hear, "Thanks for all the great questions, you guys." Tristan is right behind me. A little too close for my liking. I can smell his masculine cologne and a wisp of mint that I recognize from the other night. I hate that I am super aware of small things about Tristan. I straighten up my stance, cross my arms, and look behind me into his hazel eyes. Tristan kneels down on one knee and high-fives Hudson. "I especially liked your question, little man."

"Thanks! I like cupcakes, too!"

Tristan smirks. "The best, right?" He playfully messes with Hudson's hair and I nod to Tess to start leading the kids down to the cafeteria.

I shake my head a little as Tristan stands back up with a large smirk on his face. "I just talked to your principal and she said how excited she is that your class is taking a field trip to our practice rink so the kids can learn how to ice skate."

Shit. I kind of forgot that I talked with Bradley about setting that up. My principal, who is an avid hockey fan, was over the moon about it. I cross my arms against my chest. "Yeah, so?"

"So, why didn't you tell me that *your* class is coming for the lessons?"

"Why would I tell you?" I inquire. Bradley already knows. Why would Tristan need to know?

He crosses his arms in turn, matching my energy, except his energy feels more playful. "I figured since I am the one who usually runs those types of lessons, you would let me know. I like to be prepared for who I am dealing with."

"Well..." I say. He steps closer to me and my body jolts slightly from the close proximity. The same feelings I began to have the other night at his house are rushing through my body. I am realizing I do not mind Tristan Lawson being this close to me. I swallow hard and continue, "Now you know."

Suddenly, I feel Tristan's vibe change from playful to confrontational as Dean approaches. Almost protective. I hate when he acts like he's my brother. One is enough.

"Hey, Brooke. You look extra cute today." I look down at my outfit which consists of a bright pink maxi skirt and a white t-shirt. And of course I am wearing my signature bubblegum pink knotted headband. My bright green lanyard is hanging from my neck. Oh yeah, super cute.

"Thanks!"

"So, that Casino Night is coming up." Dean inches closer to me.

"Yeah?"

"What about it, Hastings?" Tristan chimes in. His tone is anything but friendly. He must really despise this guy. Now I want to mess with his head even more.

Dean glares at Tristan and then looks back at me. "I was just wondering if you were going."

Tristan raises his hand to his scruff and laughs, "There is no way she is going. Brooke doesn't go to team events like that. Never has."

I squint at him. *Game time, Lawson.*

"As a matter of fact, I *am* planning on going." Tess is finally back from dropping the kids off at the cafeteria. I yank her to my side. "With Tess." I plead with my eyes and we have known each other long enough to understand nonverbal communication. "But I will look for you there," I say in my best flirtatious voice I can muster.

"Uh, that's right," Tess plays along. Thank God for her. I'll debrief with her later.

Tristan's mouth is agape out of pure disbelief. "You cannot be serious." I don't blame him. He's right. I would usually never go to these types of things.

"I am serious."

"Sounds great. I'll be looking for you, too." Dean says, then pats his hand on Tristan's shoulder. Tristan flinches and looks back at Dean like he wants to throw him into the wall and make a Dean-shaped hole in the drywall. "Ready to go, Lawson? We have practice in an hour. See you soon, Brooke." Dean takes my hand and kisses the top of it.

I sheepishly smile while Tristan's jawline is clenched. He's really pissed off.

Good. I'm winning at this game.

11

Tristan

I woke up stupidly excited for today. I always like when we have kids come by so we can instill the love of the game in their little minds. I remember the first camp I went to as a kid and it was one of the best days of my life. It gives this whole career more of a purpose to give back to the community. Plus, I get to terrorize Brooke today. One of my favorite pastimes.

"All right kids, let's file in and wait for Mr. Lawson to come and instruct what to do next," I can hear Brooke's coworker, Tess, tell the kids.

Then I spot the only woman on this earth who hates my guts. My stomach turns to knots and I notice that she isn't wearing her usual knotted headband, but instead a bright pink beanie. Not a look I am used to, but I'm completely ready to embrace it.

Hastings skates up next to me, already complaining. "God, this hour is going to last forever. I can't believe Coach dragged me into this. Where is Bradley, anyway? Don't you two do everything together?"

"He's busy with Jen today. Suck it up; it's a good way to spend your free time. If and only if you get into a leadership position, you need to sometimes do things you don't want to do. So I am going to say it again: Suck. It. Up."

I plaster a smile onto my face and skate over to the other side of the rink. I can sense that Hastings is doing the same.

"Hi guys! Are you all excited to do some skating today?"

All the kids say in unison, "Yeah!"

"All right, that nice man behind the counter over there," I point toward Josh, the rental skate attendant, "will get you all set up with some skates and I'll see you out here on the ice. Parent chaperones can go ahead and get some skates as well."

Brooke is standing in the back with her arms crossed. She looks miserable. Even though she might be putting on a slight smile, she is clearly uncomfortable. I mean, I know she hates me, but I hope she lets go a little bit and has some fun. For some reason I can't get over the way she looks in a beanie. It's just so uncharacteristic about her and I am not hating it.

It's been ten minutes since the kids, the chaperones and Tess come out onto the ice. After a quick lesson, I let Hastings take over. Where the hell is Brooke? I take a lap around the rink and notice she is sitting in the stands taking pictures of the kids, with a wide grin on her face. I take a mental note of that smile since it's a rare sight for me. I get off the ice and walk over to the bleachers. Her posture shifts and smile fades but she still has her phone up and takes one more picture. "Can I help you, Hot Shot?" She clicks the side of her phone and puts it away in her puffer jacket pocket.

"Aren't you going to get out onto the ice with your students, Cupcake?" I say, leaning against my hockey stick.

"Nope, all good sitting right here. Don't worry. I'm monitoring.

And Tess and the chaperones are out there anyway. They've got it all handled." She looks out into the rink. She's acting strange.

And then I get a weird suspicion that she has never stepped foot on ice. It's a look I'm all-too-familiar with. I help out with camps with young kids to teach them about hockey, most importantly how to skate. Brooke has the same scared, doe-eyed look in her eyes that those kids do.

"Cupcake," I say in an accusatory tone.

"Hot Shot..." She mimics.

"You've never ice-skated before, have you?"

She purses her perfect lips and then bites her bottom lip and says, "No."

"Okay, I'm officially disowning your brother for not teaching you."

"It's not his fault. He always wanted to, but I was stubborn."

I squint at her and shake my head. "All right, that's it."

"What's it?" she says, clearly annoyed.

"You're going to pull up your big girl panties, put skates on and go out there on the ice so I can teach you how to skate. Or at least start teaching you how to skate. We need more than just an hour."

"Um, no I'm not."

"Either you come on your own or I am going to throw you over my shoulder and carry you down. Your choice."

Her brow furrows and she crosses her arms, standing her ground. "No means no, Hot Shot."

"Fine." I step onto the bleachers, lift her up around the waist, and throw her over my shoulder.

She screams and I feel her fists pound against my back.

"Wait, no! Tristan! This really isn't necessary. I've gone through my whole twenty-eight years of life not knowing how to skate, and look at me! I'm fine." She attempts to pull on my sweatshirt to stop me, but is unsuccessful. I am a man on a mission. God, I am going to chew out Bradley for not teaching her how to skate.

"I think it is. Necessary." I lower her to the ground and turn my attention to Josh. "Hey man, can I get—what? A size seven?" I turn to Brooke, who now looks super pissed-off with her hip off to the side.

"Eight."

"Damn, clown feet. You heard the lady. Size eight."

She mouths, "Fuck you, Hot Shot."

God I fucking wish.

She crosses her arms across her chest. "This is why I hate you! You are insufferable."

I hand her the skates. "I'll see you out there." I leave Brooke looking pissed-off, but I can't stop beaming. This is rare uninterrupted time with Brooke and I am not going to waste it. Bradley is not here to intervene or cock-block me in any way.

What seems like hours later, Brooke reluctantly places her soft hands into mine as she glides onto the ice and my heart leaps a bit. Her smooth fingers feel foreign against my calloused palms and suddenly I don't want Brooke's hands to leave mine. I can feel her entire body tense as her hold on my hands turn into a full-on death grip. She's terrified. She keeps looking down at her feet.

"Look up at me, Cupcake."

She finally meets my eyes and that's when I realize just how scared she really is. Her eyebrows are furrowed but not in a pissed-off way—this time they are curved up and her eyes are filled with tears. This is a risk for her and I know her well enough to know she hates stepping out of her comfort zone. I am actually surprised that she wore a beanie today instead of her usual headband. It's a small change, but I like it.

It means she is willing to push herself a little bit.

I guide her slowly around the rink. Her students are watching and waving. They are actually skating better than she is. But I guess that is the thing about little kids: they are not afraid to take risks. They aren't concerned about if they fall down or if they look silly doing something new.

I still can't believe that Brooke has never done this before. My heart skips a beat as she tightens her grip around my hands. She is trusting me right now. For the first time ever. And her hands are finally in mine. Despite the cold environment, I am feeling very warm inside. I am definitely having feelings I shouldn't be having about Brooke. I shake my head from the thoughts that take over and smile.

"What? I look ridiculous, don't I?" She rolls her eyes.

"No, that's not it at all. You are doing great." Then I clear my throat to save face.

"Was that an actual compliment, Hot Shot? Maybe we truly are in hell right now, because you never compliment me."

My stomach drops. "That's not true. I was just thinking about how absurd it is that you don't know how to ice skate. How is that possible? How did I not know this about you?"

"There's a lot you don't know about me." She sighs. "I've always been scared to skate. It's too unpredictable, especially the other people around you because you can't control what they do. Plus, I don't want to fall." She wobbles as the mention of falling. "That's why I like baking...it's predictable. The outcome is something you can rely on. There are usually no surprises."

I nod my head. "Hmm. Other than putting salt in your cupcakes and not telling the people eating them."

Her face scrunches up and she punches my chest, then shakes her hand from the impact. I love pushing her buttons. It's my favorite pastime. I continue before she has an opportunity to curse me out, "Well, falling is inevitable. The point is to keep getting up. You gotta take risks, Cupcake." Then a thought pops into my head and I know for a fact that Brooke is going to hate me that much more, but I'm doing it to prove a point.

I reluctantly let her hands go, skating backwards and widening the gap between us. Brooke loses her balance and falls right on her ass.

"Ow, geez what the heck Lawson?" Brooke basically growls at

me. I feel like I am getting scolded...and that makes me smile even more. To the point where I let out a laugh.

"Will you help me up, please?" Brooke says. "Instead of standing there laughing like an asshole who just witnessed his best friend's sister make a complete fool of herself?"

"I don't think Miss Beckett should be saying words like asshole," I whisper in her ear as I grab her hand and elbow and lift her up.

"Well maybe someone, who knows I don't know how to skate, shouldn't let me fall," she says through her teeth.

"I didn't let you fall. You fell all on your own. But look, you got back up. You survived the thing you were most afraid of." She finally looks intently in my eyes. She actually looks like she is letting me in, even if just for a moment. She clutches my forearms, her eyes scanning my body. Her cheeks are getting pinker and I want to file it away into my core memories, because they aren't an angry shade of pink. It's almost like she is blushing.

Before I know it, my back hits the sideboards and we aren't skating anymore. Yet, Brooke's fingers are still digging into my forearms. Her face has definitely softened since she first stepped into the rink. Her eyes divert from mine for a split second and make their way down to my own lips.

"Thank you," she says softly.

"Hold on, I don't think I heard you correctly. Did you just thank me, Cupcake?"

"Yes, I did. And now I instantly regret it based on that stupid smug look on your face."

"No, no, you can't take it back." I am smiling so hard right now that my cheeks are hurting. "What exactly are you thanking me for?"

"Having me face what I am most afraid of."

Behind me, I sense there are people skating toward us and fast. Dean must be showboating with another one of our teammates and it got a little out of control. "Guys, watch it!"

I grab Brooke's arms and whip her around. I pin her against the sideboards.

A second later, the idiots do run into me; my body presses into Brooke. Since I am not wearing my usual gear, I can feel everything about Brooke's body through her many layers of clothes. I swallow hard as I concentrate on calming my dick down so that Brooke doesn't realize how turned on I am with her body up against mine for the first time ever in our lives. That's when I notice how red Brooke is getting and I process where we are in the rink. I have pinned Brooke against the sideboard of the penalty box. And then I remember the text she sent me about having a sex dream where I was fucking her in said penalty box. My mind starts wandering with thoughts about what I was doing to her in that dream and my dick is just getting harder. I am never going to see the penalty box the same again. Now, anytime I see one, Brooke's flushed face will come to mind.

Brooke looks back at what she is pinned up against. I smile as she turns redder. She is full of embarrassment and I can't help but smile. She looks fucking adorable.

She buries her face in her hands. "Oh my God, that was so scary. I need to get off the ice...now." She peers through her hands at me. "Why are you looking at me like that, Hot Shot?"

"This particular spot reminds me of something."

She registers what I am referring to and bats her eyes wildly–do I make her nervous? "Well, stop. You are looking at me like..."

"Like what, Cupcake?" I lean a little closer. I am intrigued about the next words to come out of her mouth.

"Sorry guys, just got carried away with Jagielski. The kids bet on who would win a race."

Dammit. Is there a way to make someone magically disappear?

Dean props his arm up against the sideboard and glues his eyes on Brooke, then looks at me. "Am I interrupting something?"

Yeah asshole, you are. "No, just teaching Beckett here how to ice skate."

"Oh really? And you trusted this guy to teach you?" He nods in my direction. *Dick.* "Why didn't you ask me, Brooke? I am a much smoother skater than Lawson." *Yeah, he wishes.*

Brooke clears her throat and tucks some hair behind her ear, "Um, I don't know. These lessons were kind of last-minute and... unexpected. I think time's up anyway. I need to wrangle up the kids to go back to school." She shoots me a look that makes my insides fucking melt. I crave more time with her. "Can you move your arm out of the way, Hot Shot?"

I forgot that my arm is blocking her way out of this bubble we created for ourselves. I reluctantly move my arm. Brooke holds onto the sideboards for dear life and slowly makes her way to the entrance to the rink.

"What game are you playing, Lawson?"

I pretend ignorance. "I have no idea what you mean, man." I start picking up the orange cones we use for drills.

"I mean, why the fuck are you giving Brooke ice skating lessons? I thought you hated her."

My stomach drops. "I do." I stack the orange cones, reach down and place them on the ground on the side of the rink.

"Doesn't seem like it. You were looking at her like you wanted to fuck her brains out. I mean, I get it. That's exactly what I am going to do after Casino Night."

I grab him by his sweatshirt and pin him against the boards. "Have some fucking respect. That's Beckett's little sister." I let him go, pushing him in the process. "Why do you want her so bad, anyway? You can have any girl. Why Brooke?"

"Oh, I struck a chord with you. Interesting. Now why is that, Lawson? Is it because Brooke is like a sister to you, too? Or is it because you actually don't hate her and want her for yourself?"

I am fuming. I am showing so much restraint. I want to kick this prick's ass so badly, but he's not worth it. But one thing I know is true: if he so much as lays a hand on Brooke, I won't show any more restraint toward him.

"I hope it's the second option," Hastings continues, "because it will be so much sweeter when I win this bet. I am closing the deal with Brooke at Casino Night. Are you ready to call me captain, Lawson?"

"That's not happening, Hastings. Like I told you before, she won't break her rule. Never has and never will."

I skate toward the locker room with a smug smile on my face because that's the safest bet I could make. She won't break her rule.

She can't break her rule.

12

Brooke

"I cannot believe that you don't go to your brother's games more often. I would be at every single game if I had the chance. Hockey players are hot."

I roll my eyes at Tess. When I told her that I needed someone to go with me to see a hockey game, she did not hesitate. Tess was right when she said that my rule was dumb and I think it's time to break it. Hastings seems like a viable option, especially since he asked if I was going to Casino Night and kissed my hand before he left the other day at school. Plus, it will bother the hell out of Tristan, which is always fun.

But, I was not about to face Hastings alone. I needed my hype woman next to me. She showed up at my doorstep with Dean's jersey in hand.

"You did not have to get me Dean's jersey. I have a jersey with my own last name on it."

"Well, I figured since you are possibly interested in him, you might as well wear his jersey. He may find it hot. Hockey men love when their women wear their jerseys."

Tess apparently harassed Bradley to give us tickets close to the ice–so there we are, sitting basically right behind the Storm bench.

Another reason I don't go to games all that much, other than my rule, is that it's really hard to watch my brother get slammed into the sideboards or pummeled in fist fights. No matter how much he used to get on my nerves growing up, I don't want to see him physically hurt. But I guess that's the choice he made when he decided to pursue a hockey career.

"Welcome your Dallas Storm!" Music blasts through the arena speakers. Fans are screaming at the top of their lungs.

"Thanks for coming with me, Tess!" I yell over the chaos. The lights are flashing and I can barely hear anything over the crowd as the team starts making their way onto the ice.

"Always, girl. Oh look, there's your soon-to-be man." She points toward the ice while taking a sip of her beer. She wiggles her eyebrows like a silly school girl telling me that my crush is on the other side of the playground.

I shake my head and look onto the ice. Dean lines up next to Jageilski, and he is looking over in our direction. Then a number that I am all-too-familiar with–92–appears next to Dean. My brother follows suit next to Tristan. Dean taps Tristan on his peck and leans toward him to tell him something. Tristan's eyebrows pull together and then makes direct eye contact with me.

As the resident singer belts out The Star Spangled Banner, I try my very best to not look onto the ice at all. I have a feeling that someone is staring at me, and unfortunately I don't think it is my brother or the guy whose jersey I am wearing.

After the crowd sits down and the lights come back on, Tess leans over to me. "God, Tristan must really hate you, girl."

I gasp as if I am surprised by this news. "You don't say!" I take a sip of my beer.

"It was like daggers were piercing into your soul the whole time the national anthem was going on."

"Classic Tristan Lawson. He has no other look for me." Except for the first night I met him.

The first period seems to last forever. Neither team has scored. I swear, every time I see Bradley get slammed into the sideboards, I wince. I don't know how Jen does it. I really do hate to see my brother get hurt all the time. At least they are only on the ice for a minute tops, maybe even less. It feels like an eternity, though.

Now I am sitting up close so I get to hear all the fun expletives and trash-talking. I smile when I see someone slam into Tristan or when he trips up. He also gets this very intense look when he is on the ice that I never noticed before. He is very focused. Even though I hate his guts, I can't help but appreciate his dedication. Bradley has been talking non-stop at Sunday night dinners about how the captain's spot is about to be available and how much he thinks Tristan deserves it. He is already an alternate, so anytime the current captain is not on the ice, he is the one who takes responsibility or confronts the referee if there is an unfair call.

He is a fan favorite for sure. I scan the stands around me and 90 percent of the people are wearing Tristan's jersey. Some fangirls are even wearing the jersey with I assume shorts underneath, but at first glance it appears they are just wearing the jersey...and nothing else. I'm sure he loves that.

The buzzer goes off and the players skate off the ice. Dean waves over at me and smiles. I quickly acknowledge him with a wave and pull out my phone from my back pocket.

"I have to run to the restroom," Tess says. "I know it's not an ideal time because everyone is there, but I really need to go! Do you want anything from the concessions before I come back? More beer?"

I look at my almost-empty plastic cup and say, "Yes and can you get a pretzel with extra cheese please."

"You got it! I'll be back."

"Thanks!" I try to open Instagram to mindlessly scroll, but alas I have no service because EVERYONE is on their phones. I turn my phone over and rock my leg back and forth. Then I get a notification. I'm assuming it's a text from Tess.

I was wrong.

> Tell me the number.

Why the hell is Tristan texting me in the middle of a game? Shouldn't he be recovering or something? Wiping off that disgusting sweat that is no doubt dripping down his body?

> The number of what?

Three dots load immediately. What is he playing at? This is a weird game that I don't know if I want to play with him. Then a gray bubble appears on the bottom left hand side of my screen.

> The number of goals I need to score in order for you to take off that fucking jersey that doesn't have my name on it.

My jaw drops as I read that text message over and over again. *Take off that fucking jersey that doesn't have my name on it?* Is he serious? Why would I ever wear his jersey? Over my dead body, Lawson. But if he wants a number, I'll give him a nearly impossible one. I may not come to a lot of games, but I know all the hockey terminology. Time to get into his head.

My fingers move across the keyboard.

> I'll tell you what Hot Shot: if you get a pure hat trick, I'll do whatever you want.

About a minute passes by before a response. Maybe he realized that he isn't as good as he thought. Maybe he realized how ridiculous that last text message to me was. I smugly sit back into the arena seat.

A moment later, I get a text that makes me very nervous. Because if there are two other things I know about Tristan Lawson is that he loves to play games and he loves a good challenge. And the scary thing is, he usually wins at both.

I'll hold you to that, Cupcake.

My face grows hot again at the possibility that Tristan could pull a pure hat trick off. I am praying so hard that he doesn't, because I am terrified of what he would make me do other than take this jersey off.

I try to calm down by reminding myself that statistics are on my side with this one. There is a slim chance that Tristan will score three goals in a row with no one else scoring in between. That's why I was so comfortable betting that he would be unsuccessful.

"Are you okay?" Tess interjects, breaking into my thoughts.

I stand up so she can get back to her seat. I click the side of my phone and put it in my back pocket. She hands me my new beer and the delicious pretzel with cheese. "Yeah, I'm fine."

"Really? Because you look like someone just gave you the worst news possible."

With Tristan Lawson, I fear that's not too far off. I shouldn't have provoked him. He's dangerous when he is provoked.

ONCE TRISTAN COMES BACK onto the ice, there is an intensity in his eyes that supersedes anything that I have ever seen before. Within the first minute of the third period, he glides fluidly and swiftly towards the goal and scores. Less than a minute later, he scores again. And out of what seems like pure luck in the last five minutes of the game, he scores one more time. After his final goal and his celebratory embrace with his team, he looks up and winks at me. My stomach does a somersault. I try to convince myself it's because he won the challenge and my body is reacting to defeat—not because that wink lit a spark that I haven't felt since the night I met him.

I HEAD HOME right after the game because I have to start baking cupcakes for my coworker's child's fourth birthday party.

The second batch is in the oven when I hear a knock at my door. That's weird, I didn't get a notification that someone needed to be let in. I walk over to the door, lean against the wood, and say, "Who is it?"

"It's me, Cupcake."

I jump back from the door. Why is Tristan here? Doesn't he have to recover from tonight's game? What does he want? Another knock breaks me out of my head.

"Are you going to open the door, Cupcake, or are you going to keep me out here looking like a creep in front of your neighbors?"

Tempting. I exhale and swing open the door. At the sight of him, my heart starts to flutter and my ears get hot. And I can't shake the feeling that it isn't because of my hatred for Tristan. Did I mention how unfair it is that he looks the way he does? He smells freshly clean, with a hint of cedar and mint. He is wearing a backwards hat and his dark, wavy hair is peeking out underneath the sides. His intricate sleeves are on full display, along with the protruding manly veins on his forearms and semi-exposed biceps. My God, even fully clothed, he still evokes a silly reaction from my body, namely between my fucking legs. No matter, I am pushing those thoughts away to the ends of the earth because that would never happen in a bazillion years.

I block the entrance to my apartment. He's not coming in here that easy. Not if I have any say or control. "What are you doing here, Tristan?"

He looks down at me and his eyes turn dark when he sees that I am still wearing Dean's jersey. In the midst of racing home to beat the insane traffic from downtown and needing some baking therapy, I didn't take off that jersey. Granted, I didn't think that Tristan would check on whether or not that I did. Dammit.

"I scored a pure hat trick."

I cock my eyebrow up, trying to look tough while wearing an oversized green hockey jersey and a bubble-gum pink knotted headband. Tim Gunn would not approve.

Why did I agree to do whatever he wants? If he has his way, he is going to make me do something embarrassing in public. Or make me touch a spider–my absolute worst fear, after skating. I hate spiders. Almost as much as I hate this man standing in front of me. There is a devilish look in his eyes as he steps inside and closes the door behind him. Great. He is probably plotting something extra devious for me to do.

"All right, you win, Hot Shot. Since I lost, what do you want me to do?"

Avoiding answering the question, he moves past me and points towards the kitchen. "It smells great in here. Are you making cupcakes?"

"Um, yeah. For one of my coworker's little girl's birthday party." I lock the door and watch as Tristan runs a finger through one of the frosted cupcakes and sticks it in his mouth. The way my mouth is probably hanging open, one would think that I am watching that scene from *Bridgerton* where the Duke is licking the damn spoon, because it is giving me the same stupid tingly feeling all across my body. No one should look that hot licking his finger clean of frosting. But of course, Tristan Lawson would. It's a cruel joke from the universe that my enemy has to be so irresistible at times.

Before I can snatch the cupcake from his massive hands, he does something that stops me in my tracks. He licks around the top of the cupcake, disseminating any frosting in its wake. It paralyzes me and my face gets extra hot. Thank God it's a little warm in here because of the oven being on for the past hour or so. I can definitely blame the oven. I need to blame the oven.

"Mmmm," Tristan finally utters. "You've gotten better."

"Is this the price? You stealing a four-year-old's cupcake?"

"Not even close." He places what's left of the chocolate cupcake down on the counter and meets me halfway. My body is nearly flush against his. If I thought it was hot in my apartment before, it feels like an inferno now. "I figured since I scored three times tonight, you have to do three things for me."

Oh God, here it comes. He's going to make me streak or write on my face with a permanent marker a la Ross and Rachel in Vegas, or something equally embarrassing.

I sigh. "Okay, shoot. What do I have to do, Hot Shot?"

He licks his lips and for some reason, that small action makes me want to lick his lips, too. What is happening? This is Tristan Lawson. My enemy for the past decade. I should not want to lick his lips and discover what he tastes like. *Should* being the most important word.

I cross my arms and stick out a hip, hopefully giving off an annoyed and pissed-off vibe. I desperately hope that it covers up how turned on I am right now. "Ugh, fine, tell me what I have to do." Before he opens his mouth I add, rather plead, "But please, if I can request no spiders. I am deathly afraid of spiders."

He inhales sharply, raises his eyebrows, and inches closer to me and says, almost sultrily, "I can't guarantee that, Cupcake. You're just going to have to trust me."

My eyes flutter at how close he is getting. He is popping my innermost personal bubble, and instead of pushing him away, I am just letting it happen because I do not have the strength to fight him. Not right now.

"That's the problem, I don't trust you."

"Too bad." His eyes are so dark I swear every ounce of hazel has escaped them. Then he pulls something out of his jogger's pocket. I can't quite make out what it is until he places this object in my palm. I unravel the piece of fabric and see that it's a tie. I look back up at him and raise an eyebrow. "A tie? What is this for?"

"No more questions. Just do what I say."

Well damn. I've never been ordered around like this before, but am realizing at this very moment how much I might like it. Although I am still confused, I nod. "Continue."

He steps forward, erasing what's left of the space between us. Then he grabs the side of my arms and presses me against the counter. I sharply inhale as I lock eyes with Tristan, tightly grasping the tie in my hand. My legs are buckling at the sight of this man. He has bulked up these past ten years and his enormous arms are now locking me on either side of me, his hands gripping the counter as if his life depends on it. My breath is uneasy, mimicking my insides.

"First, I need you to take off that fucking jersey," he growls. To his credit, that is how this whole thing started. Thankfully, I am wearing a sports bra crop top underneath and don't just have a bra on. Like hell I am getting completely naked in front of Tristan Lawson. I don't care if my body is betraying me right now and desperately wanting the opposite to happen.

With the limited space between us, I manage to grab the hem of the jersey and attempt to take it off my body. It gets stuck on my knotted headband and I struggle with getting it up over my head. I hear a deep chuckle from the other side of the fabric and before I know it, the jersey is free and dropped to the floor along with my headband. Great. My hair is probably sticking up at all ends. Is this what he wants? To see me embarrassed? Because he is doing a great job.

As I raise my hand to fix my hair, Tristan's strong hand grips my wrist and stops me. "Don't. I like seeing you like this."

"Like what?"

"All disheveled. It's hot."

Did Tristan Lawson just call me hot? I don't understand what is coming out of that perfect mouth of his but I am not *not* liking it.

"Okay, jersey's off, Hot Shot. Happy? What's two?"

He grins, clears his throat and says, "Put that tie around your eyes and prop yourself up on this counter. And make sure it's tight, Cupcake. No peeking."

My heart starts to race. I want to protest because I want to see every ounce of this man that I can. I can't explain the shift that has happened in the span of ten minutes, but I have a feeling that we are past the point of no return.

I jump up on the counter, take the tie and knot it behind my head. Forget the spiders. A new fear has been unlocked. I am at the hands of my enemy and I have no defenses at my disposal. Oddly enough, I feel the safest I've ever felt in front of Tristan, despite me saying that I didn't trust him mere minutes ago.

"This is a weird request, even for you Lawson." I scoot my butt from side to side to make sure I am stable on this counter. Another chuckle escapes his lips and I can clearly visualize the stupid smug grin he has on his stupidly handsome face. I can sense him move away from me. A second later, I can smell the scent of a chocolate cupcake in front of me. Great, he's going to smash all my cupcakes in my face, take a photo and leave me to clean up the mess. He would.

"Why do you have a cupcake in your hand? You're about to smash it in my face, aren't you?"

"Stop asking questions. Only answer them." Geez bossy. Again, I am not hating it like I should. "Now answer me, yes or no."

What? "Yes or no what?"

"Uh uh, Cupcake. No asking questions, remember? Just yes or no?"

My head is screaming, *NO! Don't do it! He is the bane of your existence! He is the disgusting playboy that you've known for ten years. More importantly, he is a hockey player. The very same hockey player that made you make your hard and fast rule in the first place. Don't do it, Brooke!*

But my body is telling me something entirely different. It's screaming YES. Then I feel Tristan lean in and brush his lips against my ear. His breath causes my entire body to shiver and my breathing becomes erratic. "Yes or no. I need you to answer me, Cupcake."

Eagerly, I say, "Yes."

"Good girl. Right answer." Then I feel his fingers mess with the button on my jeans. Just when I thought I wasn't going to get naked in front of this man, I guess I was wrong.

"Tristan, what are you doing?"

Obviously not acknowledging my question, he unzips and pulls down my jeans until they are completely off my body. I thank my lucky stars that I wore cute underwear today. Lace bubblegum pink ones in fact. "I see we are into matching, are we?" Shit, he noticed too. I wouldn't have expected Tristan to notice something like that.

"We are, in fact. Do you have a problem with that, Hot Shot?" I can't help but be quippy with him after all these years.

Evading my question again, he continues, "These are sexy panties. Were you expecting someone to see them, Cupcake?"

"Maybe I was expecting a fine gentleman suitor to come by and ravish me." Okay, I need to stop binging *Bridgerton.* "You know, just like you were expecting that ice girl the other night. What was her name again? Alison?"

I wish I could see his reaction. Every other sense around me is heightened now that I can't see anything in front of me. The man isn't even touching my skin and it's tingly all over. I know that once he does touch me, I will most likely combust at this rate.

"Open that pretty mouth of yours."

I pause for a few seconds, contemplating if I should rip this damn tie off my face and tell him to get lost. But that's not what I do at all. I do as I am told. I open my mouth and the next thing I taste is frosting on my tongue. "Now lick and suck the frosting off like a good girl."

I do as I am told and even though this frosting is delicious, it's what's underneath the frosting that I am now starting to crave. I want that massive finger in a very different part of my body right now.

"Holy shit," Tristan whispers as I continue to suck on his finger, teasing him a little with my tongue. Two can play at this game, Lawson.

I release his finger, bite my lower lip and say, "Mmm. You're right, I have gotten better."

Just when I think I have the one-up on him, his hands grab my knees and spread my legs apart. I let out a gasp at the sudden motion. "I want to taste some more, Cupcake." The next thing I feel is frosting being placed in my inner thighs. The cool sensation feels amazing against my thighs that are ablaze right now. My body involuntarily inches closer to the edge of the counter, yearning for Tristan to touch me, in any way, again.

Almost like he can read my mind, I feel his hands wrap around both my thighs and his hot breath against my skin. His tongue traces the trail of frosting he made for himself, coming dangerously close to my pussy with each lick, making me even more wet than I already am. He continues on the other side and stops short after the last lick of frosting. "Fuck," is all I hear him mutter.

"Why did you stop?" My voice sounds breathy.

"I want to take you in like this."

"And how is that? Defenseless and blindfolded?" I say sarcastically.

"No, fucking beautiful and perfect."

What is happening right now? How did we get in this situation? I blame Bradley for ever meeting Tristan in the first place. I would be happily baking cupcakes right now, probably watching *The Great British Bake Off*, instead of sitting in my underwear on my countertop with the hottest hockey player in the world in between my legs, who just happens to be my arch nemesis. Not that this doesn't make me happy. It absolutely does. I am just confused. I thought he hated me.

"Can I take this tie off, please?" I plead. I need to see his face right now. I hate that I can't see his eyes. "Sure," he says, presumably still kneeling on the ground between my thighs. I rip the blindfold off, undoubtedly making my hair even more disheveled. According to his standards, I must look like a goddess by now. When I look down at Tristan, his eyes are even more ravenous. He gazes at me like I am a damn snack. And I don't hate it. No man has ever looked at me the way that Tristan is looking at me right now.

"Why are you looking at me like that, Lawson?"

He stands up and meets my gaze. "Like what?"

"Like I'm a fucking gazelle and you are a lion. Like you want to devour me."

"I do want to devour you. And I am glad you took off that blindfold because I want to see your whole face when I make you come, Cupcake."

Tristan lowers me down onto the counter and scoots me closer to the edge. He places my legs on top of his muscular shoulders and grasps my thighs even tighter. He's taking his sweet time and it's driving me crazy. He gently kisses slow trails down my inner thighs. He rubs his hand over my panties and my hips lift as I whimper.

"You like that, Cupcake?"

"Yes."

"Good." He slides my panties down my legs and throws them to the ground, alongside the rest of my clothes. I feel two of his fingers slide inside of me and I let out a moan. I rock my hips as he is fingering me. He touches my clit and continues to pound his fingers into me. "I feel your pussy getting tighter."

All I can do is nod.

"Go ahead and come on my fingers like the good girl you are."

I've never done anything like this before. I've really only had sex in a bed and it's always been so calculated. So predictable. I'm always in my head during sex. Not now. My heart is racing and I feel my entire body getting flushed by what Tristan is saying and doing to me. Even though this is anything but predictable, I want to give in. I want to let go of control for once.

And I do just that.

"That was the best fucking thing I've ever seen," Tristan

whispers. "You have no idea how long I've been waiting to see you come."

My chest is heaving and I drape my arm over my eyes. That was hands-down the best orgasm of my life.

"Now stay right there and keep your legs open for me. It's my turn to taste you." Tristan gives me a devilish grin and before I can come back with some sort of snarky statement, I feel his tongue against my wet pussy. God, this man knows how to work his tongue. He pulls my thighs closer to him and my heels dig into his back. I can hear him let out a moan and it's the sexiest moan I've ever heard in my life. It only fuels my need for him.

"Oh my god, Tristan. Don't stop!"

"Not planning on it, Cupcake. You taste so fucking good."

This man is going to be the death of me. I prop up on my forearms to see the man I've hated for so long go down on me and I love that he is practically on his knees for me and making sure that I am feeling good. He is treating me like a goddess and I've never had that in my life. So many thoughts are rolling around in my head. All the implications of this. *What does this mean? Is this just a one-time thing? Am I okay with that if it is? What if all he wants is sex? I am not that kind of girl. Never have been and even though this man is the hottest thing to walk this earth, I am not about to change for him. I want more than just this.*

"Stop."

He pulls back, confusion knitting his brow. "What?"

"Overthinking."

He growls, "I need you to come on my face, Cupcake, and you overthinking isn't going to help that become a reality. Just relax."

And just like that, his tongue is against me while his finger rubs my clit and my body releases for the second time tonight. Is he trying to recreate what he did on the ice tonight and execute a pure hat trick with me, too? I am not opposed to that at all. I collapse back onto the counter and try to slow my breathing.

"That's my good girl," Tristan says in a deep voice. God is this guy trying to ruin me with his mouth?

I exhale and lift myself up on my forearms again. Confused, I say, "You just said *my* good girl." I've never heard Tristan talk about any girl being *his* girl and he just uttered those words to *me*. Me. His sworn enemy.

Are we enemies with benefits now? Is that even a thing? Or are we more than that?

A dark grin takes over his mouth. His eyes are pitch black, consumed by hunger and passion and all the things I don't expect to see in the eyes of my enemy. "That's right, Cupcake. Because here on out, that's what you are. Mine."

Before I can even process what he said, there is a knock at my door that makes us both jump.

"Who the hell is at your door at eleven at night?"

I shake my head. I have no idea who is at my door. Then I hear Bradley's voice: "Brooke? Are you awake?"

Shit. All the blood drains from my face. "Um, just a moment!" I jump down from the counter and frantically grab my clothes from the floor.

"Should I go answer it?" Tristan says, grinning.

I jump into my jeans. "Don't you dare!" I whisper and give him a death glare. "Do you want to die tonight? Because that's what's going to happen if my brother ever finds out about..."

Tristan crosses his arms, clearly amused by my flustered state and awaiting the next words that come out of my mouth.

"About whatever just happened."

I start to put my arms through Dean's jersey and just as quickly, it is snatched from my hands.

"I never want to see you in this jersey ever again. It belongs in the fucking garbage. Not on your gorgeous body, Cupcake." He throws the jersey in the trash.

"Brooke, what the hell is taking you so long? Wait, ew, is there a guy in your apartment? Should I come back?"

My mouth slacks open as Tristan is covering his mouth, attempting to stifle a laugh. I place my headband back on my head and say, "Yes... I mean no!" My voice goes up an octave as I panic. Tristan needs to hide now. "Just a second!" I yell back at my door. My neighbors probably hate me.

I turn back to Tristan. "You need to disappear."

"There's no way out of here, Cupcake. Unfortunately, I am not a Navy Seal. I can't scale the walls of the building and make it down safely."

"Fine. But stay behind the door and I'll get rid of my brother."

We both walk over to the door and I silently instruct Tristan to stand behind the door. Surprisingly, he does as he is told. Maybe he doesn't want to die after all. I take a deep breath, flatten out my hair as much as I can and pull down my crop top as low as it can go and hope to God Bradley leaves as soon as possible.

I finally open the door and only expose my head in Bradley's sightline. "Hey Bradley, what's up, bro? What are you doing here at 11 p.m.? Isn't Jen waiting for you?"

"Why did it take you so long to answer your door? And why are you so flushed?"

That's when I feel a hand slowly slide up my leg. What the hell is Tristan doing? He clearly has a death wish. Even if Bradley doesn't kill him, I might.

"Um I was...baking." Not a complete lie. Tristan's hand keeps creeping up my inner thigh and he grasps it, stopping short of where I want his hand to end up. I have to keep a straight face. If Bradley knew that his best friend and teammate was right behind this door, touching his sister in ways that made her feel alive, it would be a bloodbath.

"What do you need? I was about done with baking and am so tired."

"Just wanted to check in with you. You kind of bolted after the game and you weren't answering your texts. Sorry, I'm just protective of you and I was honestly kind of surprised you were at the game in the first place. And wearing Hastings' jersey." He has an accusatory look in his eye. What if I was starting to date Dean? What would Bradley do?

Tristan's hold on my inner thigh tightens.

"Yeah. I just want to support you a little more. You know hockey isn't my thing but it's yours and you've always supported my dreams of becoming a baker full-time. And as for the jersey, Tess had an extra one in her car because I forgot yours before I left for work this morning. But you don't have to worry about me wearing his jersey anymore."

"Okay, well, thanks I guess. About time you come to more of my games! It means a lot that you are supporting me. I know how much you hate hockey."

I shrug. "It's not as bad as I thought."

Tristan's hand inches dangerously close to where his tongue was earlier. I need Bradley to leave *now*!

"Anyway, Brad, I am so tired. I am heading to bed. Thanks for checking up on me. It means the world."

"Okay, I'll let you go to bed. Love you sis!"

"Love you, too." I close the door, lock it and smack Tristan's hand away. "What the actual hell? Why would you touch me like that?"

Tristan grins. "Like what, Cupcake."

I squint my eyes and scoff, "You know like what. I don't have to tell you."

"I think that you do."

"I think it's time for you to go, Hot Shot. You have stayed long enough. You got what you came for." I begin to unlock the door and Tristan's giant hand stops me.

"Are you sure you want me to leave?"

No? Yes? Definitely, yes. I can't be alone with this man. It's too dangerous. Especially now that I know what he is capable of.

I look up at Tristan's face and he subtly licks his lips and his eyes are hungry again. I don't trust myself around him and I have to come to grips about who is standing in front of me. I am too scared to think of the implications of us hooking up more than we already have. I have had a preview of what this man is like in the bedroom and it has shifted everything. The solid, bolded line of hate is beginning to thin out a little.

Do I want him to leave? No. I gulp. "Yes."

I don't know what it is, but Tristan's eyes shift from hungry to defeated once those words come out of my mouth. He brushes his finger along my jawline, causing goosebumps to scatter across my body, and lifts up my chin so I can't escape his gaze. He leans in and pauses right before his lips touch mine. My body tingles from his touch and I close my eyes, waiting for his lips to land on mine. Instead he moves his face along my cheek and tickles me with his scruff, then whispers, "Okay. I know you have a long day tomorrow. Good luck at the birthday party, Cupcake."

13

Tristan

"All right, I will, Ma. Yeah, I will bring her some soup or something. I'll check in on her. Okay, love you, bye." Bradley hangs up his phone. "Shit."

"What's the matter? What did your mom have to say?"

"I guess Brooke is sick. She has a really bad cold. She went to urgent care thinking it was a sinus infection and thankfully it wasn't. I guess a lot of kids at her school have been sick. The doctor prescribed her some medicine but my mom wants me to go and check in on her since my parents are out of town and she can't go over herself."

I was wondering why Brooke was MIA the past few days. I thought she got really freaked out by what happened between us on her kitchen counter and she never wanted to see me again. But, it wasn't me. Hopefully. I need to see her.

I clear my throat. "So, when are you going over to check in on her?"

Bradley stuffs his duffle bag with dirty clothes and grabs his keys. "Right after I am done here. I will stop by the pharmacy to pick up her prescription and get some canned chicken noodle soup or something."

Brooke hates canned chicken noodle soup. I remember her being sick for one of the Becketts' Sunday night dinners years ago. Mrs. Beckett was making homemade chicken noodle soup, and she commented that Brooke hated canned soup ever since she was little. Apparently she threw it on the floor when she was in her high chair at the age of two. Even back then, she was stubborn and headstrong. "How long are you going to be over there?"

"Not very. Just long enough to make sure she is alive and then I'll head out. I don't want to catch this cold. It's been spreading around like wildfire."

"Wow. Brooke is so lucky to have such a great, caring big brother," I say sarcastically.

Evidently, Bradley doesn't catch my drift or he chooses to ignore it. "I know, right? She is lucky. Anyway, I'll see you tomorrow, bro." He reaches out and I meet his hand with mine and give him a fistbump.

I WAIT a couple of hours and then head to Brooke's house. Luckily one of Brooke's neighbors lets me into the apartment building when they see I had my hands full. Between a hot medicine ball from Starbucks and a couple of plastic bags filled with Brooke's favorite ramen and cold supplies, I can't really open the door, let alone hit the buzzer to come up. I reach apartment 309 and I hear laughing coming from Brooke's TV through the door. I also hear Brooke's cute stuffy laugh. Knowing her, she is probably watching reruns of *Friends*. I smile and knock. I hear her groan and say, "Ugh, Bradley, I literally just got comfortable. And now I have to get up from the couch and open the door and..."

The door swings open and reveals a very sick but still beautiful Brooke. Her nose is super red and her eyes look puffy. Her shoulders are wrapped in a fuzzy pink checkered blanket and her hair is in a messy braid hanging over her shoulder. She is in light gray sweatpants and an oversized shirt that says *This is a jumbo coffee morning*. There are loose tendrils framing her face. I can tell that she is surprised to see me.

She sniffles and holds up a crinkled tissue to her nose. "What are you doing here?"

"Well hello to you too, Cupcake."

She raises her eyebrows, unamused. It's scary how much she looks like Bradley when she does that.

"Um, I overheard Bradley talking with your mom about you being sick. I just wanted..." *To see that you are okay. To hold you until you fall asleep. To fucking breathe the same air as you because I miss you so damn much and I can't stop thinking about the other night.* All of the above, really, but I'll stick to the first reason. The reason most likely to not have her running away from me or slamming the door in my face. "To check on you. Sounded like a pretty bad cold to have you down and out for a few days."

Her furrowed brows soften a bit and she looks down at my hands. She points to the plastic take-out bag. "What's in the bag, Hot Shot?" she says in a stuffy voice.

I let out a small laugh, relieved she put down whatever ammunition she was holding up the moment she saw it was me at her door. "Well, first, I brought you a medicine ball. Heard these things are great for colds." Her lips curl slightly as she takes the hot Starbucks cup from my outstretched hand. Our fingers brush and it sends an electric current through my entire body. Jesus, I need her, but now is hardly the time. I'm sure I am the last thing on her mind.

"Thank you." She takes a small sip. Her tired eyes meet mine and go straight back to the plastic bag. "The bag?"

"Oh, right, I stopped by that ramen spot that you wouldn't shut up about at Sunday dinners for the past two years. You like the spicy one, right?" She slowly nods. "I thought it would be better than that disgusting canned chicken noodle soup that I'm sure Bradley brought you earlier."

There's my favorite smirk in the world spreading across Brooke's face. "You're right. Ramen is way better. Thank you." She opens the door wider, gesturing for me to come in. I walk past her couch and lo and behold, I was right. *Friends* is on. I place the bags on her kitchen counter and since I know she is hopeless with chopsticks, I take out forks from the silverware drawer. Her house smells like cinnamon apple pie and that's when I notice the candle burning on her coffee table. "You know that it's the end of winter, right? Why the hell are you burning a fall-scented candle in the middle of February?"

"What are you, the candle police? I love the smell. It brings me comfort, okay?" She wipes her nose again.

"Can you actually smell anything right now? By the sound of your voice and the redness of your nose, Rudolph, I bet you can't."

She punches my arm and then immediately shakes her hand off. When will she ever learn? "Ow, dammit. Is this your idea of making me feel better? You are doing a hell of a job, Hot Shot."

I thought that Brooke's regular voice was the best thing I've ever heard. Brooke's raspy sick voice is making a case against that fact.

"Oh so you're saying you don't want this delicious ramen? Or the Vicks vapor rub? Or the boxes of Kleenex, which by the look of your couch and coffee table, you are running out of? Or the extra box of tea that I bought you, with some local honey?" I raise an eyebrow and look down at the cutest girl I've ever known.

"I didn't say that." She takes out large soup bowls and assembles her ramen. She swipes the fork from my hand and mixes her food around. She huffs as she offers me a bowl so I can do the same thing. Then in her very raspy voice, she says, "Thank you, again."

"You're welcome."

Brooke adjusts the blanket so it covers the top of her head, causing her to look like a shepherd. She slowly makes her way back to her living room and places her giant bowl of ramen on the coffee table. I join her on the ground and I am about to dig in when I notice that Brooke looks like she is about to throw up.

"What's wrong? Do I need to go get a trash can?"

"I am scared to eat this," she says plainly.

"Why? I got the right one, didn't I?" I thought she loved this one specifically. Brooke went to this restaurant so much that she was considered a regular. Knowing this information, I described what Brooke looked like, even went so far as showing the waitress a picture, and asked what she normally gets. They recognized her immediately and knew exactly what she wanted.

"Yes. I am just scared that you put something in it."

"Brooke..."

"What? What if you thought: Hey this is the perfect opportunity to get rid of Brooke for good. She's sick and people would never suspect a poisoning or maybe they would just add it up to food poisoning going terribly wrong. Also, the other night was strategically planned out. I was playing mind games with her. Her guard is down now that we basically slept together without actually sleeping together, she won't think anything of it. I have her right where I want her. She'll trust that I am being a good guy, or she'll suspect that something is off and I'll just lie and say that her ramen isn't poisoned but it totally is." She shoots daggers in my direction.

I laugh so hard it makes my stomach hurt and tears start coming out of my eyes.

"What?" she asks, clearly annoyed by my reaction.

"You are spiraling. I am not going to poison you. I did nothing to your ramen. You are being paranoid."

"Am I?" She stirs the ramen, clearly starving. I wonder when she ate last.

"Yes, you goof. Look, I'm eating some too, okay? It can't be poisoned. Now, just shut up and eat your ramen. The broth will help."

"Don't tell me what to do." She blows on the ramen and takes a bite. Relief sets in on her face.

"It tastes normal."

"See, I told you. God you are fucking stubborn."

"No I'm not. You are." She scowls. I shake my head. This woman drives me insane and yet I can't get her out of my head. She sniffles again. I get up and grab the box of tissues I got for her earlier and open it.

I hand her a new tissue. "Here Cupcake."

She snatches the tissue out of my hand and quickly wipes her nose. "Why are you being so nice to me?"

"I'm always nice to you. You're just so used to hating me that you can't see that I am actually a nice person."

"If that's your story, Hot Shot." She sniffles. "You hate me, too."

I need to save face right now. It's not time for her to really know how I feel. I don't want to scare her off or get kicked out of her apartment. I also don't want Bradley to find out and kick my ass. Or at least attempt to kiss my ass. "Right." I go back to my ramen and actively divert my attention to her TV. "So, who is your favorite character?"

Now that she has some sort of sustenance in her system, she is thankfully distracted and her guard is lowering little by little. "Probably Monica. Although I die for Rachel's hair and fashion. If I ever win the lottery, I would buy her entire wardrobe. Or at least a wardrobe that looks similar."

"I don't think she wears nearly enough pink to pass for your wardrobe, Cupcake."

She rolls her eyes then focuses back on the screen. It's the Thanksgiving episode where they play football and try to win the Geller Cup. "Chandler's mine."

She cocks her eyebrow, "You watch *Friends*?"

"Who doesn't watch *Friends*?"

"Crazy people."

"Exactly."

"Chandler makes sense." She shrugs underneath the massive blanket covering her immaculate body. I want to be that blanket. I want to have my arms around her and be the thing that is comforting her. The thing that's keeping her warm.

"So does Monica."

"Why, because she has massive OCD, is super competitive, and is wildly insecure when it comes to her and Ross?"

Although all of those characteristics do fit the bill of Brooke Beckett, they aren't the characteristics I think of. "No, because she is caring, sweet and funny."

Brooke shoots me a shocked look, adjusts in her seat and goes back to eating her ramen.

Shit, was that too much? I try to discreetly shift the conversation. "You know it's interesting."

"What's interesting?" Her eyes don't move from her bowl. She pushes around her noodles aimlessly, almost as if she is trying to distract herself or is overthinking, which is also her speciality.

"Despite the fact that Monica hated Chandler for a bit, they ultimately ended up together."

"Well, you can't blame Monica for hating Chandler. He did call her fat." Brooke's cute little crease in between her eyebrows deepens as if she actually is Monica and someone did call her fat, which would be the craziest thing ever since she has the sexiest body in the world.

"Yeah, but he was only covering up his true feelings for her in front of her older brother." I can feel myself getting defensive.

"No way. He legitimately thought that she was fat. And it was only after she lost all the weight and had a massive glow up that he wanted her."

"There is no way you can definitively prove that. He didn't mean for her to hear that. She wasn't meant to hear that."

"Well, how is she supposed to know that? Plus, some cuts run deeper than others. If someone said something like that to me, it would be hard to get over. Especially if I liked the other person."

We sit and let the ebb and flow of TV laughter fill the silence. At some point, after we both finish our ramen – well, I finish my ramen about fifteen minutes before she does because she eats at a glacial pace – Brooke moves to start gathering up the dishes, but I stop her from getting up. "Don't even think about it, Cupcake. Sit that pretty ass of yours down on that couch and relax."

"You don't get to talk about my ass like that, Hot Shot." She raises up her bowl and I stack it on top of my own empty bowl. She has that pretty scowl on her face, one that I've grown accustomed to over the years. She still has some fire in her, even if it is doused slightly by her illness.

"Oh I think I've earned that right to talk about it like that, don't you?"

Suddenly, her nose isn't the only thing that's red. Her cheeks match and I chuckle on my way to drop the bowls off in the kitchen. I see a small brown bag is unopened, which undoubtedly has her medication inside. "Have you taken your medication yet?"

"Ugh I hate that stuff. It's the worst cold medicine in the world."

"I hate to break it to you, Cupcake, but you kind of have to take medication in order to get better." I take the bottle out of the stapled bag and read the directions. "According to the label, you need to take ten milliliters every eight hours for the next week. So if you want to get some sleep, which by the look of the bags under your eyes, you should – you might need this."

She flips me the bird.

"Look I'm kidding...kind of." I open the cap and pour the necessary amount into the clear medicine cup. I fill up a glass with water and head over to the little couch potato formerly known as Brooke Beckett. I place the medicine cup in front of her. "Here. Drink up."

Her nose scrunches up and she sticks out her tongue. "No way. I'll just let the cold pass all on its own."

"Drink it, Brooke," I say sternly. This woman is like a brick wall.

"You are not the boss of me! You are not my mother or brother, for that matter." She finally scoots up and takes the blanket off the top of her head. Her hair is sticking up from the static electricity. I press my lips together because I have a feeling that if I laugh at her one more time, she will actually throw me out of her apartment.

I lean down so that my forearms are resting on the back of her obnoxious pink couch. "You're right. I'm not and I thank God every day for that, Cupcake. Now drink the damn medicine."

"You're not going to give in, are you?"

"Nope."

"Ugh fine." She takes the cup from my fingers and downs it like a shot. She gags as the liquid makes its way down her throat. I gave her the glass of water to chase it with. I did get a whiff of the stuff and it did smell disgusting. Brooke drinks the water just as fast.

"There, now, that wasn't so bad, was it? Kind of like my company?"

"Your company is worse."

"Ouch."

"Tristan, why are you here? You knew that my brother already came by, so why are you here?"

"I wanted to make sure you weren't going to die on me, Cupcake. Despite what you say about my company, yours isn't so bad."

She curls up in her little corner like a cute little hermit. She continues to sip her medicine ball and lets out a small groan, almost like she is in pain.

"What do you need?"

"For you to go."

"You are the sweetest person I know, Brooke Beckett."

She grabs a coaster from the small basket in the middle of her coffee table and sets her white disposable cup on top of it. Jesus, she is Monica.

"Not a chance in hell I'm just leaving you here like this. Tell me, what is the thing you are wanting about right now but are too scared to tell me? I am here to help you."

Brooke peeks over at me from her corner of the couch. "Well..." She lets out a breath. "There is this thing my mom used to do when I was sick when I was a kid. I would lie on her lap and she would pat my back. I guess when I was a baby that was a way to calm me down and I would fall asleep every time. I still do. But she isn't here and I could never ask you of all people..."

"Go ahead."

"Go ahead what?"

"Ask me."

"Tristan, no."

"You can either come over here willingly or I will make you. It's your choice."

We have one of our epic staredowns. We have perfected these staredowns over time and they always make my heart explode since I have the opportunity to look into her almost purely green eyes – though there are moments when her eyes match her beautiful caramel hair and I get lost in them just the same.

She huffs, scoots her way across the couch toward me, and points at me with a serious look on her face. "Don't get any ideas, Hot Shot. What happened the other night was a one-time thing."

My stomach clenches at the thought that I will never do that to Brooke ever again. That would be my literal hell.

I raised my hands up. "Hey. I didn't say a word. Your mind went there. It must be all those romance books you love to secretly read."

"Oh it's not a secret. I wear those like a badge of honor. You men like to tease but they are actually great manuals for you all on what women want. It's kind of like a playbook in hockey so to speak. If you follow the playbook, there are more chances for a successful game, right?"

Brooke's messy braid is falling out by the second but she pays no mind to it. I like how she is not overly concerned about how she looks or acts around me. She is just Brooke. She grabs one of her many throw pillows, something that I am going to tease her about later (seriously, who needs all these throw pillows?) and places it on my lap and finally gets comfortable. I begin patting her back and I can already feel her breathing find a nice rhythm, and soon her head gets a little heavier on my lap.

"How's that, Cupcake?" I murmur.

"It will suffice for now." Before long, I can hear the faintest snore coming from Brooke. I continue to pat her back and, as always happens when this show is on, I get sucked into another episode. I've never felt this level of comfort with a woman before. I look down at the woman resting on my lap and take her in while I can. Brooke is nice like this. This version of Brooke isn't barking back snide remarks or rolling her eyes or worse, completely ignoring me. One of her hands clutches the pillow and the other rests on my knee. She is completely at ease. And so am I.

Still, it is getting late and I know she would be more comfortable in her own bed.

I slowly take the pillow out from under her head and flip her around. I drape her arms around my neck and her head limply falls against the little nook between my shoulder and my neck. I stand up and walk toward her bedroom. I laugh internally because I know that Brooke would flip her shit if she was aware of how we looked. Like a real fucking couple. Or worse, a married couple where the groom is crossing the honeymoon threshold. I lower Brooke onto her bed and take off her slippers before tucking her inside her light pink sheets and white comforter. I spot a box of tissue and place it on her bedside table.

I look at how vulnerable she is. She has her guard down and I want to tell her about the bet. Maybe now is the time? I brush her hair out of her face, tracing her cheeks and jawline softly with my finger. She stirs slightly.

"Tristan?"

I drop onto my knees and continue to play with her hair. "Yeah?"

"Stay," she says quietly.

My insides melt. Does she know there's nothing I want more at this moment? "Okay, Cupcake. Just give me a minute. I'll be back."

I go back out into the kitchen and start doing the dishes for her. I load everything in the dishwasher and decide to run it. I don't want her to wake up to a dirty kitchen. I think that is one thing we have in common. We like our houses to be clean. I find some disinfecting wipes and run them over the countertops, cabinet hardware, all the door handles, and any of the commonly touched surfaces in her apartment. I find some multipurpose spray and clean off her coffee table. Her candle is still burning, so I blow it out. After wiping down the remote, I go to turn off the TV, but before I do, I notice that it's the episode where Chandler doesn't remember which one of Joey's sisters he slept with. Damn, I've been there, and even worse, Brooke knows I've been in that shameful position. Not the part of not remembering that I've slept with my best friend's sister – because, trust me, that is the ONLY thing I've been thinking about since it happened – but the whole part about getting so drunk that I can't remember the name of the girl I've slept with. And I know that's probably one of the reasons Brooke hates me so much. I don't think she was ever into players and to be honest, I never wanted to be one. If only she knew the truth.

Back in her room, I take off my hat and set it on her dresser. I climb into the bed and she is facing me, but on the complete opposite side of where I am. This is the first time that I've ever laid in a woman's bed without having the intention of sleeping with her. Brooke's words from earlier ring in my ears: *Don't even think about it.* Regardless, I still want to make sure she feels taken care of. She looks so peaceful sleeping there beside me. I grab her hand and attempt to pull her toward me, but I feel some resistance. "Come on, Cupcake," I whisper.

"No," she mumbles. "I don't want you to get sick, Tristan. The end of the season is coming up and I don't want you to have this and have to take that awful medicine." I can tell that she is delirious because her words are slurred and she doesn't open her eyes once.

Even in her delirious state, she still has to fight against me and make up a lame-ass excuse.

Again, fucking stubborn.

I grab the back of her upper thigh as close to her ass as I can possibly get without actually touching her ass (I really want to grab her ass but I am not going to push it tonight) and pull her over until her body is flush with mine. I wrap my arms around the back of her thighs and her back. Although she is wearing sweats and a ridiculous oversized *Gilmore Girls* themed t-shirt, I find her to be in her most beautiful state. This time, she doesn't push me away. Instead, her leg wraps around mine and her hands find their way to the back of my neck. My favorite spot. I whisper in her ear, "One of these days, you are not going to push against me so much, Cupcake. And I hope that that day is sooner rather than later."

"In your wildest dreams, Hot Shot." Brooke's voice fades away and is replaced by her adorable snore.

Once I confirm that she is fully asleep, I hold her tighter and say, "I wish you could see me the way I see you, Brooke." I kiss her forehead softly. For years, I've been trying to convince myself that what I have been feeling for Brooke was really fueled by hate or at the bare minimum, a silly crush that lingered for far too long. During these past few weeks, I've seen Brooke more frequently than ever before, and it has cemented something in me that I have always known. I am just scared shitless to actually admit it to Brooke. Based on our history, the odds are not in my favor. Because of this stupid rule of hers, I've never been on her dating radar in that way and I hope to God that no one else is on her radar, especially not Hastings.

Nothing about what I am feeling is a fluke. It certainly isn't because I want to win a damn bet. My feelings for Brooke are like my love of hockey: indisputable and unmovable.

That night, I sleep the best I have slept in years.

14

Brooke

"This way, ladies," the hostess tells us, waving for us to follow her.

I finally recovered from my horrendous cold and was in desperate need of social interaction. So, when Tess suggested we go to brunch in Uptown, I jumped at the opportunity. I still haven't told Tess about Tristan coming over and nursing me back to health a few days ago. Or that he ended up spending the night.

We sit down in a patio area since Tess brought her small dog, Pippa, with her. I swear if she had the option of bringing her dog to work, she would. It is a really nice spring day and the real Texas heat hasn't set in. I think we still have another couple of months left before it feels like the surface of the sun here.

"I'm so relieved you are feeling better, B. I've missed you at work.

The kids have been extra crazy. I think they can feel that it's close to springtime. Also, they have been dropping like flies. No doubt you got your terrible cold from one of those little gremlins. I've been popping elderberry gummies like nobody's business."

I laugh. Tess takes a sip of her coffee and leans closer across the table. "So, anything interesting happen while you were recovering?"

"Well Bradley came over and dropped off what he thought was a nice little care package–canned chicken noodle soup."

"Um, does your brother not know you at all? You hate canned soup. It's official, he is going to win the award for the most clueless brother. I guess he earns some brownie points for going over in the first place, though."

"Right? Anyway, I thought that's where my night was going to end. I snuggled up on the couch and continued to binge watch *Friends*. After like one episode, I heard a knock at my door. I totally thought it was Bradley because he has my extra key fob so I didn't even check who was outside before opening the door. Guess who was there?"

"Hmmm... oh my gosh! Was it Nick coming to win you back?"

"No. Not even close."

"Then, who? You know I suck at guessing."

"Tristan." Tess' eyes widen and her mouth drops open. "He brought me my favorite ramen, a medicine ball, tissues and other cold provisions. Tess, he even bought me more chest rub!" Tess is still in her shocked mode and rendered speechless, so I continue, "Also, he might have stayed overnight. In my bed."

"What? Why would he stay? Was he trying to seduce you while you were sick?"

I bite my bottom lip. "No, it wasn't like that. I may have... asked him to stay?" That whole encounter in my room is a little hazy. The one thing I do remember clearly are his large hands grabbing me and pulling me closer to him. The heat and tingles that ran through my body had me thinking for a second that I was getting a fever. Nope. That's just how my body reacts to Tristan Lawson touching me now.

It is my new normal. I don't think anyone would ever forget the way that man's hands feel on their body once he has run them all over. I blame my deliriousness for my uninhibited actions of letting him care for me the way he did. That is a way a boyfriend would take care of their girlfriend.

But I don't let my thoughts go there. Not in a million years would I ever actually date Tristan.

And if snuggling with me throughout the whole night wasn't enough, when I woke up the next morning, he had already Doordashed some coffee—a pistachio latte, to be exact. It's not always available to order and is only around for a couple of months, if that. He somehow remembered that is my go-to coffee order in the late winter months. This gesture, along with the countless other ones he did for me the previous night, was too much for me to handle. And because I am a chicken and don't know how I really feel about Tristan, I freaked out and literally pushed him out of my apartment. I haven't heard from him since. Maybe he finally got the message that nothing will ever happen between us. Ever.

After dispelling all of this information onto Tess, she crosses her arms and gives me a suspicious look. "Wait, let me get this straight. He slept over? And you guys didn't do *anything*? You are telling me that one of the hottest hockey players in the world slept in your bed and you didn't make a move or he didn't make a move?"

"We didn't do anything *that* night." I purse my lips and avoid eye contact with Tess because I already know my comment has sparked a fire I can't extinguish.

"Brooke Beckett! What do you mean *that* night? There was another night where something happened?"

So I tell her all about the pure hat trick night. About the frosting. About all the ridiculously hot things he did to my body that no other man has ever done to my body before. When I am finally done spilling the tea, Tess' expression is one of pure excitement and intrigue.

"Woman! How did you not immediately tell me what happened

that night? I knew he had to be good in bed. Well excuse me, he sounds amazing in the kitchen with you splayed all over the counter."

"Tess!" I glance at the table next to us, where funnily enough are seated two old ladies who look as though they have been friends for decades, also just catching up, still drinking bottomless mimosas and eating pastries. Goals. I just hope they didn't overhear what Tess just said. I can feel my cheeks heat up regardless.

Tess raises her eyebrows. "So are you guys like a thing now? Oh my God, I love that for you."

I don't know? Are we a thing? I've actively avoided talking with Tristan about what happened that night because I am too scared of the implications. Also, I am fucking terrified about how my body is now reacting when anyone mentions Tristan's name or anytime I see his face. Living in Dallas, it is impossible to avoid all the billboards, and now that we are in Uptown, they have Storm posters in almost every shop window. I can't escape Tristan Lawson. And now he is in my head more than usual.

"I honestly don't know what we are." I finish my first mimosa and Tess waves down the waiter so he can pour more into my glass. I drink half the glass and tap the side of it.

"Well, I know one thing is for sure," Tess says with a serious expression.

"What's that?"

"I'm never going to see cupcakes the same again. You both have ruined them for me, but in the best way."

I blush. "Oh my God, Tess!"

She smiles. "I just love this for you. I mean, one of the reasons you broke up with Nick was because he was too vanilla. Too safe. Right?"

I shrug. "Right."

"It seems like Tristan is definitely the opposite of vanilla. In every way. You met your match with Tristan, Brooke. I don't know why you are resisting him so much. I wasn't even there and you describing what you did on that kitchen counter is what girls and let's be honest, guys dream about. I know that would be a dream I would want to come true. There's that thin line between love and hate."

"I'm resisting him so much for a plethora of reasons." Mainly because he called me ugly and not his type the night I met him. He finds every opportunity he can to tease me. He has slept with so many women I don't think I can count them on my two hands. So who is he comparing me to when he is with me? Also, he is my older brother's best friend. That's a whole other line that I don't know if I want to continue crossing. No matter how much I loved the way Tristan's hands, lips and tongue felt on my body.

I swallow hard. "Reasons I don't feel like getting into right now. Can we please talk about something else other than Tristan? What's new with you?"

"You're not getting off that easy, B. We are going to continue this conversation at a later date. But since you asked…"

AFTER BRUNCH, we need to kill some time and sober up before driving home. It also gives Tess an excuse to get a nice walk in with Pippa. We stroll around West Village and come across a storefront with an "available to rent" sign in the window. It's a corner lot with a lot of potential for my dream bakery. There is faded green trim on all the windows and an existing awning outstretched overhead. The worn brown door has a brass handle and there are remnants of where the old sign hung above the door frame. The retail shops, restaurants and small movie theater that surround the two-block radius of West Village would bring in a good amount of foot traffic. Although there is a Starbucks at the opposite corner – far enough away that I could serve coffee for my customers as well. That is part of my business plan. Even if it doesn't happen right away, I want to grow into a bakery that serves an array of coffee choices. Cupcakes and other baked goods will do for a bit before I can expand into the coffee sector.

I can see it all. I actually have a big 3-inch binder with an entire business plan and I drew up some designs for how I want the exterior and interior to look. Brooke's Bakes. It will have a bright green door with cute pink metal tables along the three big windows on each side of the entrance. Pink and green flowers will cover the main store sign and cascade alongside the big green door. I want a large, clean, white display case and counter with floor-to-ceiling white built-ins behind the counter where I can also display merchandise and extra treats. The walls will be painted a light pink shade and the floors will be light wood. There will be comfortable suede green and pink chairs around square white marbled tables with gold bases. Long, thin Edison bulb light fixtures hanging over the space. Fresh pink flowers as the centerpiece at every table. A pink neon sign with the lit-up words "How Sweet It Is..." because I love that song.

I remember when I was a little girl sneaking down the stairs to watch my parents dance to that song every Saturday night. It was their wedding song and any time this song came on the radio, they would be in the middle of the living room dancing in each other's arms. I knew what my parents had was special and I hoped that someday I would have the same thing. A man to dance with to our wedding song. A girl can dream.

"So what do you think?"

Tess' question jerks me out of my head, back to the present. She is peeking into the window. Pippa props herself on the glass, mimicking her owner.

"It's perfect." It really is, but I am already struggling with how much my apartment rent is increasing – I can't imagine how much the rent would be for a space in the West Village. "Unfortunately, I don't think I can afford it, Tess."

She walks backwards to where I am standing. "Well, the only way you can know for sure how much it will be is to call this number. Take a picture and call."

"That's true." I grab my phone from my back pocket and snap a photo of my dream space. One that I can surely never afford, but maybe I will print out this picture and put it into my scrapbook, along with what I want my dream bakery to look like.

"Promise me you are going to call, right? Because I know you, B. Don't be scared to dream big. And before you say anything, it's not a stupid dream or too big of a dream. No dream is stupid. It's scary as hell to pursue something you are passionate about. But you will never know if you can make it a reality unless you try. And you know you have the biggest support system ever with me by your side. Hell, I may even quit teaching and help you run your business. I would love to be able to still hang out with you all day and be around all the sugary goodness."

"Thanks, friend." I give her a hug.

As we continue down the sidewalk, I look back at the storefront, trying to capture this moment. Also, trying not to get caught up in it.

"I'll call tomorrow and see."

"Good. And okay, I have one question for you and you have to promise you won't be mad or annoyed that I asked this."

"Tess, when have you ever held back on anything you've ever asked me? I promise."

"Tell me again why you can't ask your brother to spot you for this? Knowing Bradley, I am certain he would help you."

I take a very deep breath. Of course this is something that has crossed my mind countless times. But deep down, I don't want to ask my brother because Tess is right: he would help me in a heartbeat. Call me stubborn, but I want to do this all on my own. I don't want to owe anyone anything. I want to prove to myself – myself more than anyone – that I can achieve my dreams just as much as my uber-successful pro athlete older brother. I know it's not a competition, but I've always been known as Bradley's younger sister instead of just Brooke. And it does wear on a person the longer that lasts. I love my brother and the fact that he wouldn't skip a beat in helping me with this venture. But I don't want to have to ask him for help.

Another factor is my mother. My mom would constantly treat this as another reason to remind me how great Bradley is and the only reason I was able to achieve my dreams was because of him. I don't want that. Hell no.

"Because I just want to do this on my own. I don't want to owe my brother anything. He also has a big wedding coming up and I know that they want kids. He is starting his life and just because I am his sister, doesn't mean that I am entitled to whatever money he makes. I could never ask him to do this for me."

Tess reaches into her purse for her keys and fiddles with them, "Okay, I understand where you are coming from. Just remember, B: it's ok to accept help from others. You don't have to pursue your dreams alone."

"I know, Tess. Thank you."

She opens her back door and lets Pippa in the back seat. She shuts the door and walks around her car to give me a hug, "Promise me that you will call them." Then she pulls back and gives me a stern look. "Don't be afraid of telling the world all that you are, B. You aren't just a teacher. You aren't just Bradley Beckett's kid sister. The more you acknowledge that you are a baker and own that identity, the universe will help guide you toward the right opportunities and people."

"I promise."

She finally lets go of my arms and walks back toward the driver's side, "Now, you're sure you don't need a ride back to your apartment?"

"I'm sure. I need to get more fresh air since I was cooped up in my apartment for a few days." I blow her a kiss. "Love you! See you at work!"

"Love you!" She climbs in, starts her car and drives away.

I start walking toward my apartment, feeling this mixture of excitement and anticipation about the future. Change is coming and for the first time in my life, I want to welcome it with open arms.

15

Tristan

My car beeps behind me as I walk into the venue. I button my black suit jacket, adjust my sleeves over my watch and pull open the doors. I am glad that my face has healed completely since my altercation with Hastings last month. This is not the night for my face to look beat up. Casino Night has always been one of my favorite nights of the year. I love anything that our foundation does to give back to the community. They always put on a great event for the community and I like how we have some time to be the dealers and interact with our fans.

The only thing different about tonight is that I wish I had someone by my side. I am sick of going to these things alone. But I don't want to take just anyone with me–that would definitely send the wrong message, and I don't want one of the many ice girls I've hooked up with to get any funny ideas.

Speaking of ice girls, I was so pissed the other night when Alison just stopped by. I had no idea she was coming over. I mean, I guess I am not surprised. That's always been our arrangement. Just show up if we wanted to hook up. Brooke looked so pissed-off and the scary thing about Brooke being pissed-off this time around was that I actually *cared* that she was pissed-off at me. Something definitely shifted inside of me that night in Brooke's kitchen. The feeling that occupied my body took me back to the day we first met. The tension between us has changed. There's still tension, but not out of hate. It's something else.

The venue looks great with all the tables set up. Pop-up bars are set up around the room. There are tables lined up along one of the back walls with all the prizes and giveaways. I decided to anonymously offer up my property in Telluride for a weekend within the next month or so. I have been meaning to go back soon. Maybe after the season ends, which hopefully isn't until mid-June. I want that Stanley Cup so bad. I haven't had my hands on that trophy in almost a decade. I lucked out and won with Boston my rookie year and a couple years ago with the Storm and honestly took it for granted. I was young and foolish and didn't realize how rare it is to be a champion. It's the hardest trophy to win. I have a feeling that this is our year. We have a good mix of veteran guys and young players who keep us on our toes, so I think we have a legit shot.

Unfortunately, the only teammate that I cannot stand walks in right behind me. He stands next to me and nods. "Lawson."

"Hastings," I respond curtly. If Brooke does end up coming tonight with Tess, he isn't coming anywhere near Brooke. I am getting an overwhelming sense of protectiveness toward her. "What, couldn't lock down a date to this thing? Women found out what an asshole you are?"

"I could say the same thing about you. I guess Alison didn't want to be seen with the team's playboy in public."

I shoot him a glare. Fucking Alison. I knew she would talk to everyone about our hookups.

"That's right, Lawson. Everyone knows that you two are fuck buddies."

"At least I'm getting some, man." I don't tell him that five minutes after Brooke ran off, I turned Alison down and told her I don't want this kind of relationship with her. I don't want to do random hookups anymore. It is getting old and I am honestly getting tired of the playboy reputation. Sure, it's helped me a little in my endorsement deals and various photoshoots, but personally, I always felt a little ashamed that my family would see those headlines and think I treated women poorly, which couldn't be farther from the truth.

People are starting to trickle in, including Bradley and Jen. "Hey did you know that Brooke is coming?"

My heart starts to race at the mention of Brooke's name. I try my best to play it off as smoothly as possible.

"Um, I think she said that she was coming with her friend, Tess."

"I'm glad that she's getting out of the house," Jen says. "She would probably be at home watching the latest episode of the *Spring Baking Championship* – which, don't get me wrong, I love watching that and recapping it with her, but she needs to dress up and come out to events like this every once in a while."

"Do you know when she is coming?" I say, almost with a panicked voice.

"Why, so you can go and hide? Gosh you guys just need to bury the hatchet one of these days."

If Jen would have asked me that question a few weeks ago, it would have been yes to go hide. But now it wasn't an "avoid Brooke at all costs" feeling. I wasn't trying to think of ways to get Brooke to give me her "death glare" (a glare that has become one of my favorite looks of hers. I don't know how to explain it, but it is the cutest death glare around). Rather, my panic comes from a "I can't wait to see her" feeling. My body is aching for her to touch me.

"Not hiding," I say. "Just wondering. Let's go get something to drink."

We all head over to one of the bars and order our drinks – whiskey neats for me and Brad, gin and tonic for Jen.

"So," Brad says, "you ready to schmooze a bunch of fancy foundation members and convince them to donate more money?"

"Ready as always."

"Speaking of, there's the president of the foundation. I'll see you around." Bradley and Jen make their way towards the president of the Dallas Storm Foundation. I'll definitely have to make my rounds at some point. That's one of the "perks" of being a high profile player–having to kiss everyone's ass so everything is on the up-and-up. I probably have to go over there at some point and apologize for what happened the other night and guarantee that it won't happen ever again. Even though I wouldn't think twice of doing it again.

Now it's just me and Hastings left standing together. More people trickle into the venue and I can't help but try and spot a bright bubblegum pink dress. Knowing Brooke, she's probably wearing a fucking knotted headband to this fancy event. I take a swig of my whiskey and let it burn the back of my throat.

Maybe she decided not to come. That will make my night that much easier. I can focus on what I have to do. I avert my eyes for a second and then I hear:

"Holy shit. Is that Brooke?"

It is Brooke. And she is not in a bubblegum pink dress. It is the complete opposite. She is wearing a dress that makes me want to fall to my fucking knees and worship every inch of her. It is black with a lace see-through bustier and a slit that practically shows off all of her left leg. I have never seen her in anything that is not pastel colored or without a headband in her hair. Her hair is a sleek low bun and she is wearing long earrings that point to her exposed neck and cleavage. She needs to wear corsets on a daily basis. She looks fucking beautiful. She can't know that, though. She would flee if she could hear my inner thoughts right now. I have to pretend that I hate the way she looks.

"The bet is still on for the captain's spot right, Lawson? You weren't serious about calling it off, right? Because I am about to lock that down tonight. I can't wait to take that dress off her." Hastings downs the rest of his whiskey and taps the bartop, indicating he wants another. He better keep his shit together tonight. We don't want to draw any more negative attention to ourselves. Even though I am holding back another punch to his face for even thinking he is going to lay a hand on Brooke tonight.

Like hell are we going through with this bet.

It's over.

"Actually Hastings, I was serious when I said this bet is off. You aren't going near her and I am never endorsing you for captain. Ever."

"Bet or no bet, I am still going home with Brooke tonight. Have fun tonight, Lawson. I know I certainly will."

Now all my hate has zeroed in on Hastings and his master plan to break Brooke's rule. She would never, though. It's her one unbreakable rule.

Shit, she is coming over here. Now it's my turn to down the rest of my whiskey and ask for another. I can see Tess, who is actually wearing a hot pink dress, dragging Brooke over to where we are standing. Brooke's eyes are wide and I can see her mouth say, "No, no, no." I glance over at Dean and I recognize the look in his eyes—hungry. He's practically undressing her with his damn eyes. I can't blame him, though. I am doing the same fucking thing.

"Well, hello gentlemen!" Tess says in a sing-song voice. "Don't you two look dapper this evening. Y'all clean up nice for a night off the ice. Much better than those sweaty uniforms and helmets."

I am trying not to stare at the unbearably gorgeous Brooke standing next to her, but I can't help myself. Brooke is fucking perfect. I've never seen this side of her and damn it, now that I know she has two sides to her, I don't want to go back to only seeing her as the bubbly (well to everyone else but me) kindergarten teacher who wears pastel colors like it's going out of style. Her signature look has been replaced for the night. She's flipped the script and it's a whole different power play than I am used to.

"Thanks beautiful, you two look gorgeous as always," Dean says. But his eyes are glued on Brooke. Well, more on her damn tits. I hate this guy. She blushes a little at Dean and I want to pummel him all over again. This time we are on solid ground and I know for a fact that I could kick his ass even more than I did the other night.

She bites her bottom lip slightly and it gets me hard immediately. *Calm down, Tristan. Think of something to distract you from those lips. You never cared about her damn lips before. Why do you care now?*

Because Dean fucking wants her and I can't let that happen.

"What will it be for you ladies?"

"Two palomas please. Right, Brooke?"

Brooke finally looks me directly in my eyes. Her lips part slightly and she scans my body. I am gripping my glass like it's my lifeline, which let's be honest, it is right now. Focusing on grasping my glass distracts me from what I really want to do: drag her out of this venue so no other man can look at her. I can't do that though...for a multitude of reasons. She clears her throat and finally says, "Uh yeah, sounds good."

"Hey Tristan!" Bradley calls from a nearby table. He is waving me over. Apology time, I guess.

"Um, I better go talk with the president of the foundation." Brooke's eyes flutter as she looks down, almost like she is disappointed? "I'll see you ladies at the blackjack tables...Tess, nice to see you again." Then I give my former nemesis the smallest acknowledgement, "Brooke." I have to save face and try to go back to hating this woman because that is the only thing that is calming my dick down right now. It's not the time to tell her the truth—that I don't hate her.

That I've never hated her.

16

Brooke

Tess and I decide to touch up our makeup before we start playing some blackjack.

"Oh my gosh, Dean and Tristan are *so* hot!" she squeals as we lean into the mirrors above the bathroom sinks side-by-side. "I mean, I know that you will never go home with Tristan, and obviously I would never because hello girl code, but all I'm saying is that if you don't go home with Dean, I might."

"We'll see how the night goes." All I want to admit to my best friend is how much I want that to happen. I *need* to go home with Dean tonight. I am so determined to break my rule. Tess was so right. It is stupid and I need to start taking risks. And I need to cleanse my palette of all things Tristan. Weird things have been happening lately between us. Things that have been making my body shiver every time I think about him.

"Ready?" We head back out and find two open seats at a nearby table. I scan the room to look for the hazel-eyed man who has been driving me crazy since he walked into my parent's kitchen a decade ago, and luckily he is preoccupied with some middle-aged women talking his ear off. He is flashing his stupid perfect boyish smile, making them weak at the knees I'm sure.

Tess and I start playing and we do pretty good. This is the first time that I've ever played blackjack. Surprise surprise. I'm not doing too bad. "I'm going to go get another drink. Do you want another?"

"Yes, please." The dealer starts dealing cards again and I smile, thinking that I haven't done this in a long time. "This" being dressing up and going out. When I told Tess that I actually wanted to come to Casino Night and change things up, she called me and squealed. She is so excited that I finally want to break my one rule. Come to think of it, I bet Bradley prefers that I have this rule. It has kept him from kicking people's asses.

When Tess and I went dress shopping for this event, I insisted that I wanted to completely do a one-eighty from my normal. Hey, if I was going to switch it up, I was going to go all in and not look back. And I am not going to lie, it has been refreshing. No headband. No pastel. No overalls covering a slightly oversized shirt with white Keds. I wanted to surprise myself and I have succeeded. Don't get me wrong, this corset is not the most comfortable thing to wear, but I feel the most confident I have ever felt in my life.

"Is this seat taken?" I turn and look up to find Dean smiling down at me. His blue eyes are scanning my body and I notice how messed up his face looks with the scars from the fight he had with Tristan. Wow, Tristan really did a number on him. I wonder what Tristan meant the other night when he said, "He is dangerously close to getting something that I want"? That statement stubbornly hasn't left my mind and I wish I could make it disappear.

"Um, no." Tess will forgive me. "It's all yours."

Dean unbuttons his jacket as he sits down, a move that I've always found to be very hot when any guy does it. "You know how to play?"

I shrug. "First time."

"Well looking at that pile of chips you have stacked next to you, you aren't doing so bad."

"Thanks." I nervously play with one of the piles of said chips. This is weird. I don't even know this man and yet I am willing to break my rule for him. I guess this is the best way to do it. It's not like any other prospects are in the mix.

"You look beautiful tonight, by the way."

My face is getting hot. *Lock it down, Brooke. Act like you have been complimented on your looks before.* There is a tinge of disappointment that I can't explain. *This hot hockey player with ice blue eyes is telling you that you look beautiful! Why aren't you responding?*

It's because that's not who I want to hear it from.

I smile extra big and say, "Thank you, Dean! You look extra handsome tonight. I've only ever seen you in your hockey gear and I think I prefer this look better."

"Ok, y'all," the dealer says to our table. "I think that it's time for me to turn over the reins to one of the players."

A chill runs down my spine because the universe hates me that much. Almost as much as I loathe the man stepping behind the blackjack table and looking at me with just as much disdain. I've never seen him look at me this fiercely before.

Tristan starts to deal the cards and avoids eye contact with me the whole time. I hope I don't lose any hands with him, but if I know anything about gambling, I know that the odds aren't in my favor whatsoever. I bite my lower lip out of nervousness at my hand. I have sixteen. I can go either way honestly.

I hear Tristan clear his throat and growl, "What's it going to be, Beckett?"

Beckett? He only calls me Beckett if he is really irritated with me or just plain indifferent. I look up and his hazel eyes are super dark and his bulky arms are spread across his torso. At some point while I was contemplating whether to hit or not, Tristan took off his jacket and rolled up his sleeves slightly, giving everyone a peek of his tattoos. His Rolex watch is glistening under the lights. I feel Dean's hand on my upper thigh and my breath hitches. I swear I hear Tristan growl again and I can tell his jaw is super clenched, even under the dark scruff on his face. He seems almost...jealous. Interesting.

I don't push Dean's hand away. One, because I like the way a man's hand feels on my body. And two, I like seeing Tristan squirm a little. I like seeing him jealous. He always has the one-up on me and now, I have the upper hand.

I reach my hand around Dean's neck and ask him, "What do you think I should do?"

"I didn't ask Hastings. I asked you," Tristan practically barks at me.

I direct my gaze back to Tristan. You could cut the tension between us with a knife. Everyone at the table is staring at us, wondering about our next move. I take it.

"I'll stay, Lawson."

Finally, there is an inkling of a smirk as he flips over his card, almost like he was expecting me to say that. Jokes on him: he ends up busting.

Dean lets out a laugh, looks directly at Tristan and says, "I guess that's the second thing you are losing tonight, Lawson." Then he tightens his grip on my upper thigh, "Good job, Brooke."

I start clapping and doing a little dance. "See, Lawson, sometimes it pays off playing it safe."

"Maybe." Tristan swipes all the cards up with his huge hand. His tongue playfully licks his lips. Then he looks directly at me, clearly forgetting that we are surrounded by people and aren't alone, and says in the most seductive way possible, "But it's not nearly as fun."

He knows what he is doing and it's working. I squirm a little in my chair as tingles travel all across my body. I have to do something to make him just as uneasy. And I know how much he despises the man holding onto my leg right now.

"You're right," I respond just as seductively. Then, I decide to do the riskiest thing I've probably done in my life. (I know that's sad, but it's true. I am the poster child for playing by the rules.)

I turn to Dean, pull him near me and kiss him on the cheek. Innocent, but deadly to the man standing across from me, clutching onto the deck of cards so tightly with one hand that they actually start to bend in half.

Tristan looks like he is about to kill a man. I've seen him frustrated before, but never like this. This is a whole new level of Tristan. He looks like the most dangerous man in the world.

It was a peck on the cheek. It's not like I made out with the guy. But even if I did, it's not like Tristan and I are together. Why should he care who I am kissing or dating?

The poor card dealer that stepped out comes back. I guess he could read the tension, too. He reaches down and attempts to pry the cards out of Tristan's steel grip. Tristan finally wrenches his gaze from me, looks down at the sweet employee and lets go of the cards. He rolls down his sleeves and practically knocks the chair over while retrieving his jacket. Although a beautiful man's hand is firmly still on my upper thigh, I can't help but notice Tristan's clenched fists as he storms away from the table, toward the silent auction set up in the back of the venue.

"Um, I think I am done playing blackjack for the night."

Dean's hand slides from my thigh to my lower back. "Yeah, okay that's fine." Then he looks up behind me and his eyebrows draw together. "They are waving me over. I think it's my turn to deal some cards over there. Come find you in a little bit?"

"Sounds good. I'll be around."

I need to go talk to Tristan anyway. What the hell has gotten into him?

17

Tristan

I had to get away from that table immediately or I was going to finish the job that I left on the ice. She fucking kissed him? I don't care that it was on his damn cheek. Her lips were on his skin and that fucking bothers me. Did the other night mean nothing?

I practice my breathing exercises to calm down my anger, when in the corner of my eye, I sense the very woman who brings me to my knees. She has no idea the effect she has on me. It doesn't help that she walked into this damn room with the sexiest dress I've ever seen on any woman. Who am I kidding? Brooke could've walked into the venue with a bright pink shirt and overalls and still commanded the room with her presence. She always has.

Just go talk to her. You need to talk to her now. Before it's too late.

I can't let Hastings go home with her.

I slowly make my way over to Brooke, who is pretending like I don't exist. Typical Brooke.

I notice she is perusing the stay in Telluride that I anonymously donated. Tapping the pen against the table while simultaneously tapping her foot in the same nervous fashion.

I clear my throat and Brooke flinches slightly.

"That looks like a nice trip," I say.

"Yup," she curtly responds without even looking up at me. I haven't been this close to her all night. She smells like summer. Coconut? Delicious.

I peek over her shoulder, my torso almost touching her perfect ass. "To be honest, I didn't take you for a gambling type of girl. But what do I know, right? You went ahead and kissed Hastings, so I must be wrong about you, Cupcake."

"Yeah, maybe you don't know me, Hot Shot. I thought that I should make it known to him that I am very interested in dating him."

What the actual fuck? "Since when do you *date* hockey players? You've never dated hockey players." What I want to say is: "I thought that was your #1 rule. I thought it was unbreakable."

"Like we've already established, a girl can change. And you clearly don't know me."

"So it seems." My jaw clenches out of frustration and annoyance. She looks so fucking hot and I want so bad for her to not be interested in Dean. Or to be Bradley's younger sister. I just want her to be Brooke.

Just Brooke.

"Why Hastings?" I seethe.

"Why not Hastings? He's hot and I am sick of playing it safe. It hasn't gotten me anywhere so far. Might as well have fun with Dean."

I fume as I register the words "hot" and "fun." That combination creates a mental image that I immediately want to erase. Especially since it involves fucking Hastings. He is winning her over and I can't let that happen.

I don't care about what I would get out of the bet. I don't care about the captain's spot. Hastings can have it. He can have whatever he wants–except her.

After signing her name on the raffle sign up sheet, Brooke turns around and I get a view of her perfect body from this angle. It is dangerous, just like my feelings for her. She playfully bats her eyelashes as she looks up at me and says, "Well, I am going to find Dean. This dress is getting a little uncomfortable and I need some help taking it off."

She smirks and starts to walk around me, but I discreetly and gently grab her arm.

She looks down at my hand and says, "Tristan, what the...?"

"The only way that dress is coming off your body is if I'm taking it off."

Her mouth falls open and her eyes rake over me. "What did you just...?"

"Was I not clear the other night, Cupcake? You. Are. Mine."

18

Brooke

I didn't get a chance to say goodbye to Tess. I didn't get a chance to say goodbye to anyone. Before I could process what came out of Tristan's mouth, he grabbed my hand and led me out to his car.

"Tristan." He doesn't utter one word, and I need him to talk to me. "Tristan, will you slow down? Where are we going?"

He unlocks his car and opens the passenger door for me to get in. Again, no words are coming out of his mouth. He looks determined and intense. It is similar to the look that he has when he is on the ice. He nods his head for me to get into the car.

I don't know what possesses my body to do it, but I get in.

He slams the door shut behind me and practically runs around the car to get to the driver's side.

I send a quick text to Tess. I feel bad about abandoning her, but I know she will understand.

> Hey Tess. I am so sorry I had to bolt. I will explain later. I hope you find a hot hockey player to go home with tonight.

Tristan, who has apparently turned mute in the past ten minutes, turns on the car and begins to drive.

I got a text back from Tess.

> Ooooo are you with Dean?? Can't wait to hear about it.

> Um, not with Dean.

> Oh you're right I see Dean now.

> OH. MY. GOD! You did not go home with Tristan fricken Lawson!!!

> Yes, yes I did. Am I stupid for doing this? I mean he is my enemy Tess!

> So what? You both need to release all that pent-up enemy energy you've been carrying around for way too long. I hope you have fun doing it 😉. You are obligated to tell me everything when I see you again. I'm serious—a very detailed debrief with coffee and donuts is a must! Promise me now, Brooke Beckett—you will take a chance on Tristan and let him do whatever he wants to do to you tonight.'

My thumbs hover over the keyboard on my screen.

> Coffee and donuts, you've got it. Are you sure you are ok with me leaving? I am the worst date ever.

I am perfectly fine. See you on Monday.

Love you!

Love you too 🩶

Tristan takes a hard right turn. He would be a dead ringer for one of the *Fast and Furious* characters. "Oh my god, Tristan! Are you trying to get us killed? Why are we in such a rush? Where are you taking me?"

Again, silence. He grips the gear stick so hard that the veins in his hands are protruding out. A new sexy thing about him that I've never noticed before. He weaves his way through the evening traffic on the highway and heads south toward downtown. Maybe he is taking me home? I do live a little outside of Uptown. But then again, he lives in one of the most luxurious communities in the metroplex. And it just so happens to be right down the street from my apartment. So it's a toss-up of where we are going.

Or maybe he's gone crazy and decided this is the night he is going to get rid of me for good. All's fair at this point in our dysfunctional relationship.

We exit off the highway and I get my question answered when he takes a right turn instead of a left.

We are heading to his house.

"Tristan, why are we here?"

Again, no response. He unlocks his door and deactivates his alarm. He motions for me to come inside where I am greeted by his two big dogs again. He herds them to the back of his massive house and slides open the back door to let them out into the backyard. He removes his jacket and drapes it along the back of the back of his couch. Tristan grabs a remote and turns on the gas fireplace. He turns on the lights but clearly has a dim setting so it's not very harsh. I place my clutch on the couch as well.

Tristan's silence is making me nervous.

Maybe being playful will kill the silence. "Is this the part where you kill me? Because if you are, just put me out of my misery already. I can't take another minute of waiting for you to explain what we are doing here and if you are, please give me the courtesy of saying goodbye to my family and friends. And I guess say goodbye to your career because then you'd be a murderer and my brother will probably hate your guts more than I ever did because you killed his only sister..."

"If you are going to break your one rule, I want you to break it with me, Brooke."

I feel whiplash, trying to process his words. I can only blink at him and ask, "What did you just say?"

He doesn't answer me right away. Instead he keeps pacing and goes back and forth between rubbing the back of his neck and rubbing his forehead.

Tristan's words are on a conveyor loop in my head. All I can do is repeat his own words back to him, "You want me to break my rule with you?" I let out a nervous laugh. "Why...why would I do that?"

"Because...I want to be with you. And not just in a 'benefits' type of way. I've wanted this – I've wanted you – since the moment I walked into your parents' kitchen ten years ago and you had flour all over your pretty face. Since the moment I put that disgusting cupcake in my mouth. The only reason I ate it all was because I didn't want to be an asshole and make a bad first impression."

I feel like my entire reality has been shattered. My legs are actually trembling. He must be fucking with me. "I am so confused right now, Tristan. I thought you hated me."

"I never hated you Brooke. Not for one moment. I just pretended to hate you because for some unknown reason, you hated me from the start. And once Bradley told me that you have this one rule that you would never date a hockey player, I had to force myself to put you out of my mind. I slept with other women, dated other women. And I know how fucked-up this sounds but they were just a distraction for me. I would've saved myself for you, Brooke."

I cannot form words right now. My thoughts are incoherent and my brain feels really foggy. Kind of like I am drunk, but I barely had anything to drink tonight.

"What was it that made you hate me so much?" Tristan continues, looking at me intently.

If he is confessing things, I guess it's my turn to be honest with him. "I, um, heard you and Bradley talking in the hallway. Ten years ago. I was in the bathroom cleaning off my face so that I wouldn't look like a complete troll to you. I thought you were the most beautiful guy I'd ever seen and I was so embarrassed that I was covered in flour and messed up my cupcakes. I was such a mess."

"Brooke..."

"I heard you. You said that I wasn't your type at all. That you liked girls with big boobs, girls who were blonde and skinny and just not—me. I was so over competing with girls like that. And not to bash anyone who fits that description. I was just so hurt by that statement because, once again, I wasn't enough for someone. I've never been enough for someone. It seemed like you were flirting with me in the kitchen and so I thought maybe, just maybe I had a chance with this super handsome guy who is ridiculously charismatic and funny." Tears well up in my eyes at a memory that has haunted me for all these years. "I thought: How did I get so lucky? My heart leaped that night when I first saw you." I wipe a tear from my cheek. "But that feeling was short-lived when you said that to my brother. I guess I was protecting myself and sort of passing judgment on you. Which in retrospect, wasn't fair. But the truth is I made that rule because of you, Tristan. Your words hurt me and I made it about hockey because I couldn't admit to anyone that I was hurt so badly."

"Oh, Brooke. That's why you hated me all of these years?" Tristan pinches the top of his nose and furrows his eyebrows. Then he closes the gap between us and grabs the sides of my face, wiping another tear away. "The only reason I said that to your brother was because I was fucking scared of admitting to him that I fucking fell for you the moment I saw you. That my brain chemistry was altered so much so that no woman has been able to live up to you. Even on the days when you were so mean to me, I wanted to throw you over my shoulder and take you home and make you mine." Then he starts to laugh a little. "God you are so fucking stubborn...always have been."

My pulse is rushing and I feel lightheaded. Tristan Lawson fell for me the moment he saw me? This is a lot of information to process. I am still so confused and a little pissed off that he waited so long to tell me. There are so many thoughts swirling around in my head. One thing I do know is that I don't want to make a huge mistake. I decide to put my guard up. Old habits. "Tristan, I don't know why you are calling *me* stubborn. You are the most stubborn man I know." This is too much. I can't risk getting hurt by this man again. I grab my clutch and say, "I appreciate you being honest with me, Tristan. I just don't know if I can do this."

I turn toward his front door, but then I feel Tristan's hand grab my arm and whip me completely around. I crash into his chest and he grabs onto my jaw and forces me to look up at him. "You aren't going anywhere, Cupcake."

"You're not the boss of me, Hot Shot. And I'm not breaking my rule." My voice gets a little shaky as I finally look into Tristan's eyes and see how intense they are. "Especially with you."

Tristan smirks, leans down, and whispers in my ear, "Are you sure about that?" Then I feel his lips press against my jaw. "Because based on the other night, I think you like what I do to you." I can feel his fingers take out the pins in my hair and let them fall to the floor as he places another kiss on my collarbone. "And I want it all with you, Brooke." He grabs my face with both hands again. He searches my eyes for my answer.

I can't lie: I want it all with him, too.

Then he presses his forehead against mine. "Please put me out of my misery, Brooke, and tell me that you want it all with me, too. But if you don't feel the same way, I'll take you home and never bother you again."

My heart leaps at what this gorgeous man is saying to me. Even with his tough exterior, I have never seen him so exposed and vulnerable. My throat feels dry, all my words dried up.

After a few moments of silence, I can feel him shake his head against me. He lets go of my face, almost as if he lost a fight that I wasn't privy to for the past ten years. "I figured I'd shoot my shot with you. I guess I'll take you home."

He starts to back away from me and that's when I drop my clutch on the floor, reach up and grab his strong jaw. His scruff tickles my hands and I force him to look down at me. "I don't want to go home." I reach on my tip toes and press my lips to his.

Tristan kisses me back with urgency. No hesitation. He presses against my lower back so that my entire body is flush with his. I can feel every ridge of his abs and one of his hands grabs my ass.

I laugh and break our kiss. "Excuse me, Lawson. What do you think you're doing?"

"Taking what's finally mine." Tristan smiles and kisses me more. This time, his tongue explores my mouth a little, making my knees buckle at the sensation that runs through my body. Memories of the other night flood my brain. I swear that tongue is going to be the death of me.

His fingers run through my hair and pull it slightly so that I am looking up at him. He's in control again and I am totally okay with that. "Last chance to back out, Cupcake. Just say the word and I'll take you home." He places a small peck on the side of my mouth, teasing me and thus infuriating me at the same time. I am about to respond, but Tristan continues, "Because once we do this, I have no intention of going back and pretending to hate you, Brooke. I do, however, have every intention of falling deeper in love with you."

I am catapulted back to the night I first met this man. Back to the first smile I ever witnessed come across his face. How his dimples became so prominent and his eyes lit up. That is how he is looking at me right now.

I knew that man was inside of him. All this time.

Tristan plays with the hair framing with my face. At some point my hands moved down to rest on his abs. I slowly move them around to the sides of this torso. My desire for him is increasing every second. But being playful has always been a part of our relationship, so I decide to tease him a bit. I lean away from him, just enough so there is an inch of space between our bodies.

"You know, someone told me tonight that it sometimes pays off to take risks. So, I'm taking a risk right now and I'm hoping it pays off." I scan his body. "Besides, you told me you were going to take this dress off me. I thought you were a man of your word, Hot Shot." I smile against his lips and I can feel him smile back.

"You're right. I am. Turn around," he whispers against my lips. I do as I'm told because I can't wait to get this dress off me. I want to feel Tristan's hands all over me. His hand goes across my chest and pulls me against him. I let my head fall back against his sculpted chest. He presses little kisses on my neck and I let out a small moan. His other hand is splayed across my lower back. I feel it travel up the path of my zipper and his fingers grab onto my zipper pull.

My hands start to shake. I am so nervous. I know that I was practically naked in front of Tristan the other night, but this moment holds more weight. Confessions have been made. It feels like I woke up from this alternate reality where Tristan hated my guts and I've been pushed into this new reality where it was all a lie.

"You bought this dress to make me jealous, didn't you? You really wanted me to take it off your perfect body, didn't you Cupcake?" Tristan bites my ear as he pulls my zipper down, slowly, meticulously. He knows what he is doing. He is driving me insane. Like always.

I reach up and grab his hair. I love that he has grown it out a little. More to grab onto. "God, Tristan. Just take my dress off already. You're driving me crazy."

"I love it when you get upset at me...that means I have your attention." The zipper pull finally reaches the zipper's end. My dress falls to my feet, exposing my black lace thong. No bra was needed for this dress. It was all built-in with the corset. I instinctively cover my boobs, remembering that I don't have the enormous boobs that Tristan is probably used to.

Tristan's hands grasp my wrists and pull my hands down to my sides. "Don't. I want to see all of you, Brooke." Both his hands find my hips and turn me around, so now I am facing him. I can feel myself blushing. This is so unfair. He is still dressed while here I am, laid bare with nothing but a thong and heels that are killing my feet. I step out of the dress and Tristan kicks it off to the side.

"Mmmm." Tristan's eyes travel across my body. I feel a surge of confidence because I can tell he likes what he sees. With his hands still on my hips, he pushes me against his couch. My butt is resting on the top of the couch and I place my hands next to me to steady myself for whatever Tristan is about to do to me.

Tristan falls to his knees and lifts up my foot.

"What are you doing?" I ask.

He unclasps the buckle on one of my heels and takes it off, his fingers briefly caressing my feet. I feel immediate relief. I am not used to wearing heels like that. I am used to wearing my white Keds all day. Heels would not bode well while running around after little kids.

"You looked uncomfortable, Cupcake. I want you to be as relaxed as possible tonight." He does the same thing to my other foot. This is the second time that Tristan Lawson has been on his knees before me. And this is also the second time I have been nearly naked in front of this man.

Just when I'm thinking it is going to be a repeat of the other night, Tristan stands up in between my legs. My chest heaves as he puts his hand under my chin and gently lifts it. He nearly brushes his lips with mine and shivers cascade through my entire body. I want more. My body is craving him. I think it has been for ten years.

His thumb brushes my chin and he licks my bottom lip. He is teasing me. He's roping me in with his unadulterated hotness and he knows it. His eyes are the darkest I've ever seen them. I can feel how turned on he is and I love how hard he is right now. I inch my hips toward him and run my hands around his torso, pulling him closer to me.

"Tristan..." I say against his lips.

He lifts my chin to meet his lips and kisses me hard this time. Like he has been waiting all his life to do this. All of our moments, good and bad, are all wrapped up in this consuming kiss. Somehow, magically, it's as if all the bad dissipated and all that is left are the good moments. This is definitely the biggest risk I've ever taken in my life. But even if it does backfire, somehow I know that it will be okay in the end. At least I took a chance, right? In any case, that is what I am telling myself at this moment, because I've never wanted anything or anyone this badly. I desperately want to know what I have been missing all these years.

My fingers find Tristan's belt buckle and start to undo it. Tristan's hand firmly grabs mine. He breaks our kiss and my eyebrows furrow. *I thought he wanted this.* He gives me a quick peck, almost like he can read my confusion and temporary self-doubt.

"Patience, Cupcake. There is something I want to do first." Tristan hooks one of his arms under my thighs and throws me over his shoulder. I laugh out of surprise, and from the thrill of being carried like this. He goes to the back door and lets in his pups, then heads upstairs. To his bedroom. But instead of going to the bed, he heads to his bathroom, which is the size of my living room and kitchen combined.

His shower has all glass walls and there is a massive bathtub at one end. I glimpse a rainfall showerhead and built in benches.

He reaches into the shower and turns it on. The bathroom starts steaming at the perfect moment. Tristan unbuttons his shirt and pulls the bottom of the shirt from his almost-too-tight-for-his-body pants. That is when I unabashedly take him all in. I just saw him shirtless a couple weeks ago, but I didn't allow myself to stare for too long. Now I feel no shame for staring, and I have a suspicion that Tristan doesn't mind it.

His chest is covered in tattoos and he has a small one on his left rib cage. I've never noticed it before. I walk toward him, partly because I want to help him finish getting undressed, but also so I can see what his tiny tattoo says.

"What's this? I've never noticed it before." I reach out and touch the tattoo. I squint and make out the initials *B.B.* "Aw, did you get a tattoo with my brother's initials? You guys are so cute. Does he know how much you love him?"

Tristan laughs and shakes his head. "Okay, you caught me. The second B is for Beckett." Then he pauses and points to the first B. "But the first B is not for Bradley. I know you always think I am fawning over your brother but, like I told you the night I met you, I am not. There's another Beckett who I hope knows how much I love her."

Wait. He got my initials tattooed on his body? "You got this for me? Why?"

"I only get tattoos that mean something to me, Cupcake. You mean everything to me."

I graze my fingertips over the small black letters. I just fell harder for this man. Since the first night we met, I've spent so much time and energy refusing to let myself fall for him. But now. Everything is different.

Tristan pulls his belt out of the pant loops and throws it on the ground. I hook my fingers into his belt loops and draw him closer to me, repeating the words he said to me downstairs: "Turn around."

He raises an eyebrow and does what he is told. I reach around his waist to find his pants' button and undo it slowly. I can feel his muscular back tighten with my touch. I decide to tease him a little and plant small kisses all over his back as I unzip his pants. I hear him groan which fuels my need for him even more. I reach back around and slightly graze his cock with my hand. He grunts and turns around to face me. He loops his thumbs around my panties and pulls them down, getting on his knees again in the process. He lifts my feet one by one and tosses my panties over by his discarded clothes. I hold onto his hair, hoping that he will place that mouth where I want him to.

Instead he stands and takes off his underwear. My jaw drops as I take him in fully. No wonder he has so much confidence. Before I pass out, I distract my thoughts and deflect into another subject: "Why are we going to shower? I thought we were going to the bed." If he is going to make me flustered, I am going to do the same to him. I boldly grab his ass and he chuckles at my candor. I don't know what has come over me. All I know is I want this man more than anything I've ever wanted.

He releases my hands from his perfect ass and leads me into the steaming shower. The glass walls look like the car window in *Titanic*. We step into the middle of the shower and let the water fall over both of us. Tristan takes a loofa and lathers it in body wash, which smells deliciously like him: mint and cedar. It's intoxicating. Like him. After it gets sudsy, he starts to rub it against my body. His body glistens and each droplet of water looks like a diamond against his protruding muscles. "You asked why we were in the shower."

"Yes, I did," I let out breathlessly.

Tristan takes hold of my torso and pins me against the shower wall. His eyes are so intense they make my pulse quicken. Soap and water are dripping down our bodies. Tristan's face suddenly twists into a painful expression as he says, "Hastings had his hands on you tonight. Before I touch you any further, we need to wash off any trace of that prick."

He kisses the side of my neck and sticks two fingers inside of me, making me squeal. I clutch onto his broad shoulders and dig my fingers into him. My other hand grabs his wet hair and pulls hard. He stops kissing the side of my neck and gives me his signature playful smile that I've seen him flash on and off the ice way too many times to count. I spread my legs more while he fingers me. His mouth finds mine and he kisses me. No, not just kisses me. Full-on makes out with me. I have no defenses left against this man. His tongue is exploring my mouth in ways that make my body ache even more for him. He wants this as much as I want this. And it's definitely not out of hate.

I break our kiss because I can't take it anymore. "I need you *now*, Tristan."

"I want to make you come first. So come for me and then I will take you to my bed, Cupcake." He presses his thumb over my clit and continues to finger me. He lifts one of my legs up and wraps it around his torso. My breathing is erratic as I move my hips to match the movement of his hand against me. I want more than just his fingers and tongue inside of me. Just that thought alone makes my body finally release and I collapse into him.

"Good girl," he whispers to me. He steps away from me momentarily so he can turn off the water. Then he lifts me in his strong arms and slowly walks out of the bathroom. "Did that feel good, Cupcake?"

"You know it did, Hot Shot."

He pauses at the foot of the bed. As he places me down onto the softest sheets ever, he suddenly looks worried. It's a rare sight – Tristan Lawson having a look of trepidation about something. Hell will definitely freeze over in a matter of seconds.

"What's wrong?" I ask, praying he isn't getting second thoughts.

"The problem is, once we do this, I know that I won't be able to stop wanting you. I am going to keep wanting you more and more. I have wanted this for so long. You are completely going to undo me, Brooke Beckett."

I stand up so our bodies are right up against each other. I love seeing Tristan like this. Unfiltered. No bullshit. No games. Not putting on a damn show for fans. I cradle his face and make him look me in the eyes. Wet tendrils are falling into his face and I attempt to push them back, but fail. Small droplets are still falling slowly down each ridge of his body, every curvature of each muscle. "Well it's a good thing that you have already undone me, Tristan Lawson. The moment you walked into my parents' kitchen. And I've wanted this for so long, too. I was just too stubborn to let my guard down with you."

"Mmmm, so you admit that you are stubborn." Tristan smiles as he brushes a piece of damp hair behind my ear. There it is. My favorite smile in the whole world.

I shake my head, smile back and say, "Shut up and fuck me, Tristan."

19

Tristan

Fucking finally.

I grab her face and crush my mouth onto hers. I take hold of her dark hair and pull and she moans—a sound that I want her to keep repeating over and over again. I want to explore every inch of her tonight. She is so goddamn beautiful and sexy and everything I've ever wanted and thought I would never have. And yet, she is here, kissing me, digging her fingers into my back, wanting me too.

I need Brooke more than I need air to breathe. Always have.

I hoist her up and carry her onto my bed as our mouths move in sync and out of sync all at once. It's a give-and-take kind of kiss and it's a dance I am all too familiar with when it comes to Brooke. We are trying to one-up each other with licks and nibbles and kisses. I am determined to lead this dance with her tonight, though.

"Put your weight on me, Tristan," she begs in between kisses. She is now tugging my hair and for a second I think I am going to explode. She is a force to be reckoned with. Luckily for me, I have been preparing to withstand her force for a while now. I just wasn't prepared for how undeniably hot she is in bed. She fucking knows what she is doing and a tinge of jealousy traverses through my veins, thinking of all the men who have touched her and made her groan like she is right now. Who made her beg for them to be on top of her. I am determined to give her everything she wants. I'm just afraid I might hurt her.

"Cupcake, I won't put all of my body weight on you. I will probably crush you."

"Eh, you're not that big." Her eyes scan all the way down my body and stop at my dick. "I wouldn't worry about it." She smirks.

She is trying to get a rise out of me, and it's working. Combined with the jealousy about other men sleeping with her and her playfully commenting on my size, it fuels me to take full control. I have a feeling she wants me to. I look into her eyes and she definitely has sex eyes. They are hungry and craving. I fully intend on giving her anything she wants.

"Is that so?" I turn her hips to the side and spank her. She whimpers, but then her beautiful smile spreads across her face. *She likes that? Noted.* "Does my girl like that?"

She nods.

"Say it." I spank her again.

"Yes, I like it," she exhales and pulls my hair even more. My God this woman is going to kill me. I grab her thigh and spread her open and lower my body onto hers. She wraps her legs around to the center of my back and digs her heels into me. I run my hand up and down her body. I love how soft her skin is and how she always smells faintly of coconut all the time. I love her curves and the fact that she has something to hold onto. She's definitely not like the other girls I've slept with, but I love that fact even more. The amount of times I've thought about grabbing onto these thighs and spreading her legs open for me are too many to count.

My cock is grazing her pussy and Brooke lifts her hips to get closer.

"Wait, Brooke."

"Why? What's wrong?" Her eyes shift from turned-on to concerned.

"Trust me, nothing is wrong. I just have to put a condom on."

I attempt to get up, but Brooke's legs trap me in. She places her hands on either side of my face and rubs her thumbs along my beard.

"Brooke…"

"I want you, Tristan. And that means all of you. I want to feel every single inch of you inside of me, Hot Shot." She kisses me and her tongue parting my lips sends shivers down my body. She bites my bottom lip and says, "Everything is okay. I got it covered."

I lower myself back down on top of her and say, "You want all of me, Cupcake?"

"Yes." The look she is giving me right now is causing my body to tense in the best way. A dark grin is plastered to her face and her eyes drift down to my cock and back to my eyes. She wants me just as much as I want her.

"Got it." I trace my fingers around her breasts and lean down and suck on her nipples. The sounds that come out her mouth are fucking music to my ears and make me want her more. "I don't want to rush this, Brooke. I want to savor every second of having you underneath me, calling my name when I am fucking you, seeing you unravel when you come for me." My fingers move slowly down her torso, making her giggle. I reach her pussy and it's so wet. I want to feel all of her too.

I ease my dick into her. "Shit, Brooke. You are so fucking tight and wet." I grab onto my headboard for leverage and push my hips into hers. The sensation I feel throughout my body is euphoric and I know from this point on, I don't want to be inside any other woman. I am always going to want Brooke. She pants and rolls her hips against mine. With my free hand that is clutching onto the sheets, I grab one of her hands and interlace my fingers with hers. I press our hands down into the mattress and continue to ram into her, slow and hard.

"Tristan," she rasps and she plants her mouth on my neck. She swirls her tongue against my hot skin and I grunt in response. I thrust into her harder and she lays her head back onto the pillow. Her eyes are shut and her mouth is parted. I lean down and bite her bottom lip and she smiles and finally opens her eyes so twin pools of hazel look back at me.

"Eyes on me, Cupcake." I let go of her hand and slide mine under her hips, lifting them up towards me, angling her just right. I hold onto the headboard tighter and rock my hips hard against her.

I go deeper and she gasps, "Oh my God, yes. Keep doing that, Hot Shot."

Tingles rush through my body as I continue to fuck the woman of my dreams. Her heels dig deeper into my back and I can tell that she is close to coming again. "Come again with me, baby." She keeps her eyes on me like I told her to and I can feel her body tense up and her breath hitch. I finally release as she does and a rush of pure pleasure courses through my body. But it's different this time. This wasn't just about lust. It was so much more than that.

I collapse onto Brooke, still being careful not to put my entire body weight on her. I know for certain I would crush her–no matter how much she wants to argue with me about it. I instead put some of my weight on my forearm next to her beautiful, satisfied face. I find her left hand again and lace my rough, calloused fingers through her delicate, soft ones. I rub my thumb against her palm, causing her to giggle.

She gets her other hand free from underneath my torso and rubs my scruff. This is heaven. This woman is an angel. A sometimes devilish one. But an angel nonetheless.

I continue to rub her palm with my thumb. "Are you okay?"

She grazes her own thumb against my bottom lip, then leans up and kisses me so carefully and softly it almost makes my heart explode into a million pieces. "I am more than okay. I've never been more okay in my life, Tristan."

I ease out of her and she exhales. Damn, she is dripping all along her thighs. I start to reach behind me for a tissue, but she grabs my bicep and stops me. "Where do you think you are going, Hot Shot?"

"I was going to get a tissue to clean you up a little, Cupcake."

She shakes her head. "I don't want you to clean me up. Not yet." Her eyes are dark and insatiable again. She wants more, and so do I. This woman is full of surprises. I lean forward and kiss her just as softly as she kissed me moments before. I don't know how I am going to control myself around her anymore.

She kisses me harder and her hands run over my arms, stopping at every curve. She traces her fingers over the tattoo on my ribcage and smiles against my lips. "I can't believe you got this for me. I'm surprised my brother hasn't questioned you about it."

"Trust me, he has."

Her eyebrows shoot up. "Really? And what did you tell him?"

"That I got it for him. He's my best bro. He gave me a funny look at first, but he hasn't asked about it again."

Her smile withers and I can tell that an intrusive thought swept into her mind. She releases her fingers from my hand and lets go of my face. She covers her face and muffles, "Oh my God, what about Bradley?"

I chuckle and pull her hands off her face. That line between her eyebrows is deepening. She has that cute worried look that I fucking love on her gorgeous face. "What about Bradley?" I kiss the top of her hand.

"He's going to kill you."

I kiss her palm and shrug. "Let him kill me. I've lived through worse things." I lean down and nuzzle my face into her neck, planting small kisses against her sweaty skin.

"That's hyperbolic," she says breathlessly. I can feel her relax with each kiss that touches her skin.

"No, babe, it's not." I bite her earlobe. "The worst thing I've ever gone through was not being your man all these years." I press my lips against her temple, "Not being able to hold you when you had a broken heart. Not being able to be there for you when you were sick." I kiss her forehead and stroke her jawline. "Yeah, I guess I was around for the big moments because I am Bradley's best friend and he invites me to everything. But I really just wanted so badly to be a part of your life. If I couldn't have you as my girlfriend, I'd at least have you in my life as an enemy." I look into her eyes, which are starting to fill with tears. I wipe away one that is traveling down the side of her cheek. "I took what I could get from you. And just for the record, I'm not scared of your brother. What I am scared of is losing you again to another man. That's never going to happen again."

Brooke pushes my hair away from my forehead and wraps her arms around my neck. She kisses me and I feel her body shift to the side as she drapes her leg around my hip. Her hands find my chest and press hard against it. I decide to give in because I want her so badly to never stop touching me the way that she is right now.

We flip over so I am now the one on my back and Brooke fully straddles me. I can feel myself all over her inner thighs and pussy and that makes me want her even more. She is a fucking sight to see. My hands grab her ass and spank it again.

"Mmmm, never stop doing that," she groans in my ear as she leans down and puts her breasts right in my face. I take each one in my mouth and suck hard. The sounds coming out of her mouth are everything and I can tell she is getting so turned on. Her hips are starting to move against me as she holds onto the headboard this time.

"Well lucky for you, I don't think you will ever have to worry about losing me, Tristan. I'm yours."

Brooke then eases down onto me and I hold onto her hips.

"Damn straight you are, Cupcake. All mine."

20

Brooke

"Do you need any help setting the table, Mom?" I walk into the kitchen and open the cabinet that has all the dinner plates. I get out five beige plates and start placing them on the table. "I take it that Jen is coming tonight?"

My mom walks out with a big bowl full of salad and places it in the center of the table. "Yes. Oh honey, we actually need one more."

That's odd. It should be five: me, Bradley, Jen, Mom and Dad.

"Bradley didn't tell you? Well I guess not, by that crease on your forehead. Tristan is coming."

The last dish slips from my fingers and shatters all over the tile floor. *Tristan is coming?* I haven't seen him since Casino Night, or rather the next morning, and that was a week ago. It has been such a crazy week at work. We have been texting every day but our schedules didn't work out to actually get together in person. My hands start to get clammy and flashbacks from that night make me hot.

"Brooke! What is the matter with you?" My mom peers at me with concern. "Don't move. There are shards everywhere. Let me get the broom."

"Sorry Mom!" I yell after her. Why is Tristan coming to dinner? He has not been to Sunday dinner in a few months.

"Here," my mom comes back with a broom and dustpan and starts sweeping.

"Mom, let me do it. You can finish setting up since apparently I have butterfingers today."

She huffs and hands me the broom. I carefully sweep the shards. Is this supposed to be a sign from the universe that tonight is going to turn out awful? That Bradley is going to sense that Tristan and I slept together? That we couldn't keep our hands off each other that night and Tristan gave me an out-of-body experience each time he made me orgasm? I hope that Tristan is on his best behavior.

No matter how hard that is for him to do.

I AM in the middle of watching a rerun of Jeopardy with my dad when the doorbell rings. Thinking it's my brother and Jen, I get up. "I'll get it!"

I open the door without looking through the peephole and Tristan is awaiting me on the other side. He has a bottle of wine and I would be lying to myself if I didn't want to immediately take him upstairs and show him how turned on I am by the sight of him. He of course is wearing a Dallas Storm t-shirt with jeans and a backwards hat.

I am wearing a short, pink, floral sundress. Tristan licks his lips and rakes his eyes all over me. "Hello, Cupcake. You actually look nice tonight."

What the hell? My stomach feels like a giant boulder just fell in it. I am about to flip him the bird, but then he leans in and whispers, "Remember, everyone has to believe that we still hate each other. You look gorgeous tonight, as always."

I smirk as he hands me the bottle of wine, breezes past me, and greets my parents.

"Tristan! It's so nice to see you!" My mom gives Tristan a big mama bear hug and pats him on the back. "It's been too long. I know you hate Brooke, but you don't hate us."

I close the door behind me and lean on it. Tristan glances over at me. "You're right, I don't hate you or Mr. Beckett. Just Brooke." He discreetly winks at me and my stomach does a full-on somersault.

My dad gets up from his chair and shakes hands with Tristan. "Nice to see you, Tristan. You're having an impeccable season."

I roll my eyes as the hockey talk is about to commence and last for the remainder of the night. I head to the kitchen to get wine glasses out. It's going to be a long evening of my dad, Tristan and Bradley talking all things hockey. At least I can chat with Jen about wedding stuff tonight. And I am grateful Tristan brought a bottle of wine. I am going to need some to get through tonight, pretending to hate the man I spent the best night of my life with a week ago.

I glance at the bottle and it happens to be my favorite type of wine. Peach moscato. I smile that Tristan remembered that small detail from years ago. I'll have to properly thank him at another time.

I open the drawer and take out the wine opener. I feel someone's body heat up against my back and sleeves of tattoos trap me against the counter. Tingles travel up and down my body. It is taking everything in me to not turn around and make out with the man standing behind me.

Tristan brushes my hair from one side of my neck, rendering it exposed, and whispers, "Did I get the right one, Cupcake?"

Goosebumps appear on my body. *Keep your composure, Brooke.* "Mmhmm," I succinctly respond, trying to focus on screwing in the wine opener correctly.

"Here." Tristan's hands cover both of mine and a jolt of electricity permeates me. Tristan begins to twist the corkscrew and even that simple act makes me hot. He presses his body up against mine and I can feel how his body is responding to my presence. This night is going to be interesting to say the least. How the hell are we supposed to get through this charade when we both want to rip each other's clothes off? The cork finally pops off just as the doorbell rings, making us both jump and come back to the reality that we are not alone in this house.

Unfortunately.

"It must be Bradley and Jen," I say as I place the cork on the side of the bottle and grab a glass.

"Yeah, must be." Tristan leans against the counter and crosses his arms as he watches me pour what is probably half the bottle into my wine glass. "Woah, slow down slugger. Save some for the rest of us. Are you planning on getting shitfaced drunk at your parents' house on a Sunday night?"

"Whatever it takes to get through this doomed evening."

"Let's be positive about this, Brooke." He takes my wrist and brings it up to his lips and softly kisses it. "At least we get to see each other. I missed you all week. Did you miss me?"

My mouth turns dry and I part my lips, about to respond, "Of course I did!" when Bradley's voice seems to be getting closer. I yank my hand out of Tristan's and smile toward the entrance to the kitchen.

"Hey bro! I didn't realize you were already here!" Tristan and Bradley make the loudest sound with their handshake, more like a clap, and give each other a one-armed hug. Why are men like this? Just hug like normal human beings!

"Damn," Bradley yells over his shoulder, "I am surprised the kitchen is still intact. And that Mom and Dad allowed you two to be alone in the kitchen. Let me check to make sure all the knives are in their proper places."

"Brad, leave them alone." Jen embraces me and then Tristan.

"Although it is a little suspicious that you two aren't at each other's throats right now."

"The night is still young," Tristan pipes in. "Anything can happen. Right, Cupcake?" The way he said "Cupcake" is unlawful. It is laced with lust and my wet panties are proof of the effect Tristan Lawson now has on me.

I decide to respond with equal lust, "Right, Hot Shot."

———

WE END up sitting next to each other. Tristan insisted since Brad and Jen would probably want to sit next to each other. "We can be civil, I promise, Mrs. Beckett," he reassures my mother as she shoots us a "you better not destroy my house tonight" look.

Just as I predicted, my dad, Bradley and Tristan talk about hockey and the upcoming games they still have left before playoffs. Apparently, they are in a really good position to make it to the playoffs this year. I can sense the excitement in both my brother and Tristan.

"So Brooke," my mom chimes in. "How is everything looking for opening up your little bakery?"

I hate when my mom says "little bakery" like it's some sort of silly wish that will never come to fruition.

I clear my throat and push a piece of chicken to the other side of my plate. I can feel all eyes on me. "Well, Tess and I saw a place that would be perfect in Uptown that is available for rent." I shrug as reality hits me all at once as I decide to not tell them how much it could possibly be. "But I still need to call them and find out more details."

Bradley butts in, "You know B, I can always spot you the money for a bit until the business starts making a profit, I don't mind."

I shake my head vigorously. "No, absolutely not. Thank you, but you have your wedding and your own life to worry about."

I can see my mom's head shaking in my peripheral vision. "I don't understand why you don't take your brother up on his offer. He's trying to help you, Brooke."

I stab the poor piece of chicken in front of me. "I don't need his help," I say curtly and look at my mom, whose eyes go wide. I rarely talk to my mom like this, but I can't take the infantilizing comments anymore. I am an adult and I don't need my older brother to take care of me. We aren't kids anymore. "I'll figure it out on my own. This is my dream and I'll open my bakery when the time is right." I need to change the subject. "So, Jen, how was the cake tasting the other day? Bradley doesn't update me on anything wedding-related." I know I am being stubborn but I have been living in Bradley's shadow ever since he scored his first goal when he was four years old.

Thankfully, the conversation shifts to the cake tasting. As I place some baked chicken into my mouth, I feel a strong hand grip my thigh. I glance over at Tristan, who is still actively involved in the conversation about his best man duties. He's evil for doing this to me right now. With my family surrounding us. But maybe that's also the fun of it all.

I purse my lips and lift my glass. As I take a drink of wine, Tristan's rough, huge hand starts traveling up my inner thigh, causing the hem of my sundress to rise up. I choke slightly on my wine, but not enough to draw attention. Tristan must be the only one who noticed because he gives my thigh a little squeeze and keeps inching closer and closer to where he wants to end up. My skin is on fire from his touch and he is dangerously close to finding out what he is doing to me. A couple more inches in fact.

He takes a sip of his own wine and smirks. He isn't even looking at me and I can tell his eyes are becoming ravenous. He is distracting himself with the wine and so am I. His fingers graze my cotton underwear. I would've worn sexier panties if I had known he was coming over tonight. Not that I was expecting us to do anything in my parents' house. He starts rubbing against my panties and I have to take another drink of wine to distract myself. I plaster a smile on my face and pretend to be invested in all the wedding talk. Even though all I can think about is Tristan. And what he is doing to me right now. And what he did to me a week ago.

It is getting too intense. I subtly reach down and swat his hand away. I stand up and say, "Excuse me, I need to go to the restroom. Be right back."

"Are you okay, sweetheart? You look a little flushed." My mom places the back of her hand against my forehead to check if I have a fever.

"It's probably all the wine. I'll be fine, Mom." I dart toward the hallway bathroom and shut the door behind me. I take some deep breaths. Tristan is not playing fair right now. He is enjoying getting me flustered in front of my family. I turn on the faucet and run my hands under the cold water, rubbing some on the back of my neck and my forehead. My skin is on fire right now. All thanks to Tristan. I close my eyes and take another deep breath. *You can do this, Brooke. We are almost done with dinner.*

I reach for the doorknob but it turns before I can even touch it. Tristan barges in and locks the door behind him.

"Tristan! What do you think you are doing? Are you trying to get caught? Do you have a death wis–?"

Tristan's lips land on mine and he feverishly kisses me. I can't help but kiss him back. He turns us around so that my back is now against the bathroom door.

"I wanted to come see how wet I made you." He says in between kisses. His hands find the hem of my dress and he starts to lift it up.

I tug my dress back down. "Tristan."

"Brooke." His hands caress my hips and upper thighs.

"Not here," I say earnestly. Then whisper, "My family is right outside this door."

"I promise I'll be quick." He starts kissing my neck. This man is absolute trouble.

"I am surprised you are flaunting that statement like it's a good thing," I tease. He squeezes the sides of my torso, making me giggle.

"Well, speed bodes well for me at the moment." Tristan smiles.

God he is ruining me with the way he looks tonight. His shirt is so tight against his chest, it makes my heart race. "Besides, I know that you don't have the greatest memory from this particular bathroom since you overheard the lie I told your brother all those years ago. I want you to have a new memory."

As much as I want this man to take me right here and now, I also want him to drive him crazy a little bit. I want to step back and not go too fast with Tristan. He is worth waiting for.

"Trust me, I do." I find both of his massive, manly hands and hold them tightly. "It's just...I don't want to rush this, Tristan." He starts to contest and I push my finger against his mouth to stop him. "I know we have waited way too long and have held back from each other but..."

Tristan places a delicate kiss on the side of my mouth. "Please, Brooke. I need you." Then his hands escape mine and he traps me against the door by putting both arms on each side of me. Even through his sleeve of tattoos, I can see large veins cover the surface of his muscular forearms and my knees weaken.

I look into his hazel eyes, which look a little more green than usual. Almost as green as they look against his kelly green jersey. "Me too. I love seeing you beg for me. I am not sure I am ready to grant your wish just yet, Hot Shot."

"Hmmm." Tristan lowers his arms. Instead of looking defeated, it appears like I fueled the fire in Tristan's eyes. "Is that so, Cupcake?"

"Yup." My conviction is starting to waver against the hot way Tristan is looking at me. His fingers tickle the side of my arms and my core tightens and breath hitches. Damn this man.

"All right, I'll play by your rules." He grabs tightly onto my wrists and pins them above my head. "Just know that at some point, I plan on breaking every single one of them."

Oh, he's good.

21

Brooke

That Friday, I invite Tess over for a long-overdue girls night. I brought coffee and donuts as promised the Monday after Casino Night, but since work has been so crazy, we haven't really had much time to talk. I haven't been able to get into everything that has transpired between me and Tristan. So I have been looking forward to our girls night all week. She brings over wine and pizza and forces me to spare no details of my nights with Tristan while I make my famous brownies.

An hour later, we are in the middle of doing clay face masks and watching our favorite romcom, *How to Lose a Guy in 10 Days*, when my phone vibrates.

I glance at the screen and see a message from Tristan. He and Bradley have a series of away games in St. Louis and Las Vegas, so the actual physical distance has almost helped keep him out of my mind. Almost.

Hey, Cupcake.

My heart starts racing and my fingers itch to text him back right away, but there is a small part of me that wants to make him wait a few minutes. I want to play with him a little bit.

"I'm going to go wash this facemask off," I tell Tess, who is mindlessly stuffing her face with a brownie.

"Okay," she muffles.

I splash warm water on my face and watch the water in the sink turn a little muddy. Just like my relationship with Tristan. How did we get here? How did someone who made me want to strangle him every time I saw him become the person who makes it harder to breathe when he is near – or far, apparently. I dry my face off with a towel and head back into the living room.

"Your phone vibrated again, B." Tess jumps off the couch and heads to the bathroom to wash off her own face.

I get a brownie from my kitchen counter and go back to the couch. I splay my pink checkered throw blanket over my legs, unlock my phone screen and open my messages.

I missed you in the stands tonight.

I am sure I have the goofiest grin on my face as I start typing back:

Oh, I'm sure you had plenty of girls cheering you on. There is no lack of fans when it comes to Tristan Lawson.

That is the understatement of the century. Images of countless girls, like that ice girl Alison who went to his house a few weeks ago, flood my brain. My stomach begins to sink because they are all the type of girls he claimed he was attracted to all those years ago. I'm sure the girls in Vegas are no different. Plus, they are in Vegas – who knows what kind of trouble these guys are going to get into.

I try to focus back on my TV. Matthew McConaughey is looking at Kate Hudson in the way all girls want to be looked at. If I am honest with myself, there is only one man who has ever looked at me like that. And he is texting me right now. My phone vibrates again and I read Tristan's response.

None of them were you.

My face gets hot as I bite my bottom lip.

"Who are you texting?"

I jump and slap my hand to my chest as my phone falls on the ground. "Oh my God, Tess, you scared the crap out of me!"

Tess comes around the couch and sits in her spot as I reach down and inspect my phone, which thankfully isn't broken.

"My bad, girl. I didn't mean to scare you." She chuckles and looks at the TV screen. "Aw man, I missed my favorite part. Do you mind if I rewind it?"

"Not at all."

She presses a button on the remote and we both rewatch "the look" scene with googly eyes. Without a beat, Tess presses on, "So, who are you texting on our sacred girls night?"

"No one," I lie, tucking some stray hair behind my ears. The sucky thing is, I am a terrible liar. And I have been friends with Tess long enough that she can spot my bullshit from a mile away.

My phone vibrates again and before I can stop her, Tess snatches my phone from my hands. She reads the screen and her eyebrows raise to a level I've never seen before, along with the grin that spreads across her face.

"What are you wearing, Cupcake?"

Tess' grin grows even wider. "Oh my god! I knew it!"

"Can I have my phone back please?" I hold out my hand. Tess gives me an up-to-no-good look, and types in my passcode. "Hey! How did you know my passcode?"

"Oh please, I've known your passcode for years." She successfully unlocks my phone and quickly types a message back to Tristan.

"You better show me before you send that mess—" I hear the swooping noise indicating that she sent whatever message already. "Tess! Oh my God, what did you send him?" I frantically reach over for my phone.

She shrugs and hands it back willingly. "Well, it's getting late and I think your night is about to get a lot more interesting." She wiggles her eyebrows at me. "I'm going to take some brownies for the road, is that okay?" Before I have the chance to look at whatever incriminating words Tess sent to Tristan, I respond, "Oh, of course, since you have been so helpful tonight."

"Trust me, I have! You'll thank me later." She grabs a tupperware container out of my cabinet and digs into the pan.

Kate Hudson is shouting the words to "You're So Vain" into a microphone. I point to the TV. "Are you sure you don't want to stay? The movie isn't over yet."

She waves me off. "You and I both know that we've seen this movie hundreds of times. I know how it ends...now as for you, I better have updates on what happens after I leave. And spare me no details...I haven't been on a date in months. Have fun with Hot Shot tonight."

I can feel myself blushing as I stand up to walk her to the door.

She wraps her arm around my neck, giving me a hug goodbye. "This was fun, B. We need to do this more."

"I agree." Tess always knows how to bring the fun into my life and calms me when I am freaking out or when my anxiety gets the best of me.

She blows me a kiss as she exits my apartment and I blow her one back. I don't know how I ever survived this life without Tess. Although now, I want to push her into a small pond like Luke does to

Jess in *Gilmore Girls* for sending a text without me inspecting it first. I hesitantly unlock my phone and see the message she sent.

Nothing.

I am going to kill Tess. I look down at my candy-striped tank top and shorts pajama set and laugh. Tristan would totally tease me about these pajamas if he were here with me right now.

Is that so, Cupcake? I would love for you to show me.

No fricken way am I sending Tristan nudes. I don't know who is around looking over his shoulder. I have to play it safe. It's in my nature.

You'll have to take my word for it, Hot Shot.

I'm afraid I can't, Cupcake. I'd rather see proof.

I don't think you can handle the proof. I am also going to finish what you started the other night. I hope you don't mind

I smirk as I open my Instagram. My brother's story circle pops up first on the story bar. I tap on it and my heart starts to race again, because it isn't my brother gracing my screen. My brother took a video of Tristan and tagged him in his story. Tristan looks stupidly hot with his signature look: a backwards hat, a Storm sweatshirt and dark gray sweatpants. The two of them are in some casino and my brother, who clearly had a little too much to drink, is sitting across from Tristan. "Hey ladies, my man Tristan over here is single and ready to mingle. DM him if you are interested." Tristan looks up from his phone and gives the camera a smile, shaking his head at Bradley.

I know we are keeping our relationship under wraps in front of my brother, but it still devastates me seeing Tristan not deny what my brother is saying. Whatever, I am not going to torture myself by replaying what I just saw in my head. I turn off the TV and gather the two wine glasses from my coffee table. I place them in my dishwasher, start it and head to my bedroom. My phone vibrates again as I turn on my bathroom light:

> You're lucky that we are not in the same room together, Cupcake. You have no idea what I want to do to you. I wish you were here 😏

I huff to myself. *Why am I lucky? So I can't see the swarm of DMs that are naturally blowing up your phone?* Whatever, it's not a big deal. He is a professional hockey player whose profile is public. My brother doesn't know anything about us. I was the one who wanted to keep it secret. I start brushing my teeth, probably a little too hard, almost like I am trying to scrub away that stupid story from my head.

> Looks like you are busy with my brother anyway. I'll talk to you later. Goodnight, Hot Shot.

I slide into my bed and pick up my book that I've literally been trying to finish for a month and attempt to start reading when my phone rings. Shit. He's calling me right now?

I place my bookmark and slam my book shut. I take a deep breath and swipe the bottom bar to answer.

"Hello?"

"Hey, Cupcake. Are you okay?" he says in his sultry, deep voice.

"Why wouldn't I be okay?"

"I don't know, it just seemed like..." his voice trails off. I can almost see his eyebrows furrowed together. He definitely has his serious face on right now.

"Like...?" I egg him on, even though I know he knows me too well to not call me out on my bullshit.

"Like you were upset. I assume you saw Bradley's story, based on your text."

"I'm not...upset. I am just not interested in seeing you smile at what my brother said." I press my palm to my forehead and squeeze my eyes shut. "About you being single. I mean we never established anything like we are exclusive or whatever you want to call it so I don't expect you to just be with me. But if that is the case, can you let me know if you are sleeping with other people? I just...don't want to get it in my head that I'm yours and you're mine if it's not true. I don't want to live off the hope of it all." I sigh, feeling exposed. "I'm sorry, it's none of my business what you are doing in Vegas." I can feel a tear roll down my cheek. I didn't even know that I was crying.

"Brooke..."

"What?" I try to cover my sniffles as best as I can.

"I am not going to do anything with anyone in Vegas. Or anywhere, for that matter. The only reason I was smiling in that video was not because of what your brother said, though it did help with the story we are telling about our relationship. I was smiling because I was texting with this beautiful girl who has fucking stolen my heart and is, in fact, mine."

I wipe another tear off my cheek as my stomach flips.

He continues, "As for sleeping with other people, not a chance, Cupcake. And just to be clear, I am nowhere near single. I'm yours and you are mine." The way he says *mine* is so possessive, it makes my body tingle.

He continues, and I swear his voice gets even lower, "Now tell me, babe, are you really wearing nothing?"

He's such a guy. I decide to put him out of his misery and snap a photo of myself in all my light-pink-and-white-striped pajama glory. I hit send and wait for him to respond.

"If you think that this isn't going to turn me on, you are mistaken, Cupcake. That candy striped look is hot."

"You better be alone in that hotel room, Hot Shot. Especially if you are going to be talking like that."

"I am alone."

"Good," I breathe out. I run my hand along my inner thigh, wishing it was Tristan's hand. My phone dings and I open a photo message from Tristan. His hoodie is gone and all I see is his sculpted tattooed chest and washboard abs and the deep V along the elastic band of his underwear that is peeking out from his dark gray sweatpants. He is sticking out his tongue playfully and I can feel myself getting so wet at the mere sight of this man. His voice is also so irresistible, I feel like my body might just combust from the vibrations of every word that comes out of that perfect mouth of his.

"You took off your hoodie, Hot Shot. And that tongue. Are you trying to tease me?"

"Oh, Brooke, you and I both know that I want to do more than tease you. And trust me when I get home tomorrow, I am coming straight over to your apartment to show you just how much my tongue misses licking every part of you. For now, I want you to be a good girl and slide your panties to the side and put your fingers inside you."

Now it's my turn to drive him crazy with the truth. "I would, except I am not wearing any."

Tristan groans and his deep voice vibrates throughout my entire body, causing my toes to curl. It's almost like he is in the same room as me. "Fuck, Brooke. This is fucking torture being away from you. My body is aching for you."

"Good thing we get to see each other tomorrow. Let's hold off until then. Would you mind waiting, Hot Shot?" As much as I want to do this over the phone, I want him next to me, on top of me, behind me...all of the above. My body is aching for him, too, and I selfishly want his hands on me and his lips grazing every inch of my skin.

I thought he would be disappointed and insist that we finish what we are doing. Instead, he surprises me with the sweetest statement: "I have waited for you for almost a third of my life, Brooke. I think I can handle it. You have no idea how much I want my hands all over you."

"Well, until tomorrow, then. I can't wait to see you. Have a safe flight back home."

"I will and I'll text you tomorrow morning, Brooke. Goodnight babe."

I smile and butterflies flutter in my stomach at the way he said "babe" so effortlessly. "Goodnight, handsome."

I tap the red button and plug my phone into the charger. I switch off my bedside lamp and pull my comforter up close to my face. I don't know how well I am going to sleep tonight because I can't get Tristan, every single aspect of him, out of my head. Tomorrow can't come soon enough.

22

Brooke

I get a notification that I have a package waiting for me in the mailroom. I pull open the large doors to the leasing office of my apartment complex. A couple of employees are at their desks.

"Hey can I help you?"

I get a quick glimpse of his nametag: Bryan. "Yes you can, Bryan. I got a notification that a package was delivered for me."

"Name?"

"Brooke Beckett."

A flicker of recognition washes over the other employee's face and it looks like she is starting to blush. I glance over at her nametag and register that her name is Kayla. "Hold on, Bryan! You don't need to go to the back room to get her package. I have it right here."

Confused, Bryan sits back down at his desk and swivels his chair around to face his computer.

"Um, is something wrong with the package that you had to hold it up here rather than with all the other packages?" I nervously laugh.

Kayla laughs back as she reaches down underneath her desk and says, "Oh no. There is no problem. It's just the guy who dropped this off wanted to ensure I give it to you directly. He said that the contents of the package were really important and he didn't want to take any chances of it being accidentally given to the wrong person."

"Okay...did this guy have a name?"

"He didn't give me a name, but he looked *really* familiar. I just can't pinpoint where I've seen him before. And just between you and me, he is really hot! He was wearing a backwards hat, had a scruffy beard and sleeves of tattoos." She blushes again and hands me a package wrapped in pink wrapping paper with a big pink bow on top of it.

I know exactly who this is from.

"Thank you for holding onto this for me. I am sure that this mystery man will be forever grateful."

I start to walk away and then the girl stops me. "Oh, he left you one more thing!" She gets up and walks toward the window where a bouquet of bright pink roses sits on the windowsill. My heart leaps as she hands me the vase. "Whoever this guy is, sure does like you. No man has ever bought me flowers and surprised me with a gift before. You're so lucky." She fawns over what I have in my hands.

I smile back at her. "Thank you."

Once I make it into my apartment, I drop my keys on the coffee table and carefully place the vase next to them. I take the box and pull on one side of the bow to release it. I tear open the wrapping paper like a kid on Christmas morning. I definitely have the same level of excitement. I lift the top of the white box. Of course there is pink tissue paper covering the contents of the package. But there is also a note lying on top.

Cupcake, I'm sorry I couldn't come by your apartment on Sunday night when I got home. I got held up with the team and some PR stuff for upcoming games. I hope tonight makes up for it. I want you to wear this underneath your clothes tonight at your ice skating lessons. I hope you like the color. ;)

P.S. There is a location change for tonight. I'll send you the address later.

I scoff and shake my head. He texted me the night he got back from Vegas saying he couldn't come by after all. It all worked out anyway since I had to get up extra early the next day. A night with Tristan would have kept me up way past my bedtime. Regardless, does he think I'm just going to do whatever he wants me to do? I don't think so.

I go to my contacts and tap *Tristan Lawson* on my list. He answers on the first ring and I can already tell through the phone he has a satisfied grin on his face.

"Hello, Cupcake."

"What makes you think that you can tell me what to wear to our ice-skating lessons?"

"Ah, I take it that you opened the package I left for you earlier. I'm glad I could trust Kayla with that very important task. Did you like what was inside?"

I move the tissue paper to the side and see some very revealing, lacy, hot pink, very expensive lingerie waiting for me in that box. "I... do...but that's not the point."

He laughs. "What is the point then, Cupcake?"

"You can't just order me around and expect me to just do your bidding and be at your beck and call."

He hums that dangerous, feminism-leaving-my-body kind of hum. My core tightens at that damn hum. "We'll see about that." I get a text message a second later with the address to the hockey arena. "I'll see you later, Cupcake. Oh and take an Uber. I'll drive you back home after we finish our lesson."

A COUPLE OF HOURS LATER, I arrive at the arena. Tristan told me to go around to a specific door and a security guard should let me in. I get to the door he indicated, but it is locked. No security guard in sight. Shit. I jiggle the door handle again and nothing. Is he playing a sick joke on me? There are no games or concerts tonight in the arena and this plaza is basically deserted, other than a few tourists taking pictures of the building. People are starting to stare at me, probably thinking I am trying to break into the arena. Forget this, I'm just going to go back to my car and save myself the embarrassment. I whip around and that's when I hear the door click open. "Miss Beckett?"

I turn back around. "Yes."

"Mr. Lawson is waiting for you. Will you follow me, please?" A large, built man is standing in the doorway propping open the door, halfway protecting the entrance while leaving space for me to slip through.

I give him a small grin as I inch my way past him in the narrow path he is leaving open for me. "Thanks." He clicks the door shut and locks it.

"This way, Miss Beckett." He extends his arm out in the direction of the rink.

I hold out my hand to shake his. "You can call me Brooke. It's nice to meet you..."

"Jackson. Randall Jackson. I've been the head of security here at Southwest Arena for almost twenty years. Mr. Lawson is my favorite athlete who has ever played in this arena and trust me, I've seen a lot of great athletes play out there on that ice. He's a good guy. No offense to your brother."

"None taken." I joke, "Did Mr. Lawson pay you to say that about him?" I smile and so does Randall.

He opens the door to the rink and says, "Nope. That is my true and honest opinion about the man. And he must really think something of you to request this private tour of the arena. We usually don't do this, but anything for Mr. Lawson. Enjoy yourself, miss."

Other than my brother, I've never heard someone talk up Tristan to this degree with so much sincerity in their voice. I don't take a lot of stock in what my brother says half the time, and I always figured he was biased because Tristan is his best friend. Hearing this glowing review from a complete stranger has more weight to it.

"Thanks. It was nice to meet you, Randall. Now I will know a friendly face when I come to watch my brother and Tristan play."

He nods in agreement and closes the door. I've never been inside the arena when it wasn't blasting music from every angle of the building. The only sound right now are blades sliding across the ice and a stick hitting a puck into the goal. Tristan is busy getting some shooting practice in. He can't help it. I have seen Tristan play hockey in his Storm uniform a handful of times now, yet I rarely see him in regular clothes on the ice. To see him in the actual place where he plays without all the gear on, yet skating just as hard and just as gracefully – it is mesmerizing. Every puck he shoots zings directly into the net. Every. Single. One. Granted, there isn't a massive goalie protecting the goal, but still. He shoots from different angles and distances and still makes it in.

I could watch him forever. Without a worry that someone is going to cross-check him against his neck like a fricken guillotine or slam him into the sideboards so hard that he falls limply to the ice or punch him in the jaw and incite a full-on brawl. He's safe right now and that gives me peace.

Tristan shoots another puck and it lands square in the back of the net. I figure I should stop gawking at him and let him know I arrived. I start clapping and whistling at him. He abruptly turns his head around and registers I'm there. "Nice shooting!" My yell echoes.

He skates over to me with a wide smile. He slows down and steps onto the padded floor.

I lean over the rail and taunt, "Is that why they call you Hot Shot?"

"I don't know. You tell me. You're the only one who calls me Hot Shot, Cupcake." He grabs the side of my neck and pulls me down and kisses me, gliding his tongue into my mouth. Shivers run across my body and suddenly, I want that tongue in a very different place. He is driving my need for him higher with every kiss. *Calm yourself down Brooke, we are here for skating lessons and a private tour evidently.*

Tristan breaks our kiss and taps on the railing. "Here, get on the railing and I'll help you down."

I climb up on the rail, straddle it and swing my other leg around it so now my butt is placed firmly on the freezing metal. Tristan places his giant, veiny hands on each side of my torso and I place my delicate, frozen hands on his shoulders. He lowers me down with ease, as if I weigh the same as a feather, which is far from the truth. I play with the hair resting against the nape of his neck and pull him down to me this time as I return the knee-buckling kiss he gave me a minute ago. I pull back so I can look at the gorgeous man in front of me. Tristan is wearing a green backwards Storm hat and a black dry-fit Storm zip-up with a gray shirt underneath and black joggers. Nothing out of the ordinary, but a deadly and favorite combination in my book. Tristan examines me in turn. I wore an oversized pink quarter zip sweatshirt, black leggings, crew socks with hot pink stripes, and pink-and-white tennis shoes.

"Did you wear what I gave you under these unnecessary clothes?" he says with a devilish grin. His hand begins to run up underneath my sweatshirt and I force myself to push his hand away. This is hardly the place for any of that. Only in my dreams is that allowed.

"Um I consider these clothes very necessary, so I guess you'll never know." I totally am wearing the lingerie he bought for me. He just doesn't need to know that yet. I raise my eyebrows while holding tightly onto his mischievous hand. His other hand grabs my butt and pulls me closer to him.

Then he places a piece of my hair that I left out of my ponytail behind my ear. "I like your hair up in a ponytail." I swing my head to the side and show off my pink ribbon that I tied into a bow, securing the ponytail. He laughs, "Of course you have a pink bow in your hair."

I shrug while playing with the drawstring of his joggers. "I thought I'd switch things up a little."

"Well, I like the switch-up. It may come in handy later." He winks at me, making my stomach somersault. *What does that mean?* He then turns around and grabs a box from the other side of the aisle. He hands it to me. "Here. Open it."

"Another package?" I feel a sudden twinge of guilt in my stomach for not getting him anything at all. "Tristan, you know I don't need you to buy me anything, right?"

"Will you just open it? And I will spoil my girl if I want to." *My girl.* I grin and take the box. I lift the lid and see hockey skates. And not standard black hockey skates. Custom pink ones. With green laces and the number 92 printed on the side. "If we are going to continue your lessons, I want you to have the best skates on the market. No more rental skates for you. Do you like them?"

"I love them! Thank you. They are perfect."

"Just like you, Cupcake." He kisses me on my forehead. Is this a dream? Because it sure feels like one. The most surreal one yet. One where I might be falling in love with my enemy with every passing moment. One where I think he is falling for me, too. "Here, sit down on this bench and I'll put them on for you."

Without protest, I sit and watch Tristan take extra care of putting my skates on properly. I can tell he does this daily. Once he is done securing them on my feet, he takes my hands and guides me onto the ice. My body jolts when Tristan yells up to the media box, "Hey Randall, my man, can you play that playlist I have queued up and do that special thing I requested earlier?"

Randall's voice booms across the empty arena. "Sure thing, Mr. Lawson."

The lights dim around us and light ricochets off the disco ball that starts turning above us. One of my favorite songs from my favorite band,The Paper Kites, starts playing. This isn't just any skating lesson. This is Tristan Lawson's version of a romantic date. This is him wooing me. And I am completely falling for it. Forget what I said earlier about maybe falling for Tristan.

I am unquestionably falling in love with him.

Tristan is skating backwards so I have no choice but to look up at him. "Are you trying to romance me, Mr. Lawson?"

"Is it working?" He tightens his grip on my hands and smirks.

It is standard for me to resort to giving him a hard time or coming back with a deflective comment. Instead, I let him in. "Maybe." I squeeze his hands back.

He continues to effortlessly glide backwards while I struggle to find my equilibrium on the ice. But even though that struggle, I feel safe. My heart is beating wildly but this time it isn't because I am afraid of the ice – it is because the man in front of me, who put so much thought into this night, is smiling at me like I've never been smiled at before.

My gaze shifts down towards the ice so I can save face. I slide a bit, but Tristan is right there to hold me up and prevent me from falling on my ass again. At least we are somewhat alone this time and not in front of a bunch of kindergarteners and their chaperones.

Tristan must sense my self-doubt. "Don't think. Just skate, Cupcake."

"Easy for you to say. You do this for a living. It is your whole world, Hot Shot." I raise an eyebrow at him and smile.

He sighs. "I used to think the only thing that mattered to me was hockey. Making it into the NHL was my dream ever since I stepped foot onto the ice when I was four. You're right, my world only consisted of hockey. The ice. The puck. The crowd." He leads us to the middle of the ice and our skating ceases. Everything but Tristan's voice seems to fade into the background. He wraps his arms around me, trapping the bottom of my ponytail under his massive, strong forearms, angling my face up so I have nowhere to look but his hazel eyes. "Until I met you."

I inhale sharply. I've never seen Tristan look so serious and vulnerable all at once.

"I wanted so desperately to get your attention with my hockey skills because for so long that was the only way I ever got attention. But I soon learned you couldn't care less about hockey. You are my biggest challenge and the best thing I could ever attain in this life. Every single goal I've scored since I met you was my own personal love note to you, Brooke."

I tighten my arms around his lower back as he presses a kiss on my forehead. I am a puddle.

He continues, "I found out over time that my hockey skills weren't going to be the thing to win you over. And for a long time I lost hope that I would ever be with you. I just considered myself lucky that I was in your life at all. The sound of your voice ignited my soul every time I was near you. The mere fact that you are on this earth is a blessing to me and motivation enough for me to be the best version of myself on and off the ice. It was because of you that I trained as hard as I did. It was because of you that I never let another woman fully in. It's not that I wanted to be a bachelor or a playboy or whatever the hell you want to call it. No other woman was good enough to have my whole heart. I didn't want to let them in because I was reserving that spot for you."

That's it. My heart no longer belongs to me. It belongs to the man holding onto me in his big, strong arms in the middle of his favorite place in the world, while my favorite song by my favorite band is playing. We can no longer fight whatever magic led us into each other's lives.

I adjust my arms to wrap them around his neck and bring his lips down to mine, more like colliding his lips to mine, almost knocking him off-balance. I need to kiss him like I need air to breathe. I want to show him how much I need him. I don't want him to doubt my feelings about him or misconstrue them in any way. My hands travel down his sculpted chest and finally find the hem of his shirt. Talk about unnecessary clothes. My fingers graze the top of his joggers and his skin sears mine.

He laughs against my lips and says, "Careful, Cupcake. We aren't completely alone."

"Well, as sweet as this romancing is, maybe we should get out of here so that we *are* completely alone," I whisper against his mouth.

"I promise you that we will go back to my house after this. But I have one more place to show you, if that's okay?"

I playfully roll my eyes and scoff, "I guess."

The next thing I know, Tristan grabs my ass and lifts me up so my legs are straddling his torso as his hands stay firmly on my butt. He squeezes a little and says, "Roll your eyes again, and see what happens, Cupcake." He skates to the edge of the ice toward the opening to the tunnel. I expect him to lower me to the ground once we are off the ice, but Tristan keeps me in his arms, walking with ease down the tunnel. He makes a turn and we enter the Dallas Storm locker room.

"Oooo is this part of my private tour? You know it has been my dream to see the inside of a locker room," I say sarcastically. Tristan sets me down on a bench, leans down to take off his skates, then begins taking off my skates. Once he places the skates off to the side, he goes over to the entrance to the locker room, shuts the door and locks it. He strides over to me, with a mischievous look in his eye that I am all-too-familiar with.

"Why did you lock the door and why are you looking at me like that?"

"You wanted to be alone, right? I just want to make sure you get what you want, Cupcake." He reaches behind me and grabs something hanging in the exposed locker. I look up and see the green strip says LAWSON.

"Yes," I say hesitantly, "but I meant alone at your house. Where you have a nice big bed...or shower...or kitchen counter." I give him an equally mischievous look. I am not holding back how much I want him. Even though Tristan is fully clothed, he is still the hottest man I've ever seen. Always has been.

He steps toward me, with what I am assuming is a Storm jersey in his hands, and growls, "I don't need a bed to do the things I want to do to you, trust me." Wild thoughts run through my imagination of what he could possibly mean and butterflies fill my stomach from the excitement of all the possibilities. "Put this on."

I unfold the green jersey and see the number 92 stitched on and his last name written across the back. I sigh and start putting my arms through the jersey. Tristan pulls the jersey away and shakes his head.

"What? I am doing what you asked. More like demanded, Hot Shot."

He grabs my ponytail and tugs a little, forcing me to look up at him once more. "Maybe I need to be more clear, Cupcake. I want you to take off that pink sweatshirt and then put this on." He wants to see if I am wearing what he bought me.

Without breaking eye contact with him, I murmur, "If you want it off me so badly, why don't *you* take it off me?"

Tristan licks his lips and smiles smugly. Taunting me back, he slowly unzips my sweatshirt and tickles the sides of my torso as he lifts it over my head. I am now standing there in a lace pink bra. "I am surprised you want me to put on more clothes, Hot Shot."

"The thing is," he brushes a kiss on my collarbone and then whispers in my ear, "I have always wanted to fuck you in my jersey, Cupcake." His words nearly destroy me as my body heats to the temperature of the sun. "Now, lift your arms up."

I do what I am told without any protest. I feel the fabric of the jersey hit my blazing skin. The bottom of the jersey hits my mid-thigh. Without pause, Tristan runs his hands underneath the jersey and drags my leggings down to my ankles. His hands bunch up my leggings and I glide my feet out of them. He curses under his breath at the sight of the matching lace panties. He kisses my upper thighs. "You wore the present I gave you. That's my good girl." His hot breath sends tingles across my body and his rough hands move up the back of my legs. My knees buckle and he's barely touched me. I know what this man is capable of and I want all of it.

He starts licking my inner thighs and I have to hold onto his shoulders to stop myself from toppling over.

"Tell me something, Cupcake. Was I shirtless?" He licks me again.

"Were you shirtless when?" I ask breathlessly, now tugging on his hair peeking through the bottom of his hat.

He groans. "In your dream. Was I shirtless?"

I swallow hard. "Yes."

Tristan takes off his hat and pulls his own sweatshirt off from the back, simultaneously taking his t-shirt off along with it. Now he is standing in front of me, only in his joggers with his hair unruly. I unapologetically ogle at his taut muscles. He closes in and pins me against the wooden panel of his locker.

I reach underneath the jersey so I can take off my panties but Tristan's hand stops me abruptly. "Don't take them off."

I crinkle my eyebrows. "But, I thought that..."

"I was going to fuck you? Don't worry about that, Cupcake." He reaches between my legs and pulls my panties to the side, brushing his fingers against me. I squirm a little and moan. Tristan grins because this is exactly how he wants me. Completely at his mercy.

He spreads my legs further and eases his dick into me. I cover my mouth to keep from screaming but his hand grabs my wrist and pins it above my head. "No one is going to hear us down here. You can scream my name as loud as you want."

He doesn't pause. He doesn't hold back. The fire in his eyes tells me that he has been craving me as much as I am craving him. I rock my hips towards him and he does not hesitate to respond. This man is consuming me with every touch and movement and kiss. He sucks on my neck as he thrusts harder into me and I squeeze my legs tighter against his body and arch my back.

"Please, don't stop." I clutch his hair with my hands.

"This is how I always want you, Brooke. With your legs spread wide open for me, taking me like a good girl and begging me for more."

I feel so outside my body but in my body all at once. There is so much pressure built up from mere days of not seeing him. Not having his hands caress my body. Not having him say my name with his deep, alluring voice.

"You're everything I've ever wanted, baby," he heatedly says and the cadence of his voice traverses across my body. I glide my tongue into his mouth and allow myself to really savor this moment with Tristan. Taking in everything he is offering up to me. Nothing is off-limits for us anymore. I let my body react to him freely, without worry that I'm too much or want him too much. I know that he wants me with equal measure.

I feel my body start to tense and my toes curl under as his tongue explores my mouth and he rams into me harder. Pleasure tingles throughout my body and I nearly collapse against him. I am expecting him to come, too, but instead he pulls out and says, "Turn around."

Still breathless, I say, "What?"

"I said, turn around," he says roughly.

I know how much Tristan loves a challenge so I decide to give him one.

I stand on my tip-toes and run my hands along every ridge of his chest, all the way down to the very cut V leading to my favorite part of his body. I whisper against his full, swollen lips, "Make me."

Without warning, Tristan whips me around and presses his very hard body against my back. His knee nudges in between my legs and spreads them apart. "Hands on the wall, Cupcake." His burly hands find my hip bones and press them back so my ass is flush up against his hard cock. He lifts the jersey up, pushing my panties to the side again with his rough, calloused fingers. His fingers slide inside me, causing me to almost see stars again in a matter of seconds. I gasp loudly.

"You are so fucking wet I can't wait to get inside you again."

"What are you waiting for, Hot Shot? I dare you to make me come again."

Tristan growls and pulls back on my ponytail. This is what he wanted to do with me. Assert his dominance. I am here for all of it.

"I'm waiting for you to say that you are all mine while you are bent over in front of me with your sexy ass up against my cock, Brooke."

I bite my lip and smile as I press my hips back, adhering to his demand. "I'm all yours, Tristan," I whimper.

His hands aggressively grab the sides of my hips as he rams into me again. The different angle makes me scream. Tristan is being dominant and possessive – as if he is releasing all the pent-up energy that has been building for the past ten years between us. I intend to match his energy because it is so damn electric and exhilarating.

One of Tristan's hands reaches down and pinches my already swollen clit and I let out another moan. I can feel myself getting wetter and I press my palms so hard into the wood panel in front of me, I think I might break through the surface. I am never going to get used to how huge Tristan is. He fills me completely and still doesn't fit all the way.

"You are so tight and wet. Are you going to come for me again, Cupcake?" He thrusts into me harder and harder as I frantically press my hips back into him, all while he is rubbing me fiercely. Tristan slaps my ass and my body vibrates with an overload of sensation.

"Tristan," escapes my mouth as pure ecstasy travels to every inch of my body.

"I know how much you love me spanking your ass, Cupcake. Do you want me to do it again?" I nod because apparently I've lost the ability to come up with actual words. He spanks me again as he manhandles me in the most delicious way. My body convulses and I completely come undone, sparks coursing through my body as I try to steady my breathing.

Tristan exhales a shuddering breath and I can feel him release quickly after I do. We both breathe heavily, reveling in the magic that just took place between us. It was earth-shattering and I am never going to try to piece back together what we used to be to each other.

"We better get going, Cupcake." Tristan slowly pulls out, adjusts my panties for me and lightly taps my ass again. Even that small gesture makes me want him all over again. He sits down on the bench before me and reaches down to get his clothes.

Before he has a chance to put them on, I go up behind him and place one of my arms across his broad, tattooed chest and the other on one of his biceps. I kiss the side of his neck and then whisper, "You are so much better than any dream I could have conjured up in my head, Tristan." I kiss him again. "And you are everything I've ever wanted, too, Hot Shot."

He turns, reaches his hand up behind my head and pulls me in for a kiss. "You are my dream, Cupcake. Always have been."

23

Brooke

I close the oven with the side of my hip when I hear my phone ding. I place the freshly baked cupcakes on the cooling rack, wipe my hands against my apron and tap my screen to see the notification:

> Just got out of practice, Cupcake. WYD?

My lips curl up at the sight of Tristan's name on my phone. My heart beats wildly as I unlock my screen and text him back.

> I have a bridal shower I am making 60 cupcakes for. Super busy. Still need to decorate all of them. Just need them to cool enough. Probably going to be a late night here at home. 🙁

Gilmore Girls is on in the background and my kitchen is a mess. Cocoa powder and flour are sprinkled all over my counters. Luckily for me, I only have one more batch left to make and then I can frost them.

> Need a taste tester? You know, just in case a mistake was made

Jerk. But a hot jerk at that.

> I think it'll be fine. A thorough inspection was made before I even put them in the oven.

> Fair enough...I miss you. I am having Brooke withdrawals.

I giggle. We literally saw each other a couple of days ago and couldn't keep our hands off each other. I didn't think I could miss someone who I see almost daily, but here I am missing a man who I avoided seeing for so long.

> It has been two days, Tristan. I hardly think you are having withdrawals.

It's totally possible since I am having the same withdrawals.

> Two days too long, Cupcake. I need to see you tonight. It's not even a want for me anymore.

My heart leaps. As much as I need to see him too, I need to get this done more. This is a really important client for me and I can't afford any distractions.

> Can we take a raincheck? I am probably going to be wiped after I frost the last cupcake.

Three dots appear, then disappear. My stomach sinks a bit, but I literally have to get this done and then I plan on vegging out on the couch and binge-watch *Gilmore Girls* for the thousandth time.

About forty minutes later, I am halfway through piping frosting on my cupcakes when someone knocks at my door. I set down the piping bag and run my hands under the sink. I take a kitchen towel and dry my hands as I pass my TV –Lorelai and Rory are in an argument because Lorelai didn't tell her she was dating again.

I look through the peephole and see Tristan standing outside my door with a bottle of wine and a plastic bag. He is the most determined man on this planet.

I check my appearance in the mirror next to my door. I adjust some rogue strands of hair and wipe some flour off my nose. I am a mess but, to be fair, Tristan's seen me look a lot worse. Then again, I wasn't sleeping with him when he saw me at my worst. I exhale and open the door.

Tristan stands there with one arm up on the doorframe, leaning in toward me. Shivers cover my body at the sight of him.

"What are you doing here, Hot Shot? I told you I was..."

"Busy. Yeah, I know." He kisses me, almost habitually, as he steps into my apartment and makes his way to my kitchen. He places the plastic bag on the one empty space on my counters and takes out two pints of ice cream. Before he can close the freezer, I glimpse the label: Strawberry Cheesecake. My favorite flavor. And he brought my favorite wine...again. This man is spoiling the hell out of me with my favorite things and I am glad he is progressively becoming one of them. He closes the freezer door and shrugs. "I wanted to come help you out. Plus, like I said earlier, I needed to see you."

He taps my nose, then grabs my chin and presses his lips to mine. The invigorating scent of mint and cedar hijacks my senses. He smiles against my lips. "You taste like chocolate."

"Well, like I told *you* earlier, I ensured that the cupcakes were up to par." I grab the bottle of wine. "Is this your master plan? To get me drunk and have your way with me, Lawson?" Secretly, I am not opposed to Tristan having his way with me.

"I would never get you drunk and take advantage of you, Cupcake. Call me old-fashioned, but that's not really my style." He sits down on one of my bar stools and assesses my mess of a kitchen.

"I know it's not. I was joking." I grab the piping bag and continue to layer icing intricately onto the top of the cupcake. "Are you sure you want to be here, Tristan? I have about thirty more of these to go and then I was just going to chill on the couch and continue watching *Gilmore Girls*. Super exciting things are happening at the Beckett residence this evening."

"Anything that involves you in the equation is always exciting in my book." He hops off the stool, walks around the island and starts washing his hands. "What can I do to help? Do you need me to frost some of these to speed up the process?" He takes the kitchen towel off my shoulder and dries his large, veiny hands. I bite my lower lip and remind myself to calm down. He literally just dried off his hands–that should not elicit such a visceral response from me, but it does.

I laugh off his suggestion to help. "I don't know if you could frost one of these, Hot Shot. It's kind of intricate work."

He closes the gap between us and takes the piping bag from me. "I got steady hands, Cupcake. I thought you knew that by now." He licks the excess frosting coming out of the bag with an unruly grin.

"Fine." I grab another piping bag and spatula white icing into the clear bag. "But none of *that* tonight, you seducer of women."

Tristan's laugh booms in my small apartment. "I'm hardly a seducer of women."

I snort. "Whatever you say, Hot Shot. I see the way women look at you. They are practically foaming at the mouth."

"I guess I haven't noticed. None of them are you, so what's the point?" He has a serious, focused look on his face as he pipes frosting almost like a pro. His tongue sticks out of his mouth and I smile because he only has that look when he is concentrating really hard on something. He is legitimately trying his best.

He must sense me staring at him, because he stops and shifts his gaze toward me. "Am I doing this right?"

I pretend to inspect the cupcake, which is perfect, and say, "That's pretty good for an amateur. I approve. You can continue."

We carry on for about fifteen more minutes. Tristan helps me wash and dry the dishes and get the cupcakes into the containers for transport. After getting the ice cream out and pouring glasses of wine, we make our way onto the couch. I plop down and start rubbing my feet.

"God, my feet are killing me. Those little monsters at school were running rampant today. And then having to bake tonight has really done me in. And I even wore comfortable shoes to work."

Tristan sets his wine glass on my coffee table. "C'mon, give 'em here." He taps the top of his lap. When I hesitate, he reaches down and grabs both of my ankles with one colossal hand and props them on his thighs. He places the perfect amount of pressure on the balls of my feet. I rest my head back against the arm of my couch and say, "Oh my goodness. Do you moonlight as a masseuse or something? That feels so good." I let out a moan.

"When would I have the time to moonlight as a masseuse? I barely have time to relax during hockey season, and I hardly get a vacation before preseason training starts back up." His thumb presses into my foot, traveling from my heel to the ball of my foot and I let out a moan again. "And you better stop doing that, Cupcake."

I grab my glass and take a sip. "Doing what?"

"Moaning like that. Add that to how you look tonight. Talk about me being a seducer. You are being a temptress right now. And I'm trying really hard to be on my best behavior tonight per your request." He moves on to my other foot and keeps his gaze on the TV.

"Tristan, I am wearing gray sweatpants, a white tank top and my hair is up in a clip. What about this image makes me a temptress?"

"Everything about you makes you a temptress." The muscles in his forearms and biceps move as he massages my feet. That simple undulation makes me shift on the couch and now it's my turn to distract my dirty thoughts about what I want Tristan to do to me.

He clears his throat. "So, what's going on in this show?"

I finally process what episode it is, and it happens to be one of my favorites. It's the season one finale, the one where Max Medina proposes to Lorelai with a thousand yellow daisies. Lorelai whispers to herself, "A thousand of them. A thousand yellow daisies," and I start tearing up.

"A thousand yellow daisies? What the hell?"

"Let me explain something to you, Hot Shot. This is probably one of the most romantic gestures of the whole show. I am not going to tell you the other one because that will spoil things and I would never do that to you."

"Okay, enlighten me, Cupcake. Why is this one of the most romantic gestures of this whole show?"

I sigh, then continue, "Because Max remembered what a proposal is supposed to look like based on Lorelai's standards that she laid out earlier in the episode. He did that for her. And this episode honestly is why I love daisies." Tristan glances at me while his hands shift to massaging my shins and calves. "How romantic would that be, a thousand yellow daisies? But I'd want pink daisies because I love them. I love the notion of a thousand pink daisies. Doing something like that for somebody – proposing in that way – I mean, swoon."

Tristan grunts out a laugh.

"Seriously," I continue, "even though they weren't together for very long, Max understood Lorelai. I mean Luke is obviously endgame, but for Max to do that grand gesture, you know, taking what she said and literally providing that for her and giving her what she really wanted? Because in the arguing scene before, she was just spewing out all the other ways he could have proposed, but subconsciously she truly wanted a man to do that for her. To show up and listen to what she has to say." I wipe a tear rolling down my cheek and look at Lorelai sitting amongst the daisies on the phone with

Max. "I cry every time she walks into that inn and she sees a thousand yellow daisies that Max bought her."

"So, it's not really about the daisies."

I look at Tristan. He is concentrating on the scene on the screen intently, and then his hazel eyes find mine.

I scrunch my eyebrows together. "What do you mean?"

He takes both his hands and scoots my sweatpants up to expose my leg. His calloused hands wrap around my left calf and his thumbs press into my shin and move up to my knee. I can't stop looking at the veins popping out of his hands and how big his fingers are. "It's about the fact that he understood her and showed up for her in a way that no man had done before."

"Yeah. I guess that's it." My heart leaps as Tristan switches to my right leg. My gaze shifts from his hands up to his forearms and biceps that are covered in tattoos. "So, I know that one tattoo is for me, but do all those tattoos represent all the women you've been with? Like all these twisted notches in your belt?" I playfully smile at him.

Unphased, Tristan vivaciously smiles back. "Why, are you jealous, Cupcake?"

Even though I was the one who started this ex conversation, I immediately want to retract back and ask in a different way. I have to stand my ground, though. "You wish, Lawson."

"Well I'm jealous as hell about all your ex-boyfriends. They got to have what is mine and I am not above envy, Cupcake. I am not a fan of sharing."

With Tristan's admission, I feel safer revealing how I really feel. "Okay, maybe I'm a little jealous. Just a teensy bit though." I squint and shrug, placing a spoonful of delicious ice cream in my mouth, and that's when Tristan squeezes right above my knee (my most ticklish spot on my body) and makes me squirm. I cover my laugh with my hand and kick my feet wildly. Tristan belly-laughs and guards his body from my kicks.

When I finally swallow my ice cream, I nudge Tristan one more time with my foot. "Ugh, I hate you, Hot Shot."

"I definitely don't hate you, Cupcake." He traces a finger over my knee. "I will do that every day if I can see you laugh like that. Your smile is my favorite thing, especially when I see your dimples." He continues to massage my legs. "And no, my tattoos do not represent all the women I've slept with. Not even close. Most of them are for my family. I have a few for my sisters. Some for hockey. My family crest with doves and a tree wrapped around the crest." He lifts his shirt sleeve to reveal "Invictus." "My grandfather's favorite poem, and in turn mine." He lifts his shirt to reveal his chiseled chest and points to the words "Leve et reluis" over what looks like a phoenix.

"What does 'leve et reluis' mean?" I inquire.

"Arise and re-illumine." He unfortunately lowers his shirt. "It's the Lawson motto. It's on the crest and I've kind of stuck to that motto my whole life. I guess that's why I am not afraid of taking risks or giving it my all out there on the ice or in my personal life. I know that if I fall, I can always rise right back up."

"Hence the phoenix," I say in awe. I didn't know what I expected his tattoos to mean, but I didn't guess they would all have such profound significance and meaning in his life. And my initials are right there too, permanently drawn on his body.

"Yeah." He reaches for his glass and takes a sip. "How about you, Cupcake? I haven't seen any tattoos on your body. Unless they are in a very inconspicuous part, but I feel like I've seen every angle of you at this point." He winks. He's not wrong. I start to blush thinking about all the positions this man has put me in.

"Nope. No tattoos for me. I am deathly afraid of needles and the sight of blood makes me squeamish. Seriously, if one of our students has a nosebleed or falls on the playground and there is any trace of blood, I defer to Tess to take care of it." I shake off the image of all of those scenarios running through my mind. "Plus it probably hurts like hell. Which one was the most painful tattoo to get?"

"All of them were painful." He finishes off his wine. "Okay, if you were to get a tattoo, what would you get and where would you get it?"

"I don't know. I guess I've never thought about it since I made a decision a long time ago that I was never going to get one."

Tristan nods and presses his lips together. He gently slides my feet off of his lap, and stands up. Even through his basketball shorts, I can still glimpse his quadricep muscles. I will never not be attracted to this man.

He adjusts his backwards hat as he walks over to the kitchen again. "I am assuming you have a pink pen somewhere?" He aimlessly opens a couple of kitchen drawers.

"Yes, in the drawer next to the refrigerator. But why do you need a pink pen?" I nervously laugh.

He finds one of the many pink pens in my junk drawer and saunters back to the couch. I raise my feet to let him sit next to me. He grabs my left foot and places a soft kiss on my ankle. He bites the cap off the pen and keeps the cap in between his teeth as he holds onto my foot steadily.

"What are you doing?" I flinch my foot. He strengthens his grip on my foot and brings it back to eyelevel.

"Hold still, Cupcake. I'm going to give you a temporary tattoo." The tip of the pen grazes the back of my ankle.

"What, are you drawing the number 92 as a way to brand me as yours?" I tease.

"Oh I already know that you are mine, Cupcake. I made sure of that multiple times. On that kitchen counter. In my shower. In my bed." He licks his lips as he continues drawing. "In that locker room. This is strictly for you." He blows softly on the pink ink and goosebumps trickle across my body. "There. All done."

I smile softly and bend my leg up to see my temporary tattoo. Tristan drew a small pink daisy behind my ankle.

"I know it's not a thousand of them, but you gotta start somewhere, right?"

He might as well have drawn a thousand of them, because the amount of butterflies that take flight in my stomach sure as hell make it seem like he did. I prop myself up and wrap my arms around his neck. "One pink daisy. I love it."

I have no more strength to resist this man. I straddle his lap and already feel him underneath me. I give him a devouring kiss and we lose ourselves in each other as if we haven't kissed each other in years. I guess we are making up for all those years we didn't indulge ourselves.

24

Brooke

Tristan texted me to wait for him outside the locker room after his game. I am leaning against the wall when I hear the door swing open. I look up from my phone and my heart sinks when I realize it isn't the man I am waiting for.

It is the man I kind of abandoned at Casino Night and I still feel guilty about it.

"Dean! Hey, how is it going?" I say a little too sing-songy.

He looks up from his own phone and registers my presence. He smirks and glances over his shoulder towards the locker room. "Hey, Brooke. You know, it's going. I haven't really seen you since Casino Night."

He is short with me, but can you blame the guy? I doubt that he wants me to tell him the truth about that night since it involves

Tristan. There is an animosity between them that I don't understand. They are both great players. Charming. Incredibly hot. Maybe that's where the problem lies...there's not enough room for all the hotness and talent on one team.

"Um, yeah, about that," I say through a lump in my throat. Ever since I was a little girl, I've hated letting people down. It's in my DNA. "Something came up and I needed to bolt. I am sorry I kind of..."

"Left me hanging? It's fine, Brooke. I made do without you there."

Ouch. I mean, I know I was flirting with him at the blackjack table, but we technically didn't go together. We met there and it's not like I was dating him.

Dean advances on me and chills run up my spine. I am really uncomfortable right now.

"I'm curious. Was it that something came up or someone?" he presses.

I swallow hard and avert my eyes towards the locker room, hoping that by some miracle, Tristan will magically appear. "Someone."

My back hits the wall. What is Dean doing? I don't like the look in his eyes right now. They are fierce and angry and intense. If Tristan or my brother were here, they would be so pissed at how Dean is treating me right now.

"Hmm." He presses one of his hands against the wall behind me and leans down. "Who is he?"

"I don't think that is any of your business."

"Well, I think that if you are going to be a tease, lead me on and fucking leave an event that I invited you to in the first place, it is in fact my business."

There is barely any room between us now and my eyes flutter as I cower to Dean. I don't like where this conversation is going.

"I don't really appreciate you talking to me like this, Dean. And I don't think my brother would be very happy that you are making his younger sister feel as uncomfortable as you are making me feel right now."

I attempt to stand my ground and not let this man intimidate me, but I don't know Dean all that well and can't really anticipate his next move. I see Randall at the end of the hallway, but he is preoccupied with talking to someone through his earpiece. Before I can move any further, Dean moves with me. "Dean. I'm sorry, but we were never really dating so I am going to say it again, I don't owe you anything. I appreciate you inviting me to Casino Night and getting to know you, but I don't have feelings for you."

His hand grabs my wrist. I try to pull away, but he is not letting me go.

"Dean, let me go."

"So, the fact that you led me on and kissed me at Casino Night means nothing to you. Got it. Well, since kissing doesn't mean shit to you, you wouldn't mind if I kissed you on the cheek, would you."

"Actually I would...mind it. I am seeing someone and I really don't think he would like you kissing me anywhere. Now let go of me."

I don't know what is holding Tristan up, but I am not going to stay here in this situation. My self-defense instincts are about to kick in if he does not back off in the next two seconds.

Dean clearly isn't listening to me because he leans close and kisses my cheek.

I jerk away. "Stop! Stop it, Dean, please."

Suddenly, Dean is no longer pressed against me. Instead he is the one against the wall, with Tristan's forearm sprawled across his chest. "What the fuck, Hastings?"

"What, man? I was just having a conversation with Brooke. A conversation that doesn't concern *you*." Dean is trying to get out of the hold Tristan has him in, but he is unsuccessful.

Tristan's wrath for this man is unhinged and I can tell that if he had the choice, and if he wasn't the face of the Storm or still making remediations for the fight on the ice almost two months ago, he would beat the hell out of Dean right now. He is holding back, but not enough to let Dean go at this moment.

"It looked like a little more than a conversation was happening." Tristan looks over at me and registers how I am holding onto my wrist, which is red from Dean's strong grip.

A switch flips immediately in Tristan's eyes. They turn dark and cold. He growls, "You touch her again, and I will fucking break your hand and then your precious hockey career is over. Do you understand me?"

Dean laughs in his face, almost like he is mocking Tristan.

Tristan's eyebrows pull together and he shifts his hands so that now he is holding Dean by his sweatshirt in the middle of his chest. He slams him against the wall as hard as he can. "Do you think I'm joking? So much as fucking look at Brooke and I will end your career."

My heart is beating uncontrollably because I have a feeling that Tristan isn't making an empty threat. Why is he willing to put his career on the line for me?

I sense someone walking toward us. Randall is on his way over, looking concerned. Yeah, join the club. Two of the best hockey players in the league are about to go twelve rounds if Randall doesn't stop it.

"Whatever. She was a waste of my time anyway."

Tristan sucker-punches him.

Randall breaks it up and gets in Tristan's face. "He's not worth it, you hear me, son? You will lose everything. Don't go low just because that is his specialty. You are better than that, Lawson."

Thank God for Randall. If it wasn't for him... I shudder at the next thought that comes into my mind.

BACK AT TRISTAN'S PLACE, I rummage through his freezer and hand him a bag of frozen peas. "We can't keep doing this, you know."

"What's 'this'?"

"Me nursing you back to health after you get into fights. Namely fights with Dean Hastings."

"It's so fun, though. Maybe you should wear those candy striper pajamas when you nurse me back to health."

"Stop deflecting."

"What, you want me to walk away when he talks to you like that?"

"That's exactly what I want you to do because you don't always need to step in and save me, Tristan. Randall was also there and could have handled the situation without you getting involved at all. You aren't superman, Hot Shot. No matter how much you might..." I wave my hands in a circle, indicating that I am talking about his body. "...look like a tatted-up version of him 24/7."

"Hmm, didn't know you had a thing for Superman. Which one? Or do you have a thing for Christopher Reeves? Ugh, please don't tell me you love Henry Cavill."

"I hate to break the news to you, Hot Shot, but Henry Cavill has always had my heart. He might just be my kryptonite." I playfully smile as I stand in front of him.

Tristan smiles and grabs the back of my knees, catapulting me onto his lap.

"Well, you're definitely my kryptonite, Cupcake." He checks my wrist. "Does it hurt?"

"A little, but I'll be fine. Listen, Tristan, you can't just go around punching people. It's not how to deal with things. Okay? I'm a grown woman, you don't have to defend me. And I don't want you to risk your career over me. It's just not worth it."

"Everything I do for you is worth it. *You* are worth it, Brooke. You have no idea how much I would be willing to risk my career —to risk my position with the team – for you."

Tristan looks away and I notice that his demeanor changes.

"What?" I ask. "What is it?"

"Nothing."

"You looked away when you said something about risking your position."

"It's nothing, Brooke. Just – you are worth every punch that I give out in defense of you. I am always going to defend you. So you are just going to have to get used to it."

"Well, I'm not going to get used to it because that's not how conflict resolution works. Sorry to burst your bubble, Hot Shot."

"Are you seriously treating me like your kindergartners right now?"

"Yes, I am treating you like a kindergartner right now because you are acting like a kindergartner. Fighting isn't the only solution, Tristan. Why don't you and Dean just sit down and talk?"

Tristan laughs. "There's no talking to Dean Hastings. He's made up his mind about who he is..."

"Apparently, so have you. Look, I don't need you to defend me. I just...don't want to see you lose everything. Like Randall said, you've worked too hard. You've done so much for your career. I'd hate to see you lose it. Especially over me. I would never be able to forgive myself."

"Well you wouldn't have to forgive yourself, Brooke because, like you said, I would make those decisions – not you. I made the choice to punch Dean tonight, not you. And I'll do it a thousand more times if that means protecting you. Because you are my girl and I am never going to be okay with Dean treating you the way he did tonight. For him touching you the way he did. No man should ever touch a woman like that – or their partner or whoever. That's not okay. And that's why I punched him."

I look into his eyes. They are so honest. He isn't just saying these things to put a bandaid on the situation. He genuinely wants to be my protector. He doesn't want me to get hurt. Ever.

Just when I thought Tristan was done saying the sweetest things to me tonight, he continues, "And the fact that he said he wasted his time on you...how is that even possible?" He pushes some hair behind my ear and grazes my jaw with his fingers. "Spending *any* amount of time with you is not a waste. It's a fucking gift."

My heart leaps at his comment. And I realize at this moment that Tristan will do anything for me. I've never felt safer than when I am with him. He has a hold on my heart that no one else has ever had before.

I press my forehead to his and say, "Thank you for saying that. I don't think you realize what a gift you are to me, Tristan."

25

Brooke

A couple days later, I'm at work when I get a text from Tristan.

Don't hate me.

Too late. 😊 what's up?

I might have let it slip while I was talking with the guys in the locker room that you won the trip to Telluride. Bradley is gonna try and convince you to invite him, Jen, me and maybe Oakley. They want it to be a group trip before the craziness of the playoffs.

Yesterday, I got a notice from the Storm Foundation that I was the lucky winner of the weekend getaway to Telluride, which I am sure Tristan had some sort of hand in. I was so excited to spend some time with Tristan and just be us without any distractions or having to tiptoe around anyone. My heart sinks a little.

Aw I was really looking forward to having that place all to ourselves. But I still want to see you. Maybe I can bring Tess?

That's a great idea. Everyone will be coupled up. So to speak.

Again, I'm sorry, Cupcake. I really wanted to be alone, too. At least we'll be able to spend time together in some way.

But if you want, you can tell Bradley no and you can just go with Tess.

No, I want you to go.

I kind of miss you, Hot Shot.

We arrive in Telluride on Friday night and drive about fifteen minutes until we reach Tristan's house. It is located on the Telluride Golf Course and it has amazing views of the surrounding mountain ridges. His massive two-story house has a pitched roof and floor-to-ceiling windows along the front of the house. The inside is equally as breathtaking. The living room has probably a thirty-foot ceiling, showcasing gorgeous wooden beams. There is a reading nook with a large light-stone gas fireplace, situated across the way from the gourmet chef's kitchen. Off to the side, a large wooden dining room table could accommodate twelve people.

All five bedrooms are located upstairs, Tristan's master bedroom having the best view of the snow-dusted mountains. Outside of his window, I see a large hot tub that could probably fit all of us comfortably. Brad and Jen take their next largest guest room, while

Tess and I share a room and Oakley takes his own room. This place is a dream and I hope that Tristan will take me back here, just the two of us.

We end up ordering takeout since we are so tired from a day of work and travel. It is so nice being in the mountains, away from the busy city. There is a calmness to the mountains that I think we all need. Everything has been so heightened lately with the playoffs, the end of the school year and of course, for me, the whirlwind that has been my relationship with Tristan.

After a late breakfast, all the guys decide to go golfing. While they are gone, Tess, Jen and I watch multiple romantic comedies, drink wine and eat so much popcorn we think our stomachs are going to explode. For dinner, Tess decides to make her famous chicken and orzo dish. Jen is in charge of making the salad, because Tess didn't allow anyone else near the stove. And of course, I am designated to make the desserts. I decide to make chocolate souffles.

Tristan and I have skillfully avoided each other throughout the majority of the trip so far. We steal heated glances at each other and of course text each other, making one another blush or smirk. But we have to be careful. Tess is the only one who knows about us, and I want it to stay that way. At least for a bit longer. I don't want to distract anyone this close to the playoffs. Maybe after the season is over, Tristan and I can come clean about our relationship.

When Tristan walks in after golf, I barely recognize him. He is wearing an entire golf outfit —I've never seen Tristan wear anything like this before. He is wearing a black polo tucked into light gray golf shorts with a belt. His hat is turned forward, showcasing his own brand, and some golf gloves are peeking out of one of his back pockets. The man can pull off any fricken outfit and be the hottest man in the room. He looks like he belongs in the fanciest country club imaginable. I am certain any country club would be thrilled to have the one-and-only Tristan Lawson grace their golf course and clubhouse with his undoubtedly impeccable golf game and charm.

I need to distract myself now. I walk over to where Jen is standing behind the island counter and offer to help chop up veggies for the salad. I grab a cucumber and an extra knife.

"Um, excuse me. Tess specifically gave me this job because I suck at all things cooking. Your brother is one lucky man," she says sarcastically.

I continue to slice the cucumber. "Trust me, he is. I am constantly amazed by the fact that he won over the coolest girl, who is way out of his league by the way. I am the lucky one because I get to gain you as a sister. Thank you for falling in love with my ridiculous brother."

She stops slicing and goes into the fridge to grab some wine. She pours the rest of the contents in our glasses and throws the bottle in the recycling bin. I slide the collective cucumber slices into the large salad bowl and set the cutting board and two knives in the sink.

Jen's arm wraps around me. "I am also very lucky to gain a sister. I am an only child, so it is going to be nice to have someone to talk to about all the boy things."

I grab my wine and we clink our glasses together: "To sisterhood."

"To sisterhood."

"All right everyone!" Tess shouts, startling me so I jump up and spill a little bit of wine on my light pink sweater. Thank goodness it is white wine. "Dinner will be ready in twenty minutes! I need all the men to set the table when you all are done showering and changing! The women are not going to lift a damn finger. Now chop chop! You all smell."

I snort. Tess is never afraid to say exactly what she is thinking. To avoid looking directly into Tristan's eyes, I decide to start prepping the souffles so they are ready to go in the oven shortly after Tess takes out her chicken and orzo dish. I go on my tiptoes and reach up to get a mixing bowl and white ramekins from the cupboard.

I've finished mixing up the batter when my phone dings in my back pocket.

> I missed you today, Cupcake.

A rush of butterflies fills my stomach. I am smiling like a damn school girl whose crush just wrote her a note saying check yes or no if you want to be my girlfriend. This was Tristan Lawson's version of one of those notes, except he wasn't asking me to be his girlfriend. We have not put any labels on our relationship yet, but more butterflies cram in amongst the others as the label of *girlfriend* sweeps across my mind.

Another ding. I look at my lock screen.

> You look beautiful by the way.

My fingers hurriedly text back:

> I kind of missed you too. And thank you.
> You're sweet for saying so.

The oven is beeping and Tess hurries over, throws on oven mitts, takes out the large dutch oven and places it on the stovetop. "Do you need the oven to stay at the same temp?"

"No, I need to lower it actually, but I got it." I adjust the temperature to 375 degrees. At least I don't need to wait for the oven to preheat. I pour the souffle batter into the ramekins, ensuring they all level out and have the same amount of batter. After making some minor adjustments, I bend over to carefully place them in the oven.

I close the oven and then feel a hand graze my lower back. "Those jeans are really working for you." I see an arm covered in tattoos open the drawer directly beside the oven. Tristan's brawny hand fumbles with some silverware. Then he leans in and whispers, "Especially when you bend over like that."

My core heats up to an ungodly level as I set a timer for twenty minutes. I usually have a sense about when souffles are done—a kind of special intuition. But I don't trust my senses tonight; they are on overload with Tristan around. My brain is filled with nothing but him.

I turn around and lean on the curved oven handle. It's definitely getting hotter in this kitchen, so I grab my hair and drape it over one of my shoulders, exposing the side of my neck. I hear a low, frustrated growl come from Tristan's direction.

"What?"

"You are making it impossible to be around you, Cupcake." He clutches onto the silverware so intensely that his knuckles turn white. I can tell that he is holding back the urge to drop the silverware on the kitchen floor, take me in his arms, and make out with me. Or at least that's what I want him to do with me. I need to make sure he knows that I am feeling whatever he is feeling right now because I have an inkling we are thinking the same thing. We haven't been alone in days and it's crazy how much that is affecting my life.

I lean toward him. "I can say the same thing about you, Hot Shot." I let myself take a good look at him. He is back in his usual make-Brooke-weak-at-the-knees outfit: a backwards hat, gray joggers and a form-fitting t-shirt. He is literally just existing and it's unraveling me.

"Now you know how I have been feeling every single time I saw you for the past ten years. It's fucking unbearable. It's even worse now that I know what I've been missing out on."

We lock eyes and any pretense of wanting to stay away from him this weekend is starting to shatter. Our stares are no longer fueled by hate. And we could never make it in Hollywood with our attempt to pretend to hate each other. My lips start to curl at our feeble attempt to shoot daggers at each other for the millionth time. Tristan crosses his burly arms, looks down at my lips and smirks. I match his stance and don't waver. I am notoriously good at these stare-downs.

"Tristan, bro, do you need help with the simple task of getting silverware? Or are you too busy thinking of ways to torture my sister to focus?" Bradley's voice snaps us out of whatever trance we were stuck in.

Oh, he's torturing me, all right. Just not in the way my brother is thinking.

Completely oblivious, Bradley steps in between us, takes the silverware from Tristan and heads to the table. "Come on, you two. I'm starving."

Tristan holds out his hand, gesturing to me to step in front of him, his silly smile still on his face. How am I supposed to move when my entire body feels like mush?

Tess ushers both Tristan and me from behind and proceeds to boss everyone around. "Okay, so Bradley and Jen, you guys sit at the ends of the table. Then Oakley, you'll come sit by me and that leaves Brooke and Tristan on the other side."

I get extremely flushed and all the butterflies vacate my stomach as I realize that I will be right next to Tristan for the next hour or so, during which time it is expected we act like our normal selves a.k.a. want to obliterate each other. I make a face at Tess because this was not part of the plan. She and I were going to sit next to each other so the undeniable tension between me and Tristan could remain undetected by my brother, or anyone else in this house for that matter.

Tess just wiggles her eyebrows and sits down across from me. *What the hell?* I mouth to her, but she simply takes the salad tongs and places some greens on her empty plate. "Dig in, everyone. I hope you enjoy it. This is my favorite family recipe. My grandmother made it all the time when I was little! Anyone need more wine?"

"Yes!" Tristan and I both say in unison.

"Okay then." Tess hands the unopened bottle to Oakley. "Oakley, would you be so kind as to open this bottle for the table."

Suddenly, I get it. I know Tess. She is totally into Oakley. That's why she switched up the seating arrangement. I giggle and shake my head. Tess and her larks. Always stirring up the status quo. She has gumption, that is for sure.

"Uh, sure." Oakley grabs the twist top bottle and in one swift move, it comes off. So easily, in fact, that all of us start laughing. I know Tess well enough that she is crushing hard on Oakley. She is not being subtle about it either.

Unphased, Tess pours wine in my wine glass, then Tristan's.

"Okay, I want to propose a toast!" she says. "Thank you so much, Tristan, for hosting us at your beautiful house here in Telluride. It is seriously such a beautiful place. And thank you to Brooke who won this giveaway at the auction at Casino Night. This was a much-needed vacation and I'm glad we can do it all together. So I guess: to Tristan and Brooke!" *Tristan and Brooke!* I try not to blush. I love the way our names sound together.

Glasses clink and everyone starts digging in.

I scoop some of the salad onto my plate and as I pass the bowl to my left, Tristan's hand grazes mine for a millisecond. I feel tingly all over. I need to keep my facial expressions in check and try to cover my already flushed face. Tristan reaches over my plate, grabs the large serving spoon full of chicken and orzo and slaps it onto his own plate. He smells amazing. My favorite Moroccan mint and cedar smell. We lock eyes for a millisecond and that is enough to make me squirm. "Do you want some, Cupcake?"

"Yes, but I am very capable of getting it myself, Hot Shot." I grasp the spoon out of his hand – a little too forcefully, because I knock over Tristan's wine glass. His freshly poured wine spills all over his lap. Shit.

"Oh party foul. Way to go, Brooke," Bradley pipes in.

I grab a napkin and say, "Thanks for the illuminating commentary, Brad." Without thinking, I start frantically wiping down Tristan's lap.

Conversation picks back up and the attention is no longer on this side of the table. Tristan's hand holds onto my wrist, ceasing my progress to clean up my mess. "Stop."

"What? I am just trying to help."

He whispers, "You are doing something else to me right now, Brooke. Please. Stop."

I look down and realize what he meant. He's right. I need to stop.

I immediately let go of the napkin and turn my body to face the table. I gulp down my wine and successfully get the main entree onto my plate without more hiccups. Tristan scoots his seat back in and I can see his dumb, delicious dimples grace his annoyingly handsome face. He enjoys me being flustered like this. Always has. Except this time, the stakes are different. Well, I guess for me they are.

Apparently it is too quiet for my extroverted brother because he says, "So, Tristan. I am surprised you didn't bring one of your puck bunnies on this trip. What's that about, man?"

By some grace of whatever is up there in the universe the timer goes off for the soufflés. I jump up and squeal a little too loudly, "I got it!" It literally could not be more perfect timing since I do not want to hear the answer to this question. Even though I know Tristan hasn't seen anyone but me since we started hooking up, I still don't want to hear a fake account of what he might be or would've been doing with someone else.

I can feel Tristan's eyes follow me into the kitchen and despite my efforts to put space between me and that conversation, I still hear every word. "Um, you know man, I just wanted to hang out and not worry about entertaining a girl."

"Entertaining a girl" huh? What kind of "entertaining"? The same "entertaining" that we have done? I suddenly get hit with the green monster of envy. I open the oven and take out my soufflés. They are perfect. I smile and place them on the stovetop. At least these didn't turn out to be a complete disaster, unlike where this night might go if Tristan continues to be, well...Tristan.

Completely irresistible. Completely hot.

Completely off-limits – at least, I need to make sure my brother thinks so.

I turn off the oven and return to my seat. "Bullshit. Tell me the truth, man." *For the love of God, Brad, let it go.*

"I don't know man. I'm getting kind of sick of hooking up with the same type of woman. I didn't want to bring someone here who I don't really have feelings for. This place means a lot to me. I want to reserve it for someone special." Tristan's warm hand finds the top of my knee and gives it a small squeeze. My heart leaps and I stuff my mouth to keep from giving away my elation.

"Aw, that's so sweet," Jen says, and then scolds my brother. "Bradley, just leave him alone. It seems like he wants to turn over a new leaf and I think that's great."

My lips curl at the way Jen's words hit my brother like a ton of bricks. She definitely can hold her own around my brother. Unfortunately, Bradley wants to push things. "So is there...someone special?"

Tristan's grip on my knee tightens. My heart has never beat so fast in my life. "Actually, yes," he says. "But it's pretty new and before you ask...it's no one you know." *Phew, we dodged that bullet.*

"Anyone up for dessert?" I say as I get up, causing Tristan's hand to leave my thigh. I can still feel the imprint of his hand seared into my jeans.

"I think anyone would be crazy to turn down your famous soufflés, B," Tess responds.

In the kitchen, I take the ramekins off the baking sheet and wipe down the bottoms before placing them on the counter.

"I'm always up for some dessert." Tristan apparently followed me into the kitchen. He leans in and kisses my cheek. "But I think you already knew that."

"Are you trying to get caught?" I whisper through my teeth. I place the soufflés on a serving platter and hold it up to Tristan. "Can you handle taking these to the table, Hot Shot?"

He effortlessly swipes the tray from my hands and makes his way over to the table. I can't resist checking him out as he walks away. His ass looks so good in those sweatpants, he is making it harder to breathe. *Act normal, Brooke. Act like you hate his guts rather than want to yank him upstairs to his bedroom.*

Everyone digs in. Tess is the first one to break the silence: "Oh my god, B! These are amazing!"

"Thanks! I used dark chocolate this time and I think I prefer it this way. It's not as cloyingly sweet."

"So, are you back to dating anyone, Brooke?" Bradley asks out of the blue.

"Who are you, Gossip Girl? Why are you so interested in who people are dating all of a sudden, Brad?" I ask, with a hard-to-miss annoyance in my tone.

"It's just a question, Brooke. Calm down. You seem a little happier lately. Well, except for right now, since you are looking at me like you want to kill me."

"Tell him, B," Tess slips out. Her hand covers her mouth immediately. Now she is the victim to the daggers coming out of my eyes.

"Oh really? Who?" Bradley looks intrigued.

"It's nobody," I respond curtly.

"Wait, is it the same guy that was in your apartment a few weeks ago?"

Tristan adjusts his seat and clears his throat. I glance over at him and he has the biggest smirk on his face. I swear we are going to get caught.

"Not that it's any of your business, but yes." I am just going to tell a version of the truth instead of coming up with a complete lie. I look back at Tess and she is mouthing, *I'm sorry.*

"Where did you meet this guy?" Bradley asks in a protective tone.

"At a professional development I had to attend in February." I stuff my mouth with the souffle. "Actually, he was the presenter. We got to talking after and we went on a few dates."

"Why didn't you introduce me when I came over that night? Did you think I was going to put the fear of God in him?"

Tristan full-on laughs. I kick him under the table.

"To be honest Brad," Tess chimes in, "I think he could actually take you. He may look a little like Clark Kent, but there is definitely a case for him having a Superman-esque quality to him, too. I mean, from what I could gather from his presentation at the school." She winks at me. Okay, she redeemed herself and her description of Tristan looking like Clark Kent is absolutely comical since she has no idea that Tristan wears glasses occasionally.

"Well, when are you bringing this guy to Sunday dinner? I am sure Mom and Dad would like to meet him, too."

"Soon. Maybe. I don't know. It's still kind of early to really tell if he is going to stick." I pause because part of what I am saying is true. "I don't want to jump into anything too fast. It's scary to jump into a new relationship. But, I can tell he is a decent guy. I think it could really go somewhere." I brush my fingers against Tristan's leg to reassure him that I am completely in this and although we are keeping our relationship a secret for now, I don't want him to doubt what we have or how I feel about him. I clear my throat and continue, "Plus, I don't want him to undergo a Beckett Sunday dinner too early. I don't want him to be scared off by Mom's invasive questions, or yours for that matter, Brad."

"I know all too well what those dinners are like as an outsider of the Beckett family bubble. Y'all are truly intimidating." Jen looks over at me and nods. "Let Brooke date whoever she wants to date. She deserves to find the same happiness that we found in each other." Then she focuses her eyesight on Brad: "In other words: butt out of it, honey."

26

Brooke

It is a perfect night to go out to the hot tub and drink wine. Tess and I are surrounded by trees, and the Edison bulbs hanging above the massive cedar-planked deck make it all the more relaxing and magical. The stars are so clear and bright, which is not something I am used to. All the city lights in Dallas disrupt the view of the stars. The mountains are silhouetted on the horizon and the base of the range is illuminated by the small town below. The world is quiet—and after that chaotic dinner, it's exactly what I need.

Tess pours the rest of the wine bottle into my glass. "But seriously, there is something about Oakley that is so appealing to me. He's so sweet and I normally don't go for guys like that. I would've gone for someone like Hastings in the past, but I like the mystery that

Oakley has to offer." She wiggles her eyebrows and smirks deviously. "Maybe I'll make a move tonight."

"May I remind you that you are a little drunk? I have heard that Oakley is a sweetheart and he seems really innocent. So if you do try anything with him, go easy on him, please." What I have heard from Brad and Tristan, he is the ultimate golden retriever and never hooks up with girls.

"I can't promise you that." We giggle.

My head feels a little hazy. I sadly have become a lightweight since college. I think my eyes are deceiving me when I see a shirtless Tristan walk up to us. He still has his hat on and the sight of this perfect, muscular man makes me warm inside. I missed him and although I am having an amazing time with my best friend, I would have loved to go on this trip just with him, so we could spend some time alone, without any distraction.

"Oh hey, Tristan. How is it going?" Tess is the first one to speak because apparently I am unable to form words. I know what Tristan has to offer now and I want all of it. I thought he was another dumb jock with a rotating queue of women at his disposal. Turns out this man has been pining for me for ten years. I have learned his only fault is not pursuing me sooner so I could've spent more time falling for him than hating him. Ironically, I hate him for that. I also want to make him suffer a little for that. I want to be the one in control this time.

Tristan's eyes look extra golden tonight in this lighting, like pools of honey. His eyes rake over me. I knew when I packed this bikini that it was going to drive him crazy. There is very little left to the imagination and by the wolfish look on Tristan's face, I have him right in my crosshairs. Wanting more.

"It's going pretty good, Tess." He takes his eyes off me for a millisecond to answer Tess' question, and then returns his gaze to me. I am going to spontaneously combust if he doesn't join me in this hot tub soon. I bite my lip and take another sip of wine, as Tristan slips off his flip-flops and adjusts his swim trunks. I watch as his thumbs slide into the top hem of his shorts, which are dangerously low—so low, in fact, that I can almost see where the lines of his V are closing in on each other. I swallow hard and nudge Tess in the side.

She laughs and places her empty wine glass on the sideboard of the hot tub. "Okay, I better get out of here before you two pounce on each other." She winks at me before getting out of the tub. She wraps herself in a towel and walks toward the house.

"Is everyone asleep already, Lawson?"

"Oakley is the only one awake right now. Brad and Jen went to their room and crashed out about thirty minutes ago."

"Oh goodie!" Tess claps out of excitement. "Now you two have fun and don't make too much noise. It would be a shame if y'all got caught." She pats Tristan twice on his immaculate pec and saunters into the house.

Tristan steps into the hot tub and glides toward me. "So...Tess knows about us?"

I shrug. "Yeah, I had to tell someone. I was going to burst! I didn't want to accidentally blurt it out at Sunday dinner."

"Now that would be an interesting Sunday night dinner conversation."

"One I am not even close to being ready for." I suddenly feel guilty for revealing our secret. I liked the bubble we created for ourselves. "Are you mad I told Tess?"

"Not at all. And don't be mad, but pretty much the whole team, other than your brother, knows how I feel about you and I guess have known for years. According to all the guys, it was obvious. They are surprised Bradley has never caught on." The steam rising from the water is not helping how hot Tristan looks right now. He looks like he is in one of his promo videos—only shirtless.

"Hmm... I'm not mad, either." I finish off my glass. Tristan takes it from me and sets it aside. He glides closer to me and pins me against the side of the hot tub. The water bubbles against his tattoos, which I am loving more and more every time I get to see them up close. I graze my finger against my favorite one on his left rib. Then I skim my finger down each ridge of his abs and playfully trace the V I was admiring earlier.

One of his hands meets mine and he says, "How many glasses of wine have you had tonight, Cupcake?"

"Tess and I drank a bottle out here so I guess, I don't know, four or five total, including what I had at dinner. Why?"

"Just want to make sure you are in your right mind to do what you want to do with me tonight. I saw you undress me with your eyes a few minutes ago."

"It's too early in whatever this is to know what me undressing you with my eyes looks like." I point back and forth between us.

"Too bad, because I know that expression all too well. I invented that look when I mentally undress you every time I see you."

This man.

I lift my legs and wrap them around his lower back, pulling him toward me. I want to feel his body against mine. I missed his hard sculpted body. I reach up and take off his backwards hat. "Although I am a sucker for you in a backwards hat, I really like grabbing your hair more." I run my fingers through his hair and press my lips to his.

His scruff tickles my face and he pushes back some tendrils behind my ears. He is soft and gentle with his movements with me. Almost like he knows I am teasing him and he is playing the same game. His tongue grazes mine and my core is liquid and all I want to do from this moment on is to keep my fingers running through Tristan's hair and pull him closer to me and not let go.

Tristan trails kisses along my collarbone, making it harder to focus. His rough calloused hands caress my back and play with the strings of my hot pink bikini. "You should not be allowed to wear this bikini, Cupcake."

"Well maybe you should take it off, Hot Shot." I playfully trace every ridge of his abs. I can feel them tighten under my touch as I go lower and lower.

He laughs against my lips. "You realize your brother is inside right? Are *you* trying to get caught? Because I'm not above taking you right here and now."

"I really don't care if we get caught anymore." My hand slides into his swim trunks and I wrap my hand around his already hard dick.

Tristan exhales sharply. "Cupcake. What are you doing?"

I start to stroke him and he lets out a moan and utters "fuck" under his breath. His mouth lands on my collarbone, sending a jolt throughout my body, similar to the one that I felt earlier tonight when his hand squeezed my thigh under the dinner table. I tighten my grip and stroke harder.

His hand grips my wrist to stop my progress. "If you continue doing that, Brooke, I'm gonna..."

"You're gonna what?" I keep my hand on his dick and bite my bottom lip. I like playing with him and I love that he lets me.

"You know what. And I'd much rather come inside of you."

I love teasing this man. I also want him inside of me more. I reluctantly let go and slide my hand back up around his neck. His eyes turn dark and his hands move along my outer thighs and hips. He growls, "I fucking love your curves, Cupcake. They definitely make my favorite things list."

"There's a whole list?" I nibble his ear. "What's at the top?"

He leans back and looks at me intently. "Your eyes. Sometimes they are like honey. Sometimes they are the prettiest shade of green. I love not knowing what they are going to look like on any given day. I look forward to what version I am going to get whenever I see you." He brushes some hair behind my ear, then presses his thumb on my bottom lip. "They are unpredictable. Just like you."

That's probably the sweetest thing anyone has ever said to me. My lips cover his again and pull him closer with my legs. I rock my body against his and I can tell that he is about to unravel and I love that I am the one doing this to him.

I press my forehead to his as my fingers gently brush the base of his neck. "No one has ever called me unpredictable. I am usually pretty measured."

He pushes his body against mine so my back is pressed firmly into the sidewall of the hot tub. His massive hands cradle my face. "Not with me."

He's right. He's always pushed me to my breaking point. Any stability I had, he would disrupt it. He met me when I was a mess. Flour in my hair and on my face. No makeup. No facade. He has always liked me, even when I was at my worst. Isn't that when you know you have found your person? Despite all my best efforts to stay away from the notion that I could ever fall for Tristan Lawson, it happened anyway. I am not measured with him, yet I feel like everything is going to work out and be okay. Monarch butterflies take flight in my stomach, and I realize from this moment on, no one else will ever live up to Tristan. He sees me for who I am, and I am finally seeing him for who he is. And he is everything.

"I want you, Hot Shot."

"You already have me, Cupcake. I'm not going anywhere." He grabs the back of my neck and kisses me. "But I think we do need to take this back to my bedroom, because I can't take it anymore."

"What do you want to do to me that we can't do in this hot tub?" I playfully raise my eyebrow and smirk at him.

"Pin you down."

I purse my lips and nod. "Hmm." I push against his chest and he gives in, allowing space between us. I step out of the hot tub and wrap a towel around me.

"Where are you going?" He rests his forearms on the edge of the hot tub. I glimpse defeat in his eyes. I grab his hat from the ledge and place it back on his head. I barely touch his lips with mine, and when he tries to grab the back of my neck to pull me closer, I quickly move away and begin walking toward the house, giggling in the process.

He pops out of the hot tub, practically creating a deluge on the deck. "You better be going to my bedroom."

I decide to tease him more. I pick up the pace and reach the sliding glass door handle. "What are you going to do about it if I'm not?" I slide the door open and step onto the hardwood floor. The living room is empty, so either Tess went to her room alone or with Oakley. Either way, I'm glad no one can see me as I quickly tiptoe toward the staircase. I hear the door close and lock and know that Tristan is not too far behind.

I giggle on my way upstairs and run as quickly as I can on my tiptoes down the hallway to Tristan's bedroom. I run in and attempt to shut the door, but Tristan reaches the door before I can fully close it. He steps into his bedroom and closes the door behind him and locks it. He rips the towel off my body, sweeps me off my feet and pins me against the door, just like he did at my parents' house a few weeks ago. But this time is different. Tristan isn't going to hold back, and I don't want him to.

"Did you think you could outrun me, Cupcake?" His hands lock my wrists above my head, firmly against the door.

"Kinda," I say playfully.

His mouth crashes into mine and he lowers my feet to the ground, holding my hands in place with one hand while his other hand travels down the length of my body. Teasing me. Taking his time with me. Payback for me teasing him outside. I like this game. I could play this game all night. His free hand reaches behind my back and unties my hot pink bikini top and lifts it up toward my wrists. He ties a knot with the bikini top while looking me straight in the eyes.

"Hmmm. You're adorable for thinking that," he whispers along my jaw as he runs his fingers back down my arms and torso, tracing the hem of my bikini. I desperately want to grab onto his hair and pull him toward me, but his other hand is still pinning my tied hands to the door. He is entirely in control now. But I want him to be. "Keep your hands up there, Cupcake."

He finally lets go of my wrists and slowly slides off my bikini. He lifts each leg to take it completely off. He stays on his knees and props one of my legs onto his shoulder. "Stay quiet for me like a good girl."

Tristan's tongue glides into me and my hips rock toward him.

This is the type of "I missed you" sex that is so worth the wait. Tristan holds onto my hips and digs his fingers into my skin as his tongue goes deeper inside of me.

"Oh my God!" I breathe out, trying to stay as quiet as I can, but Tristan is making it almost impossible.

He pauses for a split second and looks up at me with devilish eyes. "Is this what you wanted?" He licks me again.

My core is tightening more and more. He is not letting up, and my body finally releases. I try to catch my breath. Tristan is lucky that I didn't scream out his name with what he just did to me. Now, it is my turn.

"I want you to untie me so I can touch you, Hot Shot. It's not fair that you put your hands and mouth all over me, and I can't do the same."

"Who said I wanted to play fair, Cupcake? What if I love being in control?" He stands up, slowly caressing my body again. This man doesn't even have to touch me and I am so turned on by him – so when he does have his hands on me, my body goes into full blown overdrive.

"I know you do. But I do, too," I tease back.

Tristan bites my bottom lip as he unties my hands. His hands grab the back of my head and I follow suit. I have been wanting to run my hands through his hair and tug and never let go. I take off his hat and throw it off to the side. My self control is out the window. I wrap my arms around his neck and practically climb onto him and he groans. He squeezes my ass and tightens his grip on my hair. I let out a little squeal.

"Shhh, Brooke. We are definitely going to get caught if you continue making those sounds."

"So?" I crush my lips onto his lips and let my tongue get entangled in his. It is a fierce and demanding kiss. He holds me up with ease and carries me over toward his bed, which looks identical to his bed back home. He matches my kiss with every movement and I hook my legs tighter around his strong back. Tristan makes me feel safe in the midst of being wild and vulnerable. He holds space for me to enjoy every aspect of sex and not feel ashamed for wanting what I want. It is never rushed with him and he always takes care of me first. Every. Single. Time. I feel flushed and my mouth falls open in anticipation for what Tristan said he is going to do with me. So I decide to teasingly remind him, "I thought you were going to pin me down, Hot Shot."

He licks his swollen, perfect lips. "You're right, Cupcake. Just let me hold you in my arms for a minute."

I hungrily look at him. He is everything I want and could ever ask for.

He brushes his thumb against my bottom lip. My body is pulsing from what he just did to me against that door and with the anticipation for whatever else he is going to do with me tonight. He starts kissing my neck and I take out my hair tie to let my tresses fall along my back. I move my hands along his tattoos on his bulky arms. I smile as I reach each ridge, each muscle of his biceps and triceps. He tugs on my hair and it almost sends me over the edge again.

Tristan finally looks me in the eyes. There is something different in this look–it is loaded with something important he wants to say and I realize that this is what love feels like. Being completely lost in the moment with the person who, despite all your flaws, looks at you like you are the best thing life has to offer.

I don't care if I am going to be the first one to say it. It's how I really feel. "Tristan..."

"I love you, Brooke."

I smile, pressing my forehead to his. "God, I was hoping you would say that, because I love you, too."

He places his hands firmly behind my neck and on top of my head and pulls me in close. I am in his little cocoon and that's where I am planning on staying for the foreseeable future. My breathing becomes uneven again, as does Tristan's. Everything from this point on will have a different kind of weight attached to it, but I've waited long enough for that truth to be present in my life. Especially with this god of a man holding me in his arms right now.

Tristan leans in slowly, as if this is our very first kiss, and I meet him halfway. This kiss is sweet, but laced with uninhibited passion. Our bodies become pliant against each other. I want him on top of me right now.

"Pin me down, Tristan."

27

Tristan

I smile wickedly at her and lay her down onto my bed. I can tell she is wet again and I can't wait to get inside her. I part her thighs with my knee and decide to taste her again before pinning her wrists down and having my way with her. I can't help myself. I love the way she tastes and I wanted her as wet as possible before fucking her.

Brooke's eyes are closed and her perfect lips are parted. She breathes erratically as I run my tongue inside her. She reaches down and clasps my hair. Her head falls back deeper into the pillow and she keeps repeating softly, "Yes. Yes. Yes." Soon I can tell she is close again, so I stop and pull away.

She raises her head up from the pillow and gives me a cute frustrated look. "What the hell? Why did you stop?"

I just give her a devilish smile.

"Please, Tristan," she begs.

I am so desperate to get inside her, but I love seeing her like this. Completely wanting me. Yearning for me. Begging me to satisfy her. She's mine and I am going to remind her of that every chance I get. "Put your arms above your head, Cupcake."

She does as told. She wants this as much as I do. I pin down her wrists with one of my hands again and lift up one of her legs so it wraps around my hip. Her eyes are filled with lust and love and trust all at once. I am not going to mess up that trust and it's not something I take for granted.

I've barely entered her and she is already gasping. I thrust into her fully and her groans match each of my movements. She is so wet that I have to distract myself by naming off baseball teams in my head so I won't come right away. I want this to last as long as possible.

Brooke bites her bottom lip to stop herself from screaming and that fucking drives me crazy. I thrust faster and harder. Her pussy clamps around my dick. God I wish we were back home so I could hear my name escape her mouth. To stop myself from screaming her name, I lean down and suck on her breasts. Brooke groans the sexiest groan I've ever heard and I think I might orgasm right then and there.

How is this real life? How is this incredible, gorgeous, completely out-of-my-league woman underneath me right now? How did I get this fucking lucky that, by some miracle, she fell in love with me?

"Tristan," Brooke whimpers and I slow down, wanting this moment to last as long as possible. Then she says something that nearly breaks me: "Let me get on top."

Before I can even respond, Brooke takes advantage of me being thrown off guard to break free of my grip on her wrists and roll on top of me. Her hair is wild, her dark honey eyes are ravenous, and she is the most beautiful thing I've ever seen. Every curve on her body is perfect. Her drunkenness has worn off and she looks down at me with such clarity it is a little intimidating. And I rarely get intimidated by anyone. She is destroying pieces of me that I needed to be destroyed, but now I want so desperately to construct walls all around the two of us so that no one can infiltrate what we have. Because what we have is electric. This moment, with this woman on top of me, rocking her body back and forth and pressing her hand against my chest–this is fucking electric and worth protecting.

I grab her hips on both sides and hold her in place. She bucks harder again, so I slap her ass. She gasps and her torso becomes flush with mine. She covers my body with hers as she continues to ride me. I love feeling her body on top of mine. She lifts her torso off mine, holds onto the headboard and begins riding me harder and faster.

"Jesus, Brooke."

"What Hot Shot? Do you like me on top of you?"

I anchor her hips in place as I lift my hips and ram into her. Her breath hitches.

"Yes, I do, Cupcake," I murmur. "Are you going to be a good girl and come for me again?"

She comes immediately after I ask her that question. I flip her over so she is on her back again. I want her to take me deeper. I hover over her flushed body. Her chest is heaving and a satisfied smile is plastered on her face.

"Did you like me on my knees for you, licking your clit and pussy, making you come on my face?"

"Yes," she whispers.

"I'll do whatever you want me to do to you, Brooke. I always want you to be fucking satisfied. And don't you ever forget that you're mine."

She looks up at me, then tightens her arms around my neck and kisses my jawline. It is a soft kiss, one that makes my heart twist in the best way possible. I slow my rhythm down and become in sync with her breathing. That's how I always want to be with her–connected with everything she does. She wraps her legs around me and pulls me closer to her.

"I'm yours, Hot Shot."

Those words coming out of her mouth do it for me. I collapse onto her and she runs her fingertips along my back. Although it is the sweetest, most intimate thing she could do to me after sex, she is tickling me in the process. I shiver and she laughs. I pull out of her and pull her in close. I plant a kiss on her forehead and trace my fingertips all along her back. I can tell she is dozing off, so I voice the words I am most scared to say to the girl of my dreams:

"I want everything and more with you, Cupcake."

I listen to the steady rhythm of Brooke's breathing. Just when I think she's fallen asleep, a vibration disrupts the steadiness: "Me too, Tristan."

THE SUN IS BEAMING BRIGHTLY through my windows. I squint to block the sunlight. My eyes are already blurry and irritated because I stupidly left in my contacts overnight, which means today I need to wear my glasses. The very glasses that Brooke was referring to last night at dinner.

Speaking of Brooke, I don't know how I am going to move with this angel sprawled on top of me. Her head is resting right above my heart, her leg hooked over mine and her arm spanning the entirety of my chest. I kiss the top of her head and slide out from under her, careful not to disturb her sleep. She stirs and hugs the pillow. I cover her with the comforter and brush some hair back from her face. A part of me wants to wake her up and continue what we were doing last night, but she needs sleep and I need coffee. She probably does, too, with the lack of sleep and the amount of alcohol she drank last night.

I rummaged through my bag and find my black-framed glasses, a Storm shirt and sweats. Even though it is my own house and I could walk around however I want, I do have guests and I'm sure they don't want to see me in my underwear. I quietly go downstairs and start a pot of coffee. On the counter is a container of homemade strawberry pop tarts that Brooke made yesterday morning. I stuff half of one in my mouth – it's so damn good – and go to the fridge for some creamer. I hear a sleepy, "Morning." I flinch and close the fridge door, and Jen stands there rubbing her eyes.

"Jesus, Jen, you scared the crap out of me." I nervously chuckle. "What are you doing up so early?" I grab a mug from the cupboard, pour her some coffee and hand it to her. "I don't know how you take it."

"Black like my soul."

We both snort. That couldn't be further from the truth; Jen is one of the nicest people I've ever met.

She comes over to the counter and snatches up the creamer. "Bradley was snoring so loud that he woke me up and then I couldn't go back to sleep." When she is done stirring her coffee, she takes a sip and looks up at me. Suddenly her eyes widen.

I shift nervously on my feet. "Whoa, why are you looking at me like that? You have crazy eyes right now."

"I've never seen you wear glasses before. When did you start wearing them?" She is smirking like she knows something I don't.

I shrug. "I've worn glasses all my life. I just usually wear contacts. I had a late night last night and forgot to take them out. So, glasses today."

"A late night, huh? What were you doing? Talking with that girl you mentioned at dinner?"

We did way more than just talk. We actually were doing everything in our power to stay as quiet as possible. "Something like that." I pour coffee into my own mug. I'll have to get Brooke some later.

Jen points at me. "You know who you kind of look like? Clark Kent."

I chuckle nervously. "What? No I don't."

Her eyes got wider and she covered her mouth. "Oh my God! You're the professional development guy!"

Shit. "Shhhh."

"This all makes sense. You know, at dinner, I felt like something was going on between you two but then I had to convince myself that

that would *never* happen because you both hate each other's guts." Then I can see something else clicks in her brain. "Tristan...Bradley is going to kill you."

I press my palms into the edge of the counter and hang my head between my shoulders. "I know that."

"Like legit kill you."

I look over at her, pleading, "That's why this needs to be a secret until we are ready to tell him. Please, Jen, don't say anything. And I know that it is unfair for me to ask since you are about to marry him, but..."

"But, you love her."

I swallow. "Always have."

Jen walks over and places her hand on my forearm. She looks up at me earnestly. "I promise I won't say anything, Tristan. Just be careful. There's a lot at stake here for you. You're basically an honorary Beckett. Why risk this?"

"Because she's worth it."

Jen nods slowly. "Yeah, I get it. I fell for a Beckett, too." She pats me on the shoulder then walks over to the couch and grabs the remote. "Don't mind me. I am just going to carry on with my morning as if we didn't have this conversation. I also want to binge a couple of episodes of *Selling Sunset* before everyone else gets up and teases me for it."

"I wouldn't dare tease you for it. You are keeping a huge secret for me and I don't know how to repay you."

"What secret?" Jen winks at me. "I have no idea what you are talking about, Lawson. Now go ahead and get Brooke some coffee already so you can take it back to her without anyone waking up and asking questions."

I finish getting coffee for Brooke and make my way back upstairs. Even though I feel a weight lifted off me that more people are fine with us being together, I have a lump in my stomach that will not go away. I need to come clean to Brooke about that damn bet with Hastings. I need to do this before Bradley finds out about us. That way, if Brooke decides she wants to break up with me over that stupid bet –, which I didn't dream was possible, given I didn't think I'd ever have a chance with her in the first place – Bradley won't ever have to know about us at all.

I need to tell her. But I don't want to ruin this trip. We are heading home tomorrow, so I just want to have a perfect day with Brooke. Hastings isn't here to threaten telling her. No one else knows about the bet.

I'll tell her. Soon.

I open the door quietly and sneak back into my bedroom, trying not to spill hot liquid all over myself. As if the coffee gods summoned her awake, Brooke stirs as I approach the bed. It is pretty good coffee.

I sit down next to her and kiss her forehead, "Morning, beautiful. I brought you coffee. Thought you might need it. Especially since you didn't get a lot of sleep last night." I wink.

She smiles and props herself up against the pillows, dragging the sheets with her to cover her perfect body. I want to throw these sheets out the window. She reaches her hands out to grab her mug. "Thank you." She takes a sip, then studies my face. "You turned back into Clark Kent, huh?"

"I have it on good authority that you kind of like the Clark Kent look."

"Your sources are correct. I love seeing you in your glasses. It softens all that hard exterior you've got going on." She waves one of her hands around, gesturing toward my body.

"My hard exterior, huh?" I smirk at her.

Brooke's cheeks turn bright pink and her eyes turn dark as she rakes them over me. I can read what is replaying in her mind from last night because it has been on constant repeat in my own head. She takes another sip and says, "Actually, come to think of it, your exteriors aren't really that hard. It's kind of disappointing, actually." She shrugs. "You'd think for a pro athlete..." She's baiting me and it's working. I take her coffee out of her hands, set both our cups on the nightstand, then start tickling her sides.

"Please, Tristan, stop," she whispers between laughing. Her laugh is fucking everything. I didn't get too many glimpses of it these past ten years, with her hating the ground I walked on and all. Now I intend to make her laugh every day. This version of Brooke is my favorite version – no bullshit. Completely unfiltered. Completely herself. I get into the bed with her, cover her body with mine and plant kisses all across her face, which makes her laugh more.

"Promise me you will never stop laughing or showing the world your beautiful smile," I whisper to her. "Never stop being who you are."

She grabs the back of my head and brings me down to her lips and kisses me hard. White hot desire bolts through my body. I immediately get hard and we are just making out. Jesus. Is this how it is going to be? Brooke kisses me and I can't control my body like a fucking teenager. Who am I kidding? Brooke can just look at me and I get turned on. I want to continue what we are doing, but I've changed my mind from five minutes ago. I need to tell her now, or I won't have the balls to do it later. She needs to know the truth. That's the only way we can move forward with this relationship.

Although it kills me, I break our kiss. "Wait, Brooke, I need to tell you something. Well, two things actually." Brooke's eyes are dark and goddamn insatiable. *Focus, Tristan.* "Well, first, Tess and most of the guys on the team aren't the only ones who know about us."

The lust in her eyes is replaced with panic. I quickly reassure her, "It's Jen. Jen was downstairs right now and saw me in these glasses and connected the dots. I swear I didn't say anything. And she promised she won't say anything to Bradley."

Relief settles on her face. "Okay. Well, if I had to choose between her and Bradley to find out, I'd definitely prefer it to be Jen. She is already like a sister to me."

"I feel the same way. And she was really happy for us."

"Good." That spark in Brooke's eyes returns in full force. Her hand trails down my stomach and grabs my throbbing dick. Jesus Christ I need this woman right now. I attempt to take off my glasses, but Brooke uses her other hand to grasp onto my forearm. She shakes her head. "No, I want you to keep them on."

"So, you really do have a thing for Clark Kent?"

"Maybe. But I definitely have a thing for you, Hot Shot." She continues to stroke me, moving her hips up to meet my body. I will never be sick of this ever. If I get to spend mornings with Brooke like this, completely enraptured by every inch of her, every piece of her, I'll die a happy man. This is definitely not the time to tell her anything that will ruin this moment.

I reach in between our heated bodies and feel how wet she already is for me. I stick a couple fingers inside of her and rub my thumb against her clit. Her back arches up again as I ram my fingers in and out of her. Her breathing staggers. "Tristan, please. I want you inside of me again. Last night wasn't enough."

I move her hand off my cock because if she continues what she started, I won't be able to do what I want with her in about ten seconds. "It will never be enough. I'm going to be selfish as hell with you Brooke. I am going to take what is mine any fucking chance I get." I push her legs open and ease inside of her. Her fingers dig into my back. I lift her legs up and wrap them around me, bringing us even closer to each other.

I definitely have more than a thing for Brooke Beckett.

I am completely in love with her.

28

Brooke

"You are going to change out of that outfit, right honey?"

I look down at what I am wearing: a smocked, long white dress with pretty pink peonies, a dress that I thought was appropriate for an occasion like my parents' anniversary party. Evidently, I was wrong. "The only thing I am going to change is this chocolate-covered apron after I am done baking. But otherwise – no, Mother, this is what I am wearing."

She has her classic look of disapproval and continues her usual critique of me. "You made chocolate *and* vanilla, right?" My mom steps behind me and peeks over my shoulder as I am trying to ice the third batch of cooled cupcakes.

What does it look like, Mom? "Yes, Mom. I got your order and I am fulfilling your order. Don't you need to get dressed? Your guests should be here in like thirty minutes." I just need her out of this kitchen or I am going to explode and I don't want to do that today... not on her and my dad's thirtieth wedding anniversary.

"I am just making sure, Brooke. Because I told my guests what we are having so people have expectations of what we are going to be serving them. That's all."

I stand upright and blow a tendril out of my face. "I said, I got it!" Okay, I snapped a little, but that was tame compared to what I really want to say to my mother. *Back off and let me do my job. Let me show you what I am capable of.* It's always "that's all" with her.

The oven timer beeps. Finally, the last batch for the party is done. I set down the piping bag and grab a couple pot holders. I turn off the incessant beeping and open the oven door.

Since Daphne Beckett can't read a damn room, she continues, "Seriously, Brooke, when are you ever going to get your own bakery? You have been talking about this for years and I just feel like you haven't progressed at all with your plan. I mean, look at Bradley, he started his own charity and that didn't seem to take him that long to figure it out..."

That's when I feel it. A searing pain on the inside of my wrist. "Ow! Dammit!"

"Brooke Beckett! Don't you use that language in my house!"

"I burned my wrist, Mom!" The constant badgering from my mother caused me to lose focus and the potholder slipped and the oven burned the fuck out of my wrist. Tears well up in my eyes. I am too afraid to look at the damage the 350-degree-oven did to my skin.

"Mrs. Beckett, please start running the cold water."

I suddenly feel a little more at ease hearing Tristan's voice. He's here. I've been anticipating seeing him all day, and the payoff is so sweet. Although, right now I wish I wasn't in excruciating pain.

My mom turns on the sink while Tristan grabs the potholder I dropped and finishes taking out the cupcakes. "Are these the last of them?"

"Yes," I say through my teeth.

Tristan closes the door, shuts the oven off and turns his attention to me.

"Run your wrist under the cold water." Tristan's tone is serious and I can tell he is concerned because his eyebrows do that cute thing where they pull together so intensely, there is a deep line that runs down the middle of them.

When I don't listen right away, he quietly growls, grabs my wrist and puts it under the tap for me. It is the strangest sensation and I honestly don't remember the last time I burned myself. It was probably in high school when I burned my neck with the curling iron. That was fun, explaining to people that I actually burned myself and it wasn't a hickey.

My mom stands on the other side of the island and looks at us a little suspiciously. She has never seen Tristan and me actually stand next to each other without arguing like we want to kill each other.

"Do I need to hide the knives before I go upstairs to get ready?" Her eyes dart back and forth between us.

"Go on and get ready, Mrs. Beckett. Not that you really need to – you look great already."

I roll my eyes. No matter how many times my mom has told him over the years to call her Daphne, he still insists on calling her Mrs. Beckett. It is a respect factor for him. He always has to throw his charm around like it is candy at a fricken parade.

"I think we can bypass trying to kill each other today," Tristan adds.

"Okay," my mom says warily. "I'll be upstairs if you need me."

Tristan is still holding onto my wrist like I am a freaking four-year-old. "I got it, Tristan, you can let go. I'm not a child."

He steps behind me and rests his chin on my shoulder. Goosebumps disperse across my body and my core tightens. "Will you just shut up and let me take care of you this time? Just keep your wrist underneath the cold water until I say to stop, Cupcake. I'll go ask your mom where the first aid kit is."

"You don't have to." I wince. "It's in the hallway bathroom. In the medicine cabinet." Dammit this hurts so bad. The cold water gives me some relief. Never in all my years of baking have I burned myself like this. If only I hadn't been so distracted. Gosh, why does my mom always have to compare me and Bradley? We are different people and I am successful at my teaching career. Can't she just be proud of me for that? Although she doesn't outright say it, I know that she is disappointed in me not staying with Nick. He was stable and provided security for me, just like my dad did for my mom. But, there was no spark there. She doesn't understand that I want more than what she wants in a relationship.

Tristan appears with the first aid kit. "You haven't moved an inch." Then he leans into me and whispers, "Good girl." My breath hitches slightly. Tristan quickly places a soft kiss on my shoulder, causing shivers to run up and down my body. I look up at him and he winks at me. He knows what he is doing to me and it's not fair. We aren't alone, even though I desperately want to be.

I know the water is soothing my burn, but I am still terrified of looking at the damage. I start freaking out, tears leaking from my eyes.

"Just breathe, Cupcake. Everything is going to be okay." He opens the first aid kit and pulls out some burn cream and has a Q-tip at the ready.

I squeeze my eyes shut. "Do you think it will scar?"

"It might, but scars are sexy." He swipes some icing off a cupcake and licks it off his finger, reminding me of the very first night we hooked up. He still has that same devious smile and hungry eyes.

"First of all, stop looking at me like that. And second, how long do I have to keep my arm under this water?"

"For the next fifteen minutes."

"Are you serious? I don't have fifteen minutes, Tristan. I have to finish icing all the cupcakes, then go freshen up so that my mother doesn't say anything about my appearance. She already hates this dress that I am wearing for some goddamn reason. Just what she needs is for me to have my dirty apron still on while guests show up – or worse, that on some conspicuous part of my body, there is a drop of batter." I place my available hand on my forehead and lean over the sink.

"Breathe, Brooke. That's a lot going on in that head of yours. Look, I'll help with the cupcakes. As I can recall, I'm decent at that – your words, not mine."

I sigh. "You're right. I did train you well."

"As for that dress…" He wraps his arms around me, nuzzling his face into my neck. He's distracting me from the pain and I am so grateful.

"Go on," I say as the water continues to soothe my burning skin.

"Your mother's fucking insane if she thinks anything is wrong with that dress. You look incredible and beautiful, as always." He moves my hair and brushes his lips against my neck. He takes hold of my dress by my hips and presses me back against his hard body. This isn't helping my already flustered state.

"Are you stealing kisses from me, Lawson?" I breathe out, trying to ground myself with the water on my skin. "My parents – or worse, Bradley – could walk in at any second."

"Your mom is going to take at least another thirty minutes upstairs, your dad is outside getting the chairs and tables set up and Bradley is helping string more lights in the trees." He licks my neck with the tip of his tongue. "Let me at least kiss my girl like this, since kissing on the lips is off-limits, apparently."

"The only reason it's off-limits is because if you do kiss me, I'm not going to want to stop. You are too damn good at it, Hot Shot."

I hear a not-so-distant, "Hold on, I'll get it Dad!" coming from outside the french doors that lead out to my parents' backyard. Reluctantly, I elbow Tristan with my available, non-injured arm to move away from me. This is not the time for Bradley to find his best friend in the world planting kisses along his sister's very exposed neck.

To be honest, I don't know when is the right time to tell Bradley about me and Tristan. There may never be one.

Still, I'm not ready for everyone to know. Not that I am ashamed of our relationship. It will just change the dynamic of their friendship and even possibly my relationship with Bradley. No matter how flawed, he's still my brother and I love him unconditionally.

Tristan realizes that Bradley is coming into the house and pretends like he is busy folding kitchen towels. *Smooth, Hot Shot.*

"Oh hey, Lawson! I didn't realize you were already here! I need to grab a tool from the garage and the bluetooth speaker for the music tonight." After Bradley walks over and shakes hands with Tristan, he directs his gaze to me and my arm under the sink. "Brooke, what the hell happened?"

"I'm fine. I got distracted and burned my wrist. It's going to be fine." I have to constantly say those words to believe them for myself. Bradley comes over and twists my arm so he can see my wrist.

"Jesus, what was distracting you?"

"Mom kept pressing me with questions about what I was making and the potholder slipped, but I'll be okay." I don't have the capacity to talk through the real reason I am upset with our mom. Bradley will not understand because he is also part of the problem.

"Brooke."

I glance over at Tristan as he looks at his watch and declares, "Time's up."

"Finally!" I turn off the water and open the drawer next to the sink to get a clean towel. "It doesn't matter. I got it, Bradley. You better go get the stuff that Dad needs from the garage."

"Okay, are you sure you're good? That looks pretty bad, B."

Now I am even more terrified to assess my own wrist. "Mmm hmmm," I lie so he will leave me alone.

Bradley walks out of the kitchen. As soon as I hear the door to the garage click shut, I start to breathe heavily and tear up. I close my eyes tightly and say, "Tristan, can you please come over here and put that ointment and bandage on it? I can't."

I lean over the counter and stick out my arm so he can help me.

"Of course, Cupcake. But first, I need you to open your eyes. It's not as bad as you think it is. Your imagination is worse than reality when it comes to these situations. Trust me."

"Why do you know me so well?" I begrudgingly open one of my eyes to take a peek, causing Tristan to laugh. I catch a glimpse of my wrist and although it is disturbingly red, Tristan is right, it isn't as bad as I imagined.

My arm relaxes and fully gives into Tristan's hand, while his other hand gently applies the ointment with a Q-tip. I love seeing this side of Tristan–the gentle side. It contradicts everything he presents to the world on the ice. How can a guy who is so rough also be just as tender? He intrigues me in so many ways. My stomach flips at the thought that whatever is going on between us may just be the beginning, and I am going to learn so much more about him. There was so much that I didn't allow myself to see when I wanted nothing to do with him.

I can finally take a deep breath. Tristan places the bandage over my wrist. Then, just when I thought I was on solid ground, he kisses the palm of my hand, causing my stomach to do a somersault. There's that gentleness seeping through his hard exterior. It's the same gentleness that shows up when he is teaching little kids on the ice or interacting with his fans. Although he is a beast on the ice, he is a softie in every other aspect of his life.

The access door to the garage opens again and we are no longer alone. Tristan lets go of my hand. I immediately want his hand back. I grab the piping bag and begin squeezing icing onto the top of a cupcake.

"Need any help, Cupcake?"

"Nope, got it," I say coolly. I can't risk Bradley knowing or suspecting anything. Luckily, Bradley is usually too stuck in his own little world to notice anything that isn't blatantly obvious.

Back to being cold and indifferent to Tristan's presence. Instead of hating Tristan, I am hating that I can't be openly with him right now.

"All better now, B?" Bradley walks in with the supplies he needs. His eyes are glued to the bandage on my left wrist.

"Yup." I continued to ice the cupcakes at record speed. "All good." I put all my focus on the cupcakes because I know that if I look at Tristan, I will break. He looks extra handsome in his slacks and button-down shirt. He forgoed the backwards hat for today, but his thick, wavy delicious locks are slicked back, making me want to run my fingers through it and mess it all up. And then there are his sleeves, rolled up just enough to showcase his tatted-up forearms in all their glory.

He gets up from the bar stool and grabs the bluetooth speaker from my brother's hands, totally avoiding eye contact with me as well. His jaw is clenched and there is a twinge of sadness in his demeanor. I want to fix that sadness and I think – I hope— he knows that. "Your dad has been waiting for a while, bro. We better go help finish setting everything before your mom comes downstairs."

With that, the two of them exit the kitchen without a backward glance.

I know it's just for show, but there's a rock in my gut – how it seems like we hate each other still. It feels awful to have Tristan act like he hates me. Now that I know what it feels like when he doesn't, I never want him to pretend to hate me again.

THE PARTY actually turns out to be pretty enjoyable. My parents had it catered by their favorite Tex-Mex restaurant and it is nice seeing old family friends and some of my aunts, uncles and cousins. Tristan and Bradley set up a large white screen that shows photos from the past thirty years of my parent's marriage, including some incriminating photos of me and Bradley from when we were kids.

I am standing next to what is going to be the dessert table, nursing a mimosa while being completely embarrassed that my parents included photos of me playing dress up or worse – ones where I was in the bathtub naked. Why in the world would they include those photos? But in the midst of the humiliating photos are ones displaying years of affection and love. Love between my parents. Their love for me and my brother. My brother and I are a big part of the fabric of their marriage.

"You were kind of a chubby kid." Tristan's voice reverberates through my body. I glance over and see him leaning against the other side of the table, drinking his own mimosa. Dimples appear on the side of his perfect face.

"Fuck you, Hot Shot. I was a baby and babies are supposed to be chubby." I finish off my glass and grab the pitcher to refill.

Tristan steps closer to me and brushes my elbow. "There's my girl. I missed your feisty side, Cupcake. I kind of miss sparring with you."

I raise my eyebrows and look up at him. He looks devastatingly handsome right now because the way he is looking at me is how all girls want to be looked at. "Are you saying you want me to go back to hating you?" I shrug and purse my lips. "Sounds easy enough."

Tristan clears his throat and counters, "I want the complete opposite of that, Brooke. Surely you must know that."

Before I can respond, my mom waves me over to where she is standing with my dad. I flash Tristan an apologetic look and walk over to where my parents are talking to their neighbors for the past thirty years, Bob and Karen.

"There you are, Brooke! Can I just say that your cupcakes are divine? I might have stolen one from the kitchen counter when I walked in. I will have to take some home and share them with the grandkids. Do you have your own storefront yet?" Karen asks.

Flushed by the embarrassment of the word *yet*, I open my mouth to answer, "Um, actually I..."

"Oh, no, she doesn't have a storefront yet, Karen." My mom exchanges what I can only consider to be a look of, *I know right? She has been looking for years and still nothing.* "I've been trying to tell her that she will never be able to afford anything in the area she wants without Bradley's help, or even our help, and she just doesn't listen to me. Who knows if it will become anything more than a small business she runs out of her apartment? She's still just teaching right now."

That's right. *Just teaching.* I am standing right here. My heart drops and I tap my fingers against the glass. My pulse is throbbing and I might go into a full-blown panic attack. I am getting the same feeling I always got when I was a little girl, when I felt that my parents didn't see me, when they would talk about me even if I was in the room. To them, I was invisible. I bite my bottom lip and try to focus on my breathing, to stop myself from causing a scene.

Then I can hear, "With all due respect, Mr. and Mrs. Beckett, Brooke is probably the hardest-working person I know."

Tristan has somehow snuck up behind me. *What is he doing?*

"She may not have her storefront right now, but she is busting her ass, excuse my language, teaching during the day, unruly kindergarteners I might add, plus going home and running a business on the side and making it happen. Sure, making it as a pro athlete is a rarity but then again, so is your daughter. Fucking rare."

My mouth drops open and I look at my mother's eyes, which are wide with astonishment that Tristan is talking to her and my father like this. No filter. No regard for their feelings. In complete defense of me. Bob and Karen shift uncomfortably at this unorthodox confrontation of my parents.

He continues, "Her ambition is just as high as Bradley's. Success looks different for everyone and you have two different children. I'm sorry, but I think you all are insane if you think that Brooke isn't successful because she is, and you should be proud that she is your daughter."

My pulse is in my ears now and my heart is beating hard against my chest. At this rate, I am half-expecting him to profess that we are sleeping together and they can't do anything about it.

"Again, I apologize for the language. I have been around this family for a while and I just had to say something."

My parents look shocked. All these years, Tristan has never given his opinion on anything family-related before—especially with regard to me.

Before my parents can respond, Bradley's voice cuts in on the microphone, "Okay, well, I think it's time that my parents come out to the dance floor and dance to their wedding song. They have also requested anyone who wants to share this moment with them to join them."

My dad takes my mother's hand and he practically drags her away. Bob and Karen follow suit and I am left standing next to a man who is supposed to still appear to be my enemy.

Tristan takes the mimosa from my hand and sets it on a nearby table. Without hesitation he grabs my hand, almost like we have been doing it for years. He starts pulling me toward where my parents, Brad and Jen, and other guests are dancing. "Come dance with me."

My feet are glued to the ground as I shake my head. "What if people suspect something?" I look around to make sure that no one is deciphering what is actually going on between Tristan and me.

He steps toward me, still holding my hand, and places his other hand on my lower back. He pushes me forward and whispers, "We can't control what people think, Brooke. Besides, everyone else is going to be preoccupied with their own dates or their own problems or thoughts, they won't even pay attention to us. C'mon, Cupcake."

We are finally on the outskirts of the dance floor. The sun is starting to set and my parent's solar lights kick on around the backyard. The lanterns on the tables are becoming more illuminated with each passing second. Tristan twirls me around and pulls me in to where our bodies are almost touching. He smells amazing as always and there is a gravitational pull he has on me, where I want to get closer and closer every time I am near him. A couple of months ago, I wouldn't be caught dead dancing with Tristan Lawson. Now, with the way he makes me feel, I want to dance with him forever.

I see Bradley and Jen out of the corner of my eye. "What about Bradley?" I finally look up at Tristan. He is already looking directly at me and has a lovestruck look on his face again. I wonder if I have that face too.

His hand that was initially properly placed in the middle of my back trails down to where he is practically touching my butt. I reach for his wrist and pull his hand back up, shaking my head. "Behave," I mouth.

He begins to laugh and says, "I'll deal with Bradley. I'll just tell him that I felt bad for his little sister standing there all alone."

"Gee, thanks." I roll my eyes.

"What do you want me to tell him, the truth about us?"

I lock eyes with him and stare him down with my signature "don't you dare" look.

"That's what I thought," he says smugly. His hand makes its way down my back, sending shivers up my spine. My body is craving this man more than I ever thought possible. "Just dance with me, Brooke. Stop worrying and just be here with me."

I sigh. "I can't. My brain doesn't operate like that, Hot Shot. I am a perpetually anxious person. I am basically the inspiration for Pixar as they were developing the character of Anxiety in *Inside Out 2*."

Tristan snorts and pulls me closer. Now our bodies are fully glued to each other. I can't shake the feeling that Bradley is giving us the death stare or people are looking over at us funny. But when my eyes dart around the dance floor, I hate to admit that Tristan was right. Everyone is in their own little world.

"Be in our world with me, Brooke. Let's test the waters a little bit." He starts to play with my hair swaying along the middle of my back. "You have no idea how much I want to kiss you right now."

Test the waters. "Just kiss me?" I bite my bottom lip, knowing that will drive Tristan crazy.

He raises an eyebrow. "Brooke Elizabeth Beckett. We are at your parents' anniversary party."

"Are you saying you don't want to do more than kiss me?" I raise my own eyebrow to contest the one he just gave me.

Then Tristan does something that makes my heart flip and my

knees buckle. He brings my hand he is clasping with his and holds it against his chest. I can feel his heart beating almost as fast as mine. It's such a small, intimate gesture, but it's melting me. I am a puddle and I don't know how to piece myself together after this. Tristan has shattered every image I have conjured up in my head of him. He says softly, "You know I do, Brooke. And as much as I love how naughty my girl is right now, I am not ready to share what we have yet with anyone. I want to keep you all to myself for a little longer."

The song is near its end and I step away from him. Because the truth is, even taking Bradley and my parents out of the equation, I want to keep him for myself too for a little bit longer. I joke to stop the tears of pure bliss from escaping me, "I guess that might be best, since my parents already want to knock you out for standing up to them. And using the words 'ass' and 'fucking' in front of their neighbors."

Tristan laughs.

The song ends and I remember my mom wanted the desserts to come out after their second "first dance." I nod back toward the house. "I need to get the desserts set up. Thanks for the dance and for saying what you said to my parents."

My hand parts from his, but not without a little restraint on his end. "I'll always stand up for you, Brooke. People should recognize how special you are." His hand finally lets me go and finds its way into his pants pocket. "Like I said, you are fucking rare."

29

Tristan

Two Weeks Later

"Here's to making it to the playoffs, y'all!" Jageilski says as the entire team raises their shot glasses in the air. He is already so far gone that he found my cowboy hat in my closet and decided to put it on for the evening. He thinks he is a real Texan now, even though he is the most Canadian out of all of us Canadians on the team. "Oh and to Lawson hosting us tonight. Cheers!"

"Cheers," I say before I take a shot of tequila. That's the third shot I've had tonight. I want to celebrate with my teammates, but they have also been a distraction for me. I can't stop thinking about my girl. She is like an addiction. I crave her more and more after each time I am with her. She said she was on her way about thirty minutes ago. I know it doesn't take that long to drive over to my house from her apartment. My stomach is in knots not having her in my arms, but I know we have to be on our best behavior tonight since Bradley is here.

I feel arms wrap around my waist. What is Brooke doing? This is a little much if we are trying to keep things a secret still. Maybe she decided that the charade of us not being together is over. Thank God because I can't wait to kiss her anytime I want to.

When I look down at my waist, I don't recognize the arms hugging me tightly. I pull them off me and turn around.

It's Alison.

"Alison." I force myself to smile. I don't want to be a dick but I told her that whatever was going on between us, which was basically booty calls, was over the night she showed up unannounced while Brooke was taking care of me.

I guess I wasn't clear enough.

"I haven't heard from you in a while, Tristan."

"I've been really busy. You know, playoffs are right around the corner and I need to stay focused on my game. I don't have time for any extra curricular activity at the moment." I repeat the same thing I told her that night. Little does she know that the person I would love to spend all of my spare time with hasn't shown up yet.

I am getting nervous now. There is supposed to be a pretty bad storm tonight and although Brooke doesn't live far from me, there are stupid drivers out there who seriously don't know how to drive in the rain.

"Well, you've worked really hard. And you've made it to the playoffs. How about we go upstairs so you can blow off some steam and relax." She steps toward me and places her hand on my chest. My body has absolutely no reaction.

"As nice as that offer is, Alison, I am actually not single anymore. I'm seeing someone right now." I didn't break any rules. I never mentioned Brooke's name, even though I want to shout it from the fucking rooftops.

Her hand finally leaves my chest and she looks disappointed. "I thought you didn't do relationships."

Somehow, over the loud music playing, I hear my front door close and my dogs run over with their tails wagging enthusiastically. The nervous knots in my stomach start unraveling as I take in the woman walking into my house. Brooke slowly walks through the foyer in a kelly green dress and black heels, and of course she is wearing a green knotted headband. She has a bottle of my favorite whiskey in her hand and she starts scanning the room.

There's my girl.

I look back down at Alison and say, "Well, I guess a guy can change. If you'll excuse me, Alison, there is a guest I must go see and welcome into my house."

I roll up my sleeves and adjust my watch as I walk over to the woman who has become my daylight. Every single aspect of Brooke lights up my life and now that I have been exposed to both the sassy and sweet sides of her, I want to tell the world that she is mine.

I nod and say obligatory "heys" to the other guests until I finally reach her. She gives me a coy look and does a cute little spin in her pretty green dress. I am down bad for this woman.

I glance over at Bradley, who is canoodling with his bride-to-be, to ensure we are in the clear. Brooke holds out the bottle of amber liquid. "Congratulations, Hot Shot. You made it. Are you happy? Oh and did you notice that I wore a green dress to support you all." My favorite smile spreads across her face.

My stomach flips and my craving for her completely takes over my body. I lean in to whisper, "Thank you for the whiskey. Now, be a good girl and meet me upstairs, Cupcake. I'll be there in a minute."

I take the bottle of whiskey from her hand and back away from her. Her breathing quickens and her cheeks become pinker than they already were. Her equally pink lips part and her pupils are dilated. "Okay," she finally whispers. She also looks over at Bradley to ensure he didn't see her walk in. Once she realizes that she's in the clear, she makes her way upstairs. Her green dress is dangerously swaying back and forth against the back of her thighs.

I quickly put the whiskey in my liquor cabinet and make my way upstairs.

When I enter my room, Brooke is looking out my window down at my backyard, which is full of party guests. I shut the door behind me and lock it. I come up behind her and wrap my arms around her waist. She rests her head on my chest and places her hands on my forearms, locking them into their position. I bury my face in her neck and start giving her a trail of kisses. The faint smell of coconut is invigorating and my tongue touches her hot skin.

She laughs. "Do you like your present, Hot Shot?"

I pull her away from my window, turn her around, and back her into a wall. I graze my fingers along her jawline and then her bottom lip. Her hands grasp my shirt against my lower back and she pulls my body closer to hers so that every available surface of our bodies are touching each other.

"If my present is you, then yes."

I place one hand on her lower back and hug her tight and my other hand takes hold of her chin. She raises herself on her tiptoes and her mouth catches mine and her hands reach up onto my shoulders. I can feel goosebumps cover Brooke's body as my hand leaves her jaw and traces down her side before squeezing her ass. She whimpers against my mouth and hungrily goes back in for more. Her hands are now clutching onto my hair, forcing my mouth to never leave hers. Fine by me.

Thunder claps and it starts to pour outside. My house lights flicker and I hear faint gasps and small screams coming from downstairs.

Brooke finally breaks our kiss and the words coming out of her mouth buzz all over my skin as she whispers against my lips, "Should we head back downstairs?" Her lips return to mine sending an electric current down the rest of my body. "Your guests may need their host if the power goes out." I feel the heat of her body peel slowly away from mine.

"They can wait." I grab her ass with my other hand, lift her and pin her to the wall. I press my body into her so she can't escape. She looks at me with hungry eyes and her fingers trace the raised lines of my tattoos. I squeeze her ass again and growl, "I can't."

My mouth takes hers roughly, passionately. I want to devour every inch of this woman like I have been for the past couple of months.

I will never get enough of her.

My hand starts sliding her dress up and just when I reach the seam of her panties, a knock interrupts us.

"Hey Tristan, bro, you in there? The guys want to do another shot!" It's Jageilski again. Goddamn it.

I look up at the ceiling and whisper, "Fuck me." I reluctantly lower Brooke down to the floor. Her hands don't leave my body, but instead work their way around and cup my ass. She then squeezes it and looks into my eyes.

"Maybe later." Brooke bites her lip and smiles devilishly at me.

I raise my eyebrows. "Brooke Beckett." I straighten out her dress and push her hair back behind her shoulders. "I didn't realize that my girlfriend would be such a tease." I start heading toward my door to see if we are in the clear. But her hand holds onto mine tightly and stops me in my tracks. She looks at me incredulously, her mouth agape as if she is in shock.

"Why are you looking at me like that, Cupcake?"

"Did you just call me your girlfriend?"

I swallow hard. Shit. I haven't officially asked her. I guess in my mind, she has been my girlfriend since Casino Night. Maybe a part of me never wanted to bring it up because it would be challenging her rule.

Fuck the rule.

"Yeah, Cupcake, I did. Is that okay?"

She cups my hand and brings it to her lips and brushes the smallest kiss on my fist. My heart races for a completely different reason now. What if she doesn't want to be my girlfriend? That scares me more than any opponent I am about to face in these playoffs.

There is banging on my door again.

"I'll be right down Jagielski! Give a guy a minute!" *Please, give a guy who has arrived at that one pivotal moment in any new relationship a fucking minute.*

I look back down at Brooke and all I see is a film of tears over her eyes. And they aren't sad tears; they are happy ones. "It's all that I've ever wanted. Yes, boyfriend, it's okay."

A wave of relief washes over my body. I take her face in my hands again and kiss her softly. I press my forehead to hers.

"Should we head downstairs?" she whispers.

I groan. "Ugh, I guess so. I think we are in the clear." I slowly unlock and open my bedroom door. "You go first. I'll come down in a minute, beautiful."

Unfortunately, we still have to keep things between us a secret for a little while longer. Just until we figure out how to tell Bradley.

I do wait a full minute, then make my way downstairs. I see Brooke over by a pillar, grabbing a drink from one of the wait staff. I scan the room as I take my last step and notice that Dean is talking with Bradley. Bradley's face goes from happy to completely pissed off as he registers whatever Dean is saying. I discreetly continue to keep my eye on Bradley and Dean as I pour myself a glass of whiskey. I flash smiles here and there at my guests and make sure that everyone is comfortable since everyone had to come inside from the backyard. The rain is really coming down now.

I cautiously keep my distance from Brooke, even though her very essence is like a gravitational pull I can never escape. I am at her mercy now. In every way. I take a drink of whiskey and watch as Brooke laughs at something Jen just told her. The way her head falls back and tendrils of her hair brush against her back. The way her eyes squint, causing deep lines to appear. The way her dimples magically appear. Everything about her is my favorite thing about her.

Then, I feel a large fist make contact with my mouth. I fall to the floor from the blindsided punch, dropping the glass in the process. Glass shatters everywhere. I look up and see who punched me.

Bradley.

"Oh my God! Bradley, what the hell is wrong with you?" Brooke rushes over to us, her eyes ablaze at her brother.

"How long?!" Bradley yells down at me.

I slowly get up off the ground, wiping my lip.

"Have you gone insane? How long what?" Brooke gets onto her tiptoes and into Bradley's face.

Bradley ignores her and looks directly at me with fire in his eyes. The very same look that I used to see in his sister's eyes. Shit, he knows about us.

"How fucking long?" he snarls at me again.

I stand up fully, my nose almost touching Bradley's. I glance over at Brooke apologetically. *I have to tell him,* I try telling her with my eyes. I look my best friend and girlfriend's brother straight into the eye and confess, "Since Casino Night."

Reality hits Bradley like a ton of bricks. His fury intensifies so much that he grabs me by my button-up shirt and pushes me hard against the wall. I know that I am stronger than Bradley, but I deserve this. I broke the bro code. The rule that *he* established a long time ago.

"Bradley! Stop it!" Brooke yells, trying to pry Bradley's fists off of my shirt. She is as unsuccessful as anyone other than Thor trying to wield his hammer.

"Nope. End this right now!" He finally directs his deadly gaze onto the love of my life.

"Bradley, let him go! You're making a scene. Stop!" Brooke punches the sides of Bradley's torso.

Unaffected, Bradley looks irately at Brooke. "No, you stop, Brooke! Stop seeing him!"

"I'm not going to stop seeing him." The cute little line in between her eyebrows makes its timely appearance.

"The hell you're not."

"I'm a grown-ass woman and I can date whoever I want." Brooke keeps tugging at Bradley's forearms, trying to release his iron grip from my body.

"Dean told me everything, man! I know all about the fucking bet!"

My stomach fucking sinks. I look around and find the dirtbag of a human, Hastings, crossing his arms smugly as he watches my life crumble in front of me. He has no idea what I am about to lose. I selfishly took the greatest risk of all and I busted.

Brooke furrows her eyebrows even more and gazes directly into my eyes, that no doubt look defeated. "What bet? What the hell is he talking about, Tristan?"

"Brooke..." I start to say, but Bradley cuts me off.

"Tell my little sister about the bet you made about her dating a hockey player." Bradley looks back over at Brooke. "Hastings bet that if he could get you to break your rule, he would take the captain's spot from Lawson."

"Is that true?" Brooke looks into my eyes, which I avert from hers immediately, giving her the confirmation. "Is that the whole reason you started dating me? So that you wouldn't give up your precious captain's spot?"

I look down and shake my head. Bradley is still pinning me against the wall. I don't know what to say. There is no clever angle or sarcastic comment to joke myself out of this situation.

She scoffs. "Well then, guess what?"

I finally have the balls to look at her. Her hazel eyes are clouded with a film of tears, some of which fall down over her cheeks.

"You can have it. Congratulations, Hot Shot, the captain's spot is secured for you."

With that, Brooke runs off out of my house. I seize my opportunity to escape Bradley's grasp and run after her.

The rain is torrential. I can barely make out Brooke's bright green dress, clinging to her body. Her hair is completely drenched.

"Brooke!" I yell, sprinting after her.

"Stay away from me, Tristan!" She takes out her keys and I can hear her car beep. She pulls the door open, but I desperately slam it shut.

"Please, let me explain."

"There's nothing to explain. You were just playing a game this whole time. I guess I should have known. Because that's what we do, isn't it? Play games with each other, right?"

"No, that's not what this is about!" I grab her arm and turn her around to fully face me. "It may have started out as a bet..."

"Unbelievable." She tries opening her door again. I immediately shut it.

I block the way to her door handle. "It started out that way, but Brooke you have to believe me when I tell you that my heart has always been with you. I never thought you would break your rule about dating a hockey player so I thought that..."

"You could mess with my fucking heart to save your prestigious status? To have a one-up in your career?!"

"I did it because I love you, Brooke. I couldn't stand another man even looking in your direction. For ten years I've been distracting myself so that I wouldn't deck every man who touched you. Who kissed you. Who so much as held your hand."

We stand there silently for what feels like an eternity. It's fucking freezing out here. The rain is not going to let up anytime soon. Deep down, I know that Brooke's resumed hatred for me isn't going to let up anytime soon, either.

Her eyes are steel. "That doesn't change the fact that you were willing to gamble with my emotions. Nothing has changed in ten years. God, just when I thought you weren't a son of a bitch, you go ahead and fool me again."

She bumps into me and I finally let her open the car door. Before she shuts the door, she says the four words I hoped I would never hear from her:

"Stay away from me."

30

Brooke

I am tapping my fingers on the table as I wait for Bradley to show up. A couple days after the whole playoff party fiasco, he texted asking if I wanted to grab dinner. Apparently, he wanted to see how I am doing.

How am I doing? Oh, since your best friend and former bane of my existence made a damn bet about me and my dating life and made me fall for him in the process? Miserable. Pissed. Confused. Heartbroken. Does all of the above count as an answer? Because I am feeling every possible emotion right now and have been since my brother uttered those fateful words, *"Tell her about the bet."* Those words have been haunting me almost as much as Tristan's perfect face. I can't get him out of my head, no matter how hard I try.

Bradley is fifteen minutes late and I'm lifting my phone to call him when I hear, "Oh I see her, thank you!" I look up and see my brother make his way to the table from the hostess stand, where the hostess is now looking at him like he is a piece of meat. Ew. I always find it disgusting that anyone would look at my brother like that.

He leans down and kisses my cheek. "Hey B. Sorry I'm late. I had a hard time finding a parking spot. You look good."

I look like shit. He's just trying to be a good brother. "You're a terrible liar. Always have been."

"I mean, considering everything..."

I glare at him and since he has known me all his life, he knows not to continue with whatever he was going to say.

The waitress comes over. "What can I get you?" she asks Bradley.

"Just some water for right now, thank you. I haven't really looked at the menu yet."

"I will get that for you shortly. You still good, hon?"

I nod. She gives me a smile before walking to the beverage station to get a pitcher of water. I think she can read me like a book. Everyone who has caught sight of me can probably tell I am having a rough go of it.

"So, what did you want to talk to me about, Brad? We don't normally get breakfast together like this." I don't want to beat around the bush with this. Truthfully, I am pissed off at him, too.

Our waitress drops off the water glass and says, "I'll be back in a few to take your order."

When she is out of earshot, Bradley leans across the table. "Look, before you lay into me, I'm sorry about what happened at the playoff party. I shouldn't have punched Tristan like that. There was probably a better way to handle that behind closed doors. I didn't need to make a spectacle."

I slowly nod. Tears are forming but I fight them back with all my might. I've cried enough these past few days. I feel like I'm going to run out of tears and not be able to cry again. I am turning into Cameron Diaz's character in *The Holiday* at this point.

"But, you have to understand, B, I was just so pissed off at the whole situation. The fact that he made a bet that included you. The fact that you both were lying to me about dating each other. The fact that you were sleeping with my best friend."

I cross my arms. "Would you have reacted any differently if I went up to you before the playoff party, and said I was dating your best friend?"

Bradley's hand tenses up and I can tell he is getting uncomfortable. "Probably not."

"See, that's exactly why I didn't want to say anything until we were ready, Brad. You would have made a spectacle either way. I was also terrified about the mere possibility that Tristan and I being together would alter your friendship with him in any way. I know how much he means to you."

"B, you're my sister. You mean more to me than anyone. Well, I guess besides Jen. Yeah, Tristan is my boy, but you're my OG, sis."

The waitress appears again. "Are y'all ready to order?"

I shake my head, so Bradley says, "Is it okay if I get your attention when we're ready? I'm so sorry, we still haven't even looked at the menu."

"Sure, take your time." She graciously leaves us to sit in this super awkward – and in my opinion, unnecessary – conversation.

Then Bradley utters the words that I am dreading:

"I want to talk about Tristan."

"On that note, I'm leaving." I start to stand up, but Bradley places his hand on my hand and looks at me, pleading with me to stay. I remember that look all too well. He would do that when we were kids and teenagers, when we wanted something done without saying anything to each other or without our parents knowing.

"Please, Brooke. Sit down."

I take a seat, sighing. "I don't want to talk about this."

"Brooke, c'mon. You should just forgive him."

Is he serious? I scoff, "What? Why have *you* forgiven him? He hurt me, Bradley."

"I know he did, but he did all that...Ugh it's going to sound twisted and is probably going to come out wrong...but he did that because I can tell that he fucking loves you, Brooke."

Those words make the dam break. I can't hold back my tears. I believed Tristan loved me for the past couple of months. It was my blissful reality, but then a new one set in the moment Bradley exposed Tristan's dirty little secret. I place my palm to my cheek and wipe away the tears.

Bradley's eyes are earnest. "He loves you. And I don't want you to push away someone who loves you the way that Tristan loves you."

I try to blink away the stubborn tears.

"And Brooke, the whole thing about the captain's spot, I can tell you right now that I've heard some rumors that he doesn't care about that. Not anymore."

When I speak, my voice wobbles. "Well he shouldn't have done that in the first place. It doesn't change anything at all for me. He toyed with my heart to try and advance in his career. How can you be okay with this?"

"I guess because I know that he really does love you. I know what that is like, Brooke. When you meet someone who completely alters your whole world. Someone that you would do anything for. The fact that he probably did all of it to protect you from Hastings and his bad intentions... that's the only way that I am okay with it. And I know how much you are missing him because you've been kind of a bitch the last few weeks."

"Way to kick a girl when she is down, Brad." I unroll the silverware and wipe my face with a cloth napkin.

"I think it's because you love him, too. You are just too damn stubborn and full of your own pride to take him back. No matter how much you think you hate him or how much you are hurt, Brooke, I think he is the one for you. I think he always has been. He looks at you like I've never seen any other man look at you."

Now I am full-on crying because I don't want to feel this way about a man. Sitting in these feelings sucks. Having my brother say these things about his best friend brings forth a new reality that even though his initial reaction was not ideal, he is ultimately okay with this whole situation and that all along, my brother *has* been paying attention.

"He supports your dreams," Bradley continues. "He even stood up to Mom and Dad. That's...that's huge. I always suspected that he had a thing for you. And it wasn't fair of me to step in and put up that boundary that he could never be with you. That wasn't my call to make. I couldn't imagine if someone told me that I couldn't be with Jen. And I know Tristan is a loyal enough friend to never cross that line with me, but the universe pushed you two together anyway, even with my boundary. The universe doesn't give a shit about plans or boundaries. "

Even though he is saying all of these sweet and validating things, there is one thing that has been bothering me for a while now, and I finally have the courage to speak it out loud. I sniffle and say, "And why didn't *you* defend me with Mom and Dad? You were always there when Mom would belittle me and compare me to you. Why didn't you ever step in and say something to them? Especially to Mom."

Bradley hangs his head. "I honestly don't know how to answer that. I'm sorry. I should've. I'm your big brother and I should've protected you."

"It's not just about protection. It's just being there for me, that's all. You know I always wanted them to be as proud of me as they are of you. But it was obvious to see that they weren't. Because you got all the attention. I am not saying they never praised me or said 'good job' on my accomplishments. It's just – I lived in your shadow my whole life, Bradley. You're my big brother and you are super talented at sports and make tons of money and are crazy successful. You know? And then you have the perfect relationship with Jen –"

"It's not perfect," he interjects. "She's pretty pissed at me right now with this whole situation."

Jen has my back. "It's damn near perfect, okay. Meanwhile I am over here single after I let go of a relationship with Nick that wasn't really fulfilling what I needed to fulfill. Instead of being proud of me for that, Mom is judging me for it. Mom chose Dad and I was maybe going to marry someone like Dad, and I thought he was going to be it for me because that was standard in our household, but I guess I always wanted more and I feel like I am criticized for that and put down for that. You know, I have dreams too and I feel like I am a pretty good baker and just because it wasn't an innate talent and I actually had to work for it and sharpen my skills, doesn't mean it's any less important... and I need Mom and Dad to see that."

Bradley looks defeated by my words. It's a look on my brother that I am not familiar with at all. He always stands tall and looks so confident in everything he says or does. Seeing him like this shakes me almost as much as the moment Tristan told me that he has loved me since the first time he saw me.

My brother is really listening to me.

I go on. "Yes, Tristan defended me, but it should've been you. And I am not holding it against you because I love you. I just need you to know that you should've been there more. You should've seen the way they would talk to me. An intricate weaving of little comments that built up. Invalidating everything that I've worked for – and did you know I am one of the best kindergarten teachers in the district? I love those kids and I love baking and I am really trying to make it work and it's not like I need your help with that. I want some acknowledgement that I am doing okay too, you know?"

Bradley lets out a long breath. "Shit Brooke, I don't know what to say. My whole life is wrapped up in hockey and yeah, I always liked the attention, but I should've looked out for you and we should have celebrated your accomplishments and dreams more as a family. I am so damn proud of you, sis. You have no idea how proud. And I know Mom and Dad are proud of you, too. They may not say it all the time, but they care. I am not defending Mom in any way because I know that she has hurt you with her comments and she does unfortunately compare us, but I think she sees a lot of herself in you."

I dab the napkin against my cheeks. "What do you mean?"

"She had dreams, too, before she had us, B. I think she wants you to have more than she ended up with. Not that she's not happy. I know she loves us and Dad, but she didn't get to pursue her dreams and was a stay-at-home mom. She sees so much potential in what you can become. She might be projecting her feelings and fears onto you. Not saying that's fair, but us Becketts have a way of putting up walls by deflecting or ignoring our emotions. Or like me and you, we like to set rules and follow them to avoid getting hurt. We avoid facing our fears. I'm learning that life doesn't care about the rules you have for yourself or for others. Things that are inevitable in life are going to happen. It's out of our control."

I sniffle again. "I don't like being out of control."

I think about what my brother is saying about my mom. Maybe her constant criticism is her twisted way of trying to protect me. Maybe it is her way of projecting her fear of me possibly failing or being judged, or maybe she even wants more for me than what the cards dealt her in life. I think there is a lot for us to talk about, but I want to feel better emotionally before I even think about tackling my relationship with my mother. There's a whole other relationship that Bradley is asking me to consider right now and I just don't know if I can ever forgive Tristan or let him into my heart again. He has hurt me twice. And this time was so much worse. He had every chance to tell me about the bet, and he didn't.

"I know you don't like feeling out of control, B. Neither do I. But sometimes you have to take a risk and take a chance on things that you are unsure about to find out if they are worth it. That applies to people, too, little sis."

My lips curl slightly at the ends. My tears are beginning to subside so I finally have the head space to process what is on the menu. "We better decide on what we want to eat, Brad. Our waitress is going to be so annoyed that we haven't even glanced at the menu."

Bradley's hand reaches over the table and pulls down the menu. "What?"

"You and Tristan are inevitable, Brooke. It's been that way since day one. It was stupid of me to ever try to come between you two."

It is like the air got knocked out of me. I didn't expect my brother to say those words...ever. He never thought much of any of my boyfriends before Tristan, and Tristan has always been off-limits to me as much as I was to him.

Bradley's words mean so much, and yet this is so painful because my relationship with Tristan is so complicated and he's hurt me on more than one occasion. I question the whole inevitability of us at all.

When I don't say anything, Bradley says, "Do me a favor and I promise I won't ask for any more favors again for a while."

I snort. "I doubt that." I make eye contact with our waitress and indicate we are ready. Then I turn back to Bradley. "Okay, what is the favor?"

"Give him a second chance."

31

Tristan

I am broken.

The past two months have been some of the worst months of my life.

Even hockey holds no happiness for me. We fought tooth and nail to get to this point, but I do not feel the satisfaction that I should be feeling. Guilt and anger and sadness fuel every single decision and action I make on the ice. All of that energy worked itself out on the rink and now here we are, in the last series in the playoffs against Colorado, one of the best teams in the NHL. The Stanley Cup is finally within reach again, but an unending cycle of memories, good and bad, fill my head with Brooke in every waking hour and even at night. I dream of her, wake up reaching for her in bed. During games, I often catch myself looking in the stands, foolishly wishing she was there, hoping to see her standing outside the locker room with a ridiculous hot pink headband.

I should have told Brooke about the bet the moment she walked into my house on Casino Night. Hell, I should have told her about the bet the moment I made it with Hastings. I've lost count of how many times I've wanted to punch his smug face since the night Brooke ran out of my house and never looked back. Yet, as much as I want to fully blame Hastings for the demise of my relationship with the girl of my dreams, I know it's my fault. I agreed to the bet because deep down, I *did* want the captain's spot and I really did not want Hastings to lead this team. More importantly, I wanted to protect Brooke from anything that may harm her because I love her.

Each time Sunday rolls around, I want to crash Sunday dinner and profess my apologies and love for Brooke, but I am too scared to face any of the Becketts right now. I royally fucked up and I can't sweet-talk my way out of this one. My heart has never hurt like this. I've also never loved anyone like I love Brooke. Because I do still love her. Even though I've lost her.

I lost everything that truly ever mattered to me, save for hockey, in one night: my best friend, my second family and the girl I wanted to call mine forever. Bradley hasn't spoken to me, except if needed on the ice, and I don't even know how to salvage that. We've gotten in disagreements before, but it always got solved with a handshake and an, "It's alright man. We good?"

We aren't good. Not this time. This time, there was much more at stake. What Jen said in Telluride was true. I should've listened to her. I would be spending the night with Brooke in my arms instead of tossing and turning, wishing she was next to me.

I hear something that snaps me out of autopilot: "Lawson. Can I see you in my office?"

Coach caught me at a good time. I was about to put on all my gear and skates for warm ups. I go right past all my teammates, even Bradley, without so much as a handshake or even acknowledgment they are there. I know what this meeting is about. If someone would've asked me a few months ago what I wanted most, I would have without hesitation said this damn captain's spot and my hands on the Stanley Cup again. But my priorities have changed. Not that I don't still want those things – they just aren't as important anymore.

"Have a seat. I'll make this quick."

I sit and cross my arms.

"I have a tough decision to make. There can only be one captain on this team. I can't deny the leadership that you have exhibited throughout your time here with the Storm. You are clearly the favorite, Lawson. You and Hastings are unmatched talent in the entire league. Personally, I always thought you were better. One of you has to stay the alternate. This is your time to vouch for yourself. Cast your vote, so to speak."

My heel is tapping the ground with restless energy. There is a huge lump in my throat because I never thought I would say these words. Ever since I picked up a hockey stick, this has been my dream. Until I met her. "Go ahead and give it to Hastings."

Coach looks shocked. "Can I be so bold as to ask why you would give up this opportunity?"

"Because it blinded me from what truly matters in my life. Yes, this is a career, but it's not going to last forever. I know what I am capable of and I am a damn good hockey player. I have been living my dream of playing in the NHL for almost a decade and to wear that C on my jersey would be an honor..."

"So, why are you letting Hastings take the spot? When you clearly deserve it more."

"It is not up to me to determine if I deserve this spot. It's up to the team and up to you, sir. I am just saying that if you make the decision to give it to Hastings, I will accept it and respect it. I'm sick of playing games and fighting with Hastings about this. I hope that if it's the other way around, he feels the same way, but I can only control how I feel. Adamski is irreplaceable. His shoes are going to be impossible to fill. If I am granted this responsibility, I will strive to be the best leader I can for this team. I may not do things the way Adamski does things, but I will lead nonetheless."

"Well that's all I needed to hear. I am going to converse with your teammates one more time and you'll know our decision soon." He raps his knuckles on his desk, switching gears. "Let's have a good game, Lawson. We are up three games to none. This is the last series before we head to the finals. Let's put the nail into this coffin tonight. I really want that cup."

"So do I." I finally stand up and shake my coach's hand. "I'll try my best, sir."

I SIT down on the bench in front of my equipment. I take my shoes off and pull my shirt over my head.

To my surprise, Bradley comes and sits next to me, already dressed for warm-ups. "Hey man, how are you doing?"

Bradley is talking to me now? He hasn't spoken a word to me, outside of our normal communication on the ice, since the playoff party. "I'm fine."

"Yeah, say that to your face. I can see how intense your jaw is clenched through your beard. You look like hell. You, my friend, are not fine."

I shake my head and strap my protective gear on my shins. I guess this is my opening to talk to Bradley about what happened, now that things have settled down and it doesn't look like he wants to pummel me. "Look, man, I am so sorry about Brooke and the bet. Almost right after I made the bet with Hastings, I wanted to take it back. He just wouldn't let up. Please know that I tried to break it off. Things just spiraled out of my control because I was too cocky about attaining the captain's spot. And too cocky that Brooke would never break her rule."

I glance over at him. He is still looking down, tying his laces on his skates, but I can tell he's listening.

So I continue. "I promise that I never wanted to hurt Brooke. She means so much to me. I know that I fucked that all up and don't have a chance with her again. I also care about you, man. You're my best friend, Bradley."

Bradley slightly nods and finally makes eye contact with me. "So you tried to call off the bet before I found out?"

Some relief infiltrates my chest and the large pit in my stomach doesn't feel so big anymore. "Yeah, multiple times. And I honestly thought that at some point he gave up on the whole idea because he wasn't saying anything to Brooke or to you. But I was clearly wrong."

"You could have told me, you know. About the bet." He pauses. "And about Brooke. I just thought we were closer than that. We tell each other everything, bro."

"I know. I got scared. You, Brooke, your whole family mean a lot to me and I didn't want the dynamics to change. And I knew you would be pissed off about the bet and the notion of me dating your little sister."

"Well, yeah. But, still. You should have told me."

"You're right. I should have. And I don't even care about the captain's spot. I know what matters to me more than any leadership role. That's what I just told Coach. I'd give it up to have you back in my life again. To have Brooke back in my life again."

Bradley nods, grabs my shoulders, and looks at me dead in the eyes. "You are an idiot if you think you are giving up that spot, bro. You deserve it. Hastings doesn't deserve shit. You are the face of this organization... and *almost* as good a player as me."

We both chuckle. Then he pulls me in for a hug.

"Thanks man," I utter.

I get black tape from the top shelf of my locker and start taping my stick with it.

Bradley bumps into me again. "Hey, I don't think I have outwardly said this but you know that I forgive you, right? For the whole Brooke thing."

Jagielski and Oakley walk over to us. "And what are we

discussing over here? How much you screwed up with Brooke?" Oakley says as he tries to sit next to me in all of his massive goalie gear.

I shoot him a look. To be fair, things did blow up in front of everyone at the playoffs party.

Bradley pipes in, "Yeah, basically. But you know what, bro?" He turns to me. "I know that Brooke is back to hating you, but I can tell my sister misses you. She is extra mopey, and she is baking nonstop – not just for her side gigs. You know my sister, she bakes like this when she is angry or sad. It's kind of like her therapy. I think she is still in love with you." Then he rolls his eyes and says, "God only knows why. I mean, personally, I don't see the appeal."

I laugh. "God, you are such a dick, bro."

"So what's the plan?" Bradley says.

"What plan? Like for the game?" I knot up my laces.

Bradley, Jagielski and Oakley look at each other like they all share a secret I am not privy to. Jagielski says, "Dude, the plan to get Brooke back."

"Yeah, it's time," Oakley adds.

"Time for what? Guys, did you not hear Beckett? Brooke hates me. There is not going to be a plan. My only plan is to go destroy Colorado out there so we can make it to the finals." I get up and start walking toward the locker room door.

Oakley steps in front of me and doesn't let me pass.

"Oakley, what the hell are you doing? I need to go warm up man, we all do!"

"Just sit your ass back down, lover boy." He pushes me onto the bench.

"Did you just call me lover boy?"

"Yeah, because that's your nickname from now on. Now listen to us!" Oakley insists.

Jagielski chimes in, "Like we were trying to say before you rudely interrupted us, it's time...for the grand gesture!" He does what I can only describe as jazz hands when he utters the words "grand gesture".

"Okay, you all are insane!" I start to stand up, but Bradley and Oakley sit me back down. "Look, I don't know how many times I have to tell you...Brooke hates me and I haven't heard from her since two months ago. Not since that playoff party."

Jagielski shushes me with his finger on my lips. "Beckett also said that Brooke still loves you, you dumbass."

I swipe Jagielski's finger away and point to him. "Don't ever do that to me again, Jagielski. And besides, even if that is true, she is not speaking to me. How am I supposed to even do this 'grand gesture'," I air quote, "if she isn't talking to me?"

Bradley inhales sharply, stands up, and holds out his hand for me to apparently take. I slap my hand in his and stand up.

"We'll figure that out," he says. "We're your boys! We are going to help you get your girl, aka my little sister, back."

I can't ignore the surge of hope that fills my chest, but I try to tamp it down. I need to be realistic here. Brooke hates my guts and God knows that girl can hold a grudge.

We all grab our sticks and head out into the tunnel, then onto the ice. The crowd gets louder as we approach the arena. A Blink-182 song is already blasting through the speakers. It's time to lock in on what I really want. Surprising enough, the Stanley Cup looks more achievable than getting Brooke back. I wonder what these guys have up their sleeves.

32

Brooke

Talking with Bradley really made me reflect about my relationship with my parents. More specifically, my mom. I don't want to harbor resentment toward them, and they need to be aware of how they treat me. I am glad that Tristan stood up for me, but I need to be the one to fully resolve this tension between us.

I have a key but I don't want to scare them, so I knock on the door of my parents' house. They are not expecting me but I can't wait until Sunday dinner to talk to them. I've actually missed quite a few Sunday dinners because I couldn't face my brother or my parents. I wasn't ready to talk to them about any of the drama that ensued with Tristan. That whole relationship, I was not ready to resolve. I don't know if I ever will be.

My dad finally opens the door. He looks surprised. "Brooke."

"Is it okay that I just stopped by like this? I know you weren't expecting me to come by today."

My dad opens the door wider and steps aside to let me in. "Brooke, you know you are always welcome to come by." ESPN is on the TV but the volume is low, almost like white noise. It reminds me of my childhood. My dad closes the door behind us and then brings me in for a giant hug. "This will always be your home."

Once he lets me out of the biggest hug he's ever given me, he grabs my shoulders and leans down so his eyes are level with mine. "Now, you listen to me, Brooke. I have always been so proud of all of your accomplishments. I am sorry you never felt that from me or your mom."

"It's not that I never felt it from you."

"It wasn't enough. You obviously felt dismissed by us, and we never intended for you to feel that way. I am not making excuses, but it's impossible to be there for your kids all the time. We love you both equally. Are we proud of Bradley for everything he has accomplished in his life? Of course. But we are equally as proud of you. I need you to know that."

Tears are welling up. I didn't expect my dad to say this to me. He has always been so reserved with his feelings. That is just who he is. I wipe a rogue tear with the sleeve of my pink pullover. "Thanks, Dad." I sniffle. "Where's Mom?"

"In the kitchen making dinner. You must have been on her mind because she is making your favorite: grandma's famous spaghetti and meatballs." My grandma was full-blown Italian and she made the best spaghetti and meatballs. Whenever we would go over to her house, she would always make it for us and she would whisper in my ear so that Bradley wouldn't hear, "I know it's your favorite, cara mia" and then wink. The bowls she served the spaghetti in were so giant, they could pass for mixing bowls. I smile at those memories.

The meatballs must be in the oven because the kitchen smells heavenly. It transports me back to my grandmother's kitchen. Water is boiling on the stove and from the doorway, I watch my mom dump a box of spaghetti in. She sets a timer and then moves on to stir the simmering sauce. She lifts the wooden spoon and tastes the sauce, then adds a little dash of sugar to the mix. It is scary how much she resembles my grandma.

I clear my throat. "Hey Mom."

She whips her head around. "Oh, Brooke. Hi honey. I didn't know you were coming by." She wipes her hands on her apron and walks over to where I am standing and brings me in for a hug. She holds on a little longer than normal. "Are you staying for dinner? I am making..."

"Grandma's spaghetti and meatballs. Yeah, I can see that. It smells delicious. And yeah, I'll stay for dinner. Thanks."

There is definitely some tension between us. My mom doesn't look like her usual self. This isn't the confident, headstrong woman I grew up with. She looks scared and a little sad. This is the first time since I can remember that she doesn't comment on how I look – which as of late, hasn't been the best.

I sit at the island and like my mom always does without asking, she places a glass of water in front of me, knowing that I need it. "Thanks." I tap the side of my glass nervously. *Rip the bandaid off, Brooke.* "Mom, I actually came by to talk with you about what..." I pause because even saying his name out loud is like stabbing my heart. "...Tristan said at y'all's anniversary party."

My mom is avoiding any sort of eye contact with me and busies herself with stirring the pasta and the sauce and manning the meatballs in the oven. "Was it true? Is that how you feel? Like your dad and I aren't proud of you?"

"To be honest, Mom, yeah. And it sucks for me to admit that to you. I never want to be ungrateful for the parents you are, but it has been hard for me to always be second to Bradley in basically every aspect in my life."

"Now, Brooke..."

"No, Mom let me finish. I never get to get a word in edgewise with you. I know that I am an adult and have always been the quiet one in the past. But I am not going to sit around and pretend that I am okay with the fact that no matter what I accomplish with my own career or my aspirations, in your eyes it will never live up to what Brad is doing with his life. Mom, I am one of the best teachers in the district and I am not one for tooting my own horn. When I got recognized for that, you and Dad were too busy to show up to that ceremony. Sure, it wasn't breaking a record in a pro sport like Bradley did, but it was just as important…to me. And I know that I've been talking about opening up a bakery for almost ten years, but it takes time to do it the right way. Opening up any type of restaurant is risky and I want to make sure everything is right and, more importantly, that it feels right to me. Just because it hasn't happened yet, doesn't mean it's not going to happen ever. This is a giant leap of faith and I don't want to screw it up. I think I am so scared of screwing up because I know how much of a failure I'd be in your eyes, Mom. I know that if I do fail, you would be so disappointed in me."

Tears are really making their appearance now. I plow on. "This includes relationships. I understand that you are disappointed that I broke up with Nick. He checked off everything on paper. I know that, deep down, you just want me to find someone to share a life with…like you did with Dad. And in a way, being with Nick reminded me of you and Dad. He never mistreated me. But there was something missing and I felt like I couldn't really be myself around him. I was content, but I wasn't head over heels for him. There is a difference, and I deserve to be head over heels for someone. There was no real spark there. Trust me."

My mind betrays me and wanders to the one man who ignited that spark in me. "All I want is for you to acknowledge my accomplishments with as much excitement as you do Bradley's. And Mom, I don't want you to worry about me being alone. I am surrounded by family and friends and the right man will come along when I least expect him to."

My mom just stands there and nods. Without saying anything, she drains the pasta in the sink. Just when I think she is going to carry on and make dinner without acknowledging my big speech, she walks around the counter and gives me a hug. "Can I talk now?"

I nod through my staggered breathing. As soon as my mom's hands touch my back, I break. There was so much I was holding in throughout the years – to finally release it, feels so nice.

My mom then does the same gesture my dad did to me in the living room: she takes my shoulders and looks directly at me. "Brooke, I am so sorry. Do you hear me?"

I nod, tears still covering my face.

She continues, with tears in her own eyes, "Your dad and I are immensely proud of you and what you have accomplished. I might seem harder on you because I know that you will be successful and I don't want you to give up on your dreams. But I went about it the wrong way and I am sorry. Your brother's career just took off and it was so easy to get swept up in the excitement of it all. And then he found the love of his life in Jen and I just wanted Nick to be it for you so badly. I don't want you to be alone because I know that you deserve to be loved by a man who worships the ground you walk on, Brooke." Then she cradles my face with her hands, just like she used to do when I was a kid and we were having a heart-to-heart. "Honey, I am so proud of you and love you immensely and I promise I will be better at telling you that."

"Thanks, Mom. I love you, too. Thanks for listening and hearing what I have to say." It is my turn to embrace her. Although this conversation doesn't solve everything, I know it is a step in the right direction with our relationship.

She pats my back and steps back from me. "I need to check on the meatballs. I can smell when they are done." I must've inherited my spidey sense of knowing my baked goods are done before the timer even goes off. It's just a feeling.

Mom reaches into the fridge and pulls out a bottle of wine. "Want a glass?"

"Mom, you never have to ask me that question. I'll get the glasses and pasta bowls out."

As I am placing the giant pasta bowls out on the table, my mom says as she is grating parmesan cheese, "I have to admit, I wasn't surprised that Tristan stood up for you like that."

My heart drops to the bottom of my belly. "What do you mean?"

"I mean, I think that Tristan is the man who worships the ground you walk on, Brooke."

Trying to stifle the butterflies in my stomach, I detract by saying, "Did Bradley call and tell you to say that? I swear he never lets up."

"Bradley didn't tell me anything. I can see true love when it is right in front of me. Though it was a mortifying moment to be lectured in front of our friends, and I really didn't appreciate the foul language he used, a part of me was proud of Tristan for showing up for you. A real man shows up for the people they love, Brooke. He showed up for you. I think he's loved you for ten years."

"It doesn't matter now because we aren't together anymore. He did something that hurt me, Mom. I don't know if I can give him a second chance." I place pot holders on top of the dining room table.

"Brooke, I hate to break it to you, but men are not perfect. Far from it. Even the most loving relationships have their ups and downs and people mess up. It's human nature. The real question is: did you find what you were looking for with Tristan? Because I really do think that he is the missing piece for you. Sure, he might drive you crazy. But I've always loved how he's challenged you throughout the years. He unleashed a spark in you that I always knew was in there."

I fiddle with the silverware in my hands. "I'm scared to let him in again, Mom. I didn't want to fall in love with him, but it happened anyway."

My mom places her hand on mine. I look into her eyes and she tells me plainly, "I know it did. I think you are perfect for each other. And if you want my opinion: it's about damn time."

A laugh escapes me.

"Oh but Brooke," she adds, "that's just my two cents. In the end, of course, this is *your* life and *your* decision. I'll be here for you whatever you decide."

My dad yells from the living room, "Hey! The news is doing a segment on the Storm! Maybe your brother will be on here to talk about game seven!"

Mom and I hurry in to watch. Part of the segment does feature Bradley talking about the strategy the team needs to implement during the game and how badly he wants the cup. Just when we think it is over, the anchor says, "While we're on the Storm, we have new footage to share from an Instagram Live that is currently going viral." The news station cuts to the viral video and my jaw drops when I see who is gracing my parents' television screen.

33

Tristan

Game Six of the championship round and we are ruthless out there. I don't think I've skated so hard in my life. I've already lost one important thing in my life, probably the most important; I was not about to lose the most coveted trophy in sports. Even though we are playing on the other team's turf in Colorado, we come away with a necessary victory.

After the game, I shower and put on fresh clothes. When I am leaving the locker room, our social media coordinator, Amy, approaches me.

"Do you have time to do some media, Tristan? It's for Instagram Live and I am going to record it so we can keep the footage for later."

"Sure, Amy." I run my hand through my damp hair and straighten my shoulders.

"Okay, are you ready?"

I don't know. Am I ready? This is the time to do what the guys and I talked about. My heart is pounding so hard, I am convinced Amy can tell how nervous I am. I am more nervous about what I'm about to say than I am about the upcoming final game of the series. I nod and flash Amy a smile. "Ready as I'll ever be."

A white ring light turns on above Amy's phone and she gives me a thumbs up. "Tristan, congratulations on the win tonight."

"Thank you." I force a smile through my clenched jaw.

"How does it feel to be one game away from attaining the Stanley Cup?"

"It's an incredible feeling. You know, I had the unique opportunity to win the cup a few years ago and I am ready to bring the cup home again to Dallas. This city needs a win and I am going to do everything I can in my power to get it."

"I think the fans can agree to that. What are some things you think the team needs to do in order to win in Game Seven?"

I shake my head and shrug a little. "Colorado is a great team so we have to stay focused, play our game and not let up on the fight. I know Oakley has been amazing attending goal, so we need to help him offensively by not letting scoring opportunities pass us by."

"Do you think heading back home to Dallas is going to increase y'all's chances of winning on Monday?"

I sigh. "That's always the hope. I mean, we still need to show up and play our best game. Hopefully the fans fill those seats and encourage us throughout the game. It's always a great crowd, but there is something about playoff crowds that help with momentum, you know?"

"Yes, well you heard it from Tristan Lawson himself. Go get those tickets and show up on Monday night! The game starts at 8 p.m at Southwest Arena."

I need to say what I need to say before Amy heads off to interview someone else.

"Tristan, thank you so much for talking with –"

"Wait, Amy. Uh." I stand up, rub my face and take a deep breath. "There's, uh, something I need to say."

Amy's eyes widen with surprise, but she nods and refocuses the camera onto me.

I take a deep breath. "You know, for a long time, winning the Stanley Cup was my only dream. I've had the Stanley Cup before and I know what that is like. It's one of the best feelings in the world. I have grown up a lot since winning my last cup. But I have other dreams now and there is one person who has become my dream and I don't know if I could ever get that dream back. Um, so I would like to say something to her, if I can."

Amy nods behind the camera with complete intrigue in her eyes.

"Brooke, if you're listening to this, I'm so sorry. I put my career before you and that's not what a man does. A man chooses his life outside of his career. A career is just a thing you do. It's not the life that I want to live if it's without you. It won't mean anything, even winning the Stanley Cup, which that's the ultimate goal in hockey, right? To win the elusive trophy. The hardest trophy you can ever win. But I'm afraid that in the process, I lost the girl I want the most in this world. The girl I have loved since I was nineteen years old." I look down at my feet, trying to hold back the tears.

Amy leans in a little closer to catch the request that is going to possibly change my life forever.

"Brooke, if you forgive me, I'll be waiting for you at center ice in Southwest Arena at 7:55 p.m. before our last game of the season. A game we are going to win." I look back at Amy. "We are going to get this cup, Amy, but I want to get my girl back first."

WHEN I'M PREPPING for the final game a couple days later, I learn from Amy that the video went viral. The amount of shares and tags on our Instagram account with a trending hashtag of #Bristan surpassed anything the social media team ever shared before.

"This is huge, Tristan! We've never had three million views on any reel or live or literally anything we've ever done before! She has to have seen it, right? And trust me, that helped sell out this game tonight. Anyway, I am rooting for you!"

Has Brooke seen the video of me laying my heart out on the line? That has been the question percolating in my brain since I poured my heart and soul out for everyone to witness. I am trying my best to focus on winning this game, but Brooke's beautiful face keeps interrupting my focus. Oh and the intrusive thought that she won't even show and she will hate me and avoid me forever. I can't have that. I just can't.

"Good luck," Amy says. "I hope she shows up."

God I hope she shows up tonight, too.

We make our way onto the ice for warm-ups and I've never been so nervous. The moment I step onto the ice, the crowd erupts to a noise level that I haven't heard in all the years I have played in this arena. Fans are holding up signs that say things like *Brooke and Tristan 4 ever* and *Brooke + Tristan = Endgame.*

I center my attention on the puck and go through our usual drills of contesting our goalie and circling around the rink. My teammates tap my shoulder when I pass them as a means of encouragement. I force a smile back at them, partly trying to convince myself that I'm not completely insane to request this from Brooke. Is there any hope that she even saw my message? I guess it's a risk. But I know that I didn't get this far in my career without taking a risk on myself, and I needed to take this risk to try and save the once-in-a-lifetime love that I have with Brooke.

The announcer tells everyone to rise and remove their hats for the national anthem and I make my way to my spot next to Bradley. I lower my head to ground myself. The words of the anthem fade as I focus on my breathing. The only thing preventing me from falling over is my breathing.

Earlier today, I asked the people running the scorekeeper's box to start the timer for five minutes right after the anthem. Cheering from the crowd resumes, and that's when I snap out of my own head and realize the national anthem is over. I look up at the center scoreboard, suspended over the rink, and see that a countdown for five minutes has replaced the normal twenty minutes displayed for the start of the first period.

The crowd continues to get louder and louder on their own. No prompt from the announcer. No graphic on the scoreboard telling them to do so.

"They're cheering for you, you know." Bradley bumps my shoulder. "They're rooting for Brooke to show up. As if you couldn't steal their hearts anymore than you already have."

My brows furrow a little. "What if she doesn't show, man?" My heart feels like it is going to burst out of my chest, from excitement and a sense of preemptive despair. I swallow the huge lump in my throat.

Bradley looks at me so earnestly. "All I have to say is that no matter what happens tonight, you are still my best friend. I know things are complicated between you and my sister, but honestly, when has it ever *not* been complicated between you and Brooke?"

I smile at his comment because of the truth behind it. It's always been complicated with us. Since day one. The only difference between now and then is that I love her even more.

Bradley pats my shoulder. "You shot your shot, bro. It's her turn to respond. Good luck, man."

I make my way to the center ice and the timer starts counting down. I keep my eyes on the tunnel, waiting and hoping and praying to see a pink knotted headband appear out of the darkness and for Brooke's face to illuminate in the spotlight that is inevitably going to be shining on her. I sway to keep myself in the moment and try not to focus on the seconds ticking down.

The timer is already down to one minute and there is still no sign of Brooke. *This was a stupid idea. You should've never listened to those dumbasses in the locker room the other day. She probably ignored the video altogether and stopped following the Dallas Storm on Instagram. Shit, did she even follow us in the first place? I should've checked that before I even went along with this plan.*

Thirty seconds remain on the timer. The crowd is as loud as ever and they start chanting my name. This time it isn't because I scored a goal or because I slammed someone into the sideboards. This time it is personal.

"C'mon, Cupcake," I whisper to myself with five seconds left on the scoreboard. My heart sinks all the way down to my stomach as it finally reaches zero.

Cold, stark zero.

Fuck. She didn't come.

A hush falls around the arena as reality sets in. I lower my head in defeat. As much as I was trying to prepare myself for the worst, deep in my heart I really thought she would show up. She had to have known it took a lot for me to admit all of those things in a very public way. I wanted to give her a grand gesture because that's what she deserves. I just hope the next man who comes into her life spoils her like I planned to. I guess I'll never have that chance again.

Disappointment rushes through my body and leaves me with a heavy pit in my stomach. This is worse than losing this game. I lost the one person who challenged me more than anything else in my life.

Suddenly the crowd goes wild. I glance around and see everyone pointing to the tunnel. My heart leaps.

There she is. In my jersey. Wearing a green knotted headband this time.

The most surprising thing of all is that she is actually skating out toward me. In all the countless times I imagined this moment, I always pictured me skating toward her when she showed up at the tunnel entrance. I was ready to lift her in my arms and never let go. I never imagined my girl on the ice, skating out to me. She is still a little wobbly, but she doesn't look down once. She keeps her eyes on me with the biggest smile on her face.

Brooke has the ability to drown out everything else around me. Even a crowd of twenty-thousand people going crazy before the championship game. I know from that moment on that she will be my touchstone. My rock that will forever keep me in check and ground me. She took a chance on us by showing up.

She's almost made it to me when she loses her balance. I reach out and catch her hands. God I've missed these hands. I've missed her smile. I've missed her caramel hair. I've missed her hazel eyes. I've missed everything about her.

When she regains her balance, she wraps her arms around my neck. I finally snag her around her lower back and tug her toward me so that her gorgeous body is flush with mine. I don't care if twenty-thousand people are watching us. I am going to kiss my girl.

I trace my thumb along Brooke's jaw and take every inch of her in. I lean down slowly but her lips crash into mine, and my body relaxes for the first time in weeks because Brooke is in my arms. From the second her mouth covers mine, I know that she missed me too. It isn't a quick brush of our lips. It is an all-consuming kiss, loaded with years of wanting and needing. And now we finally have each other.

I tug her closer to me as she tightens her grip on the hair brushing the nape of my neck. She opens her mouth and I sweep my tongue over hers and she moans. I try to tear my lips away from her, but Brooke kisses me harder. I laugh against her lips. She finally breaks our kiss and looks up at me, smiling with her whole face.

"You came," I murmur.

"Very risky move, Hot Shot." She continues gliding her fingers along my neck, her eyes landing on my lips and back up at my eyes. "Betting that I would come here tonight."

I tuck some hair behind her ear and smile. "You gotta take risks if you want things to change, Cupcake."

It's a damn shame I have to play this hockey game because all I want to do is throw her over my shoulder and take her home to my bed. Show her how much I missed her. "You learned how to *really* skate, Cupcake. When did you take lessons? I know I didn't teach you."

"Bradley may have helped a teensy bit." She squints her eyes and almost presses her thumb and index finger together.

I look over at Bradley and he is smiling like a fool. *Why the hell did he not tell me he was teaching Brooke?*

Almost as if Brooke can read my thoughts, she whispers in my ear, "Because I told him not to say anything to you. Tristan, I was so hurt by what you did and I wasn't sure I would ever see you or talk to you again. I wanted to prove to myself that I could follow through on at least one of the risks I took, especially since you were out of the picture. I thought that I was afraid to fall on the ice, but I think the real reason I was afraid to skate was because it was so closely linked to you and I was terrified of letting you in at all. I was afraid to fall, but despite my best efforts to keep you out of my head and out of my heart, I ended up falling for you, Hot Shot." She brushes a kiss on my lips again. "I'm still in love with you, Tristan. But I'm so terrified of letting you in again after everything."

I take her face in my hands, "Look I know that I did that stupid bet with Hastings, but I can't say I regret it. Because if it wasn't for that bet, I wouldn't have really told you how I feel and we wouldn't be standing here right now. I'm still in love with you, too. My love for you is the only constant in my life. I'm just so happy you are taking another risk being here tonight, Brooke. I promise you that I won't make you doubt me or my intentions with you ever again."

She nods. Tears are rolling down her flushed cheeks and I wipe them away. I know how much she is putting her heart on the line with me. I am not going to screw this up. If I have to make it up to her for the rest of my life, I will.

She grabs my jersey in the middle of my chest with both hands and pulls me down so our noses are touching. She bites her lower lip before speaking, which makes my insides fucking melt like they always do when I'm in Brooke's presence. "Yeah, you're right. I took a risk when I came here tonight. Good thing the risk was worth it."

She collides her mouth with mine so hard that she almost knocks me off-balance. It starts to turn into a messy, fervent kiss. I hear whistles and cheers from the crowd. I begin to think that Brooke forgets where we are because she basically attempts to climb up my body. She grabs onto my hair and pulls it slightly. She is kissing me like it's the last time and I am kissing her like it's the start of forever. Brooke laughs and lets out a small squeal as my hands travel from her face to her butt and I lift her up. "Tristan, you better not let me fall," she says in between her unrestrained kisses.

"I'm never letting you go, Cupcake." I continue to kiss my girl with unrelenting fervor when I feel a tap on my shoulder.

"Um sorry to interrupt this love fest, you two. But we kind of have a game we need to start," Bradley interrupts what is probably the best moment of my life. To be fair, he is reminding me that I am about to fight like hell for the second-best moment of my life.

He hands me my black helmet. I lower Brooke to the ice. Her eyes crinkle as she looks up at me with a smile that completely wrecks my whole world. I fucking love that smile.

"Plus, it's kind of nauseating watching you make out with my sister." Bradley grimaces as he puts on his own helmet and skates away.

The arena lights come back on and the clock on the jumbotron sets to twenty minutes. I hold onto Brooke's hand and lead her toward the entrance to the tunnel. Once she reaches the black padded surface, I release her hand. She turns toward me and grabs my helmet. She gestures to lean down. When I do, she secures the helmet on my head and taps it twice. Her hazel eyes meet mine as her hand caresses my chest and traces the Storm emblem on my jersey.

"Go get 'em, Hot Shot."

I wink at her, causing that smile to return to her gorgeous face, as I skate back and find my way to center ice for the second time tonight. I take my position for the faceoff. The main referee is about to drop the puck and funnily enough, all the pressure built up from the anticipation for this game, this integral game in my career, is lifted. I realize that no matter what that scoreboard says, no matter how many goals I score, no matter how many assists I do, or whatever else happens on this ice – there is someone in those stands who is going to love me anyway. I know whose face I am going to search for every time in the crowd. Forget the trophy. Brooke has always been everything I've ever wanted.

Brooke

A tie is covering my eyes...again. My only guidance is Tristan's voice. I clutch onto his hand for dear life. "What is it with you and ties? Are you trying to channel Christian Grey or something?"

I can practically hear him smirking. "Are you into that sort of thing, Cupcake? Based on past experiences, you seem to like it when I take control."

"Maybe I *am* fantasizing about Christian Grey while you are doing those things to me," I tease. I totally am not fantasizing about anyone. Why would I when I am dating the hottest hockey player on the planet?

Tristan pulls me closer to him and takes the tie off my eyes. He's smiling down at me with my favorite smile. "You take that back right now."

I look straight into his eyes. "Nope." I still love messing with him. I don't think that is ever going away in our relationship. It keeps things interesting.

I look to my left and notice we are in front of the storefront that I scoped out months ago with Tess.

"What are we doing in front of this empty storefront, Tristan?" Then I gasp dramatically. "Is this where you are actually going to murder me? Was that your plan all along? To seduce me and then once I fall in love with you, you kill me Dexter style? West Village is a little conspicuous, though." I smile.

Tristan grabs the sides of my face and intently looks at me. "You know, for someone with such a sunny and bubbly disposition, you sure have some dark thoughts. I bet it's all of those true crime documentaries you watch on Netflix before bed. I am voting to veto those from now on."

"They are so interesting though."

"They are ruining moments like these for me. Here I am trying to be romantic and you confuse it with me wanting to murder you. I will never have that thought, Cupcake. So get that out of your head."

"You could've fooled me with the blindfold and your weird behavior all day. What's going on with you? Can you please enlighten me how an empty storefront is romantic?" I check out Tristan fully for the first time tonight. When I arrived at his house, he immediately insisted that I put the tie over my eyes. He said he had a surprise for me and that I needed to trust him. I was not able to bask in his hotness like I am able to right now.

I never want him to stop wearing his hat backwards. It literally makes me weak at the knees every time I see him. A white short-sleeved hooded shirt is hugging his torso and arms, and the way his pants are fitting him makes me breathless.

"Will you just read the sign rather than undress me with your eyes, Cupcake? I promise you can actually undress me later."

I wanted to decline that request but just to satisfy him, I pry my hungry eyes away from his body and look up.

"Oh my God." The sign screwed into the side of the storefront says: *Brooke's Bakes.* There is a vinyl sign hanging underneath that says: *Coming Soon.*

Tristan comes up behind me, wraps his arms around me and says, "It's for you."

"Tristan, this is too much..."

"It's not nearly enough, Brooke." He turns me around and holds up my chin so that I am forced to look into his eyes. It takes me back to when he called me his girlfriend for the first time. Full of hope and promise and pure happiness. "This is your dream. I get to live my dream every time I step onto that ice. I know what that feeling is like and I want you to have the same feeling. Not that you aren't an incredible teacher, but I can see the passion you have on your face anytime you've ever talked about opening up a bakery. Or rather, cupcakery."

Tears well up in my eyes and I press my lips together to push down all the emotions I am feeling at this moment.

"You deserve to live out your dream, too, Cupcake. Besides, you can't back out now. I bought this property. For you."

"Wait– you *bought* it? Tristan, that's insane. What if it fails? What if..."

Before I have the chance to completely spiral with all the what-ifs, Tristan grabs my hand and says, "Come on, let's go inside."

He pulls out a set of keys from his jeans pocket and unlocks the door. It's completely dark when we walk into the empty space. Tristan walks toward the back of the building and plugs in a cord. Twinkle lights turn on overhead and I see a checkered blanket in the middle of the concrete floor. There is a cake stand full of cupcakes and a present wrapped up with a pretty pink bow.

"What is this?" I smile and the tears come back. I walk toward the blanket and point accusingly, "And where did those cupcakes come from? I sure as hell didn't bake them."

"Will you just sit down?"

I cross my arms and stick out my hip. "Nope. Not until you tell me where you got these second-rate cupcakes from."

Tristan laughs, shakes his head and picks one of the cupcakes up. "Just try one."

"No! I am kind of pissed off right now. How dare you cheat on my cupcakes. You have a lot of ner.."

Tristan smashes the chocolate cupcake into my mouth. "God, you are still the most stubborn woman I've ever met. Can I talk now please?"

I am about to spit out the traitor's cupcake but realize it tastes familiar. I chew a little more and look up at Tristan, who smugly has his arms crossed. He raises his eyebrows, silently telling me, "I told you just to try one."

I wipe my lips and lick any remnants of cupcake off my finger.

"I made them for you, Cupcake. It's your recipe." I must have not wiped off all of the cupcake from my face because Tristan uses his thumb to get the rest.

I'm utterly speechless. Tristan has never baked anything in his life. Don't get me wrong, I have learned that he is an amazing cook, but baking is not his forte.

"These are actually pretty good, Hot Shot."

"Well I practiced my baking on the down-low. Kind of like what you did with learning how to ice skate. The guys won't stop giving me shit about it in the locker room but hey they aren't complaining about all the trial cupcakes I've brought in for them." Now his face is turning red. "I wanted them to be perfect. So, what do you think? Did I succeed?"

I bend down and grab another one from the platter. I tisk, "Pretty close to perfect. Here, try them for yourself." I smash the cupcake in his mouth and laugh.

"Mmm." His tongue licks the sides of his mouth, almost in a seductive manner. "Well I will admit that they aren't as good as yours, but at least they don't taste completely like salt."

I push against his chest and he doesn't budge one bit. I swear this man is made of marble. "If it was so disgusting, why did you eat it all?"

"Like I told you the night I confessed my true feelings for you: I wanted to make a good impression. That cupcake was the worst thing I've ever tasted, but I would eat an infinite amount of them if that means I can end up right here with you."

Tristan grazes my lips with his fingertips and kisses me, lightly, delicately, in a way that is so uncharacteristic of Tristan. Something else is on his mind. He's distracted. Maybe it's the upcoming season. He is the captain now, after all. It's a lot of responsibility. I take the reins and grab the hair along the nape of his neck, pull him closer to me and kiss him harder. Whatever he is worried about, I want to assure him that it's going to be okay. My hands then start to travel down to the hem of his shirt and I begin to lift it.

His hands stop my progress and he breaks the kiss first. "Wait."

My eyebrows raise out of pure shock. "Is Tristan Lawson hitting the pause button on sexy time? What has gotten into you?"

He picks up the wrapped gift. "I have another surprise for you, Cupcake."

I take the box from his enormous hands and shake it, trying to figure out what it is.

"That's not going to help."

"Doesn't hurt to try." I pull on one corner of the bow. "You are just full of surprises tonight, Lawson."

I rip the wrapping paper off and open the top part of the box. All I see is a kelly green Storm jersey with number 92 stitched on the arms. I kneel down and set the box on the ground and pull out the jersey. It's literally the same one I already have. How is this a surprise? I decide to fake it to spare his feelings. "Wow! Tristan! This is so nice. I was just thinking that I needed a duplicate of the jersey I already have. You know, in case I spill something on it, or, um, it's in the wash or something when I need to wear it. Thank you, babe!"

Tristan kneels down in front of me. "It's not a duplicate, Brooke."

I huff out a laugh and hold the jersey up in front of me to inspect it further. "Tristan, I hate to break it to you, but this is the exact same jers..." I turn the jersey around so now I am looking at the back. Above the large number 92 I see the name: *Mrs. Lawson.*

My heart starts beating really fast. I drop the jersey and gaze at the man who is kneeling right in front of me. We are finally at the same level. No games. No trying to one-up the other. No hate. In fact, just the opposite.

"Hey guys!" Tristan yells behind his shoulder. "Come on in!"

"Who are y...?" The doors to the kitchen swing open and I see my brother wheel in a cart full of vases of...pink daisies. Followed by Jen and Jageilski and Oakley and the rest of the Storm with carts of their own that must have dozens of flowers on each one. They are all giving me goofy smiles and I swear some of them have teary eyes as they place pink daisies all around us, then disappear back into the kitchen. Once they are done, Bradley salutes Tristan and makes a heart with his hands for me before he and Jen disappear behind the swinging door. I hear the back door close and lock, and Tristan and I are alone again.

I feel like I am dreaming and I never want to wake up.

"Tristan Lawson, you did not just get me a thousand pink daisies." Tears are rolling down my face at an uncontrollable rate. I look around at the sea of pink, overwhelmed by the man sitting in front of me.

"You're right. I didn't get you a thousand pink daisies. I got you 3,980 of them. One for each day I have been in love with you."

I exhale and more tears flow out. My hands are shaking from the exhilaration of this moment. The anticipation that has been built up for so long. The man I have wanted from day one has always wanted me too. He's *loved* me since day one.

"I had to one-up that damn Max Medina somehow. If he was the standard, I wanted to exceed it, Cupcake."

"Tristan," is the only word I can form. He leans in and leisurely kisses my forehead, lifting my chin while wiping tears away with his thumb.

"Brooke. I know that this has been a long time coming. Us finally being together. Partly because you are as stubborn as all hell and partly because I was an idiot for letting my fear impact my decisions. I'm not going to let fear get in the way of what I want again."

His jaw clenches and he takes my shaking hands in his steady ones.

"I know that you despise change and hate taking chances when you aren't sure what the outcome is going to be. I know that opening a restaurant is the biggest risk in business, but I am willing to back you up all the way because I am betting on the fact that your business is going to thrive. You're the best baker in this city and I don't care that I'm biased. I also know..."

He reaches into his pocket and pulls out a large princess cut diamond ring, so beautiful it makes me breathless.

"...That marriage is fucking scary. The odds are definitely against us, and it's probably the biggest risk of all."

Tears are rolling down my face uncontrollably as I watch this beautiful man kneeling in front of me, crying while he is laying his heart out on the line. This is a risk for him, too, and I know he is nervous doing this. I reach out and caress the side of his cheek, wiping away the tears falling from his sincere eyes.

"I hope that you will go all-in with me on this risk, baby girl, because I don't want to do this life without you. I want to share my successes, my failures, the happiest and saddest times of my life with you by my side. I want our kids to have your pretty smile and gorgeous eyes. I want them to have my killer skating skills and shooting ability." We both start to laugh, but then he continues, "I want them to see the love their daddy has for their mama on a daily basis. They will never doubt the love I have for you. I don't know what my life is like without you in it. You're the sweetest risk I've ever taken, Cupcake. And I hope that I'm yours. Will you marry me, Brooke Beckett?"

I take Tristan's hands in mine and lean in and kiss him. Then I press my forehead to his, taking this moment in. One that replaces all the bad moments I've had with Tristan. One that replaces any hatred I once thought I had for him. One that I will remember forever.

I angle my body back and look into his eyes, "Yes, baby, of course I will marry you. I fell in love with you the moment I saw you too, Tristan Lawson. I cannot wait to be your wife."

He slides the ring on my finger.I take his face in my hands "And I'm so glad I took a chance on you, love."

Tristan's strong hands start to wander all over my body and I take this opportunity to straddle him. I love feeling his hard body underneath my thighs. His teeth nip at my neck. "I can't wait to call you my wifey."

I rock against him slightly at the sound of that word coming out of his mouth. My hands are finally allowed to reach for the hem of Tristan's shirt and pull it over his head. His hat falls off in the process. I grab the hat and place it back on his head, backwards–my weakness and he knows it. His hot hand slips underneath my shirt and unhooks my bra in one motion. His hand then trails up and down my back, causing my body to shiver.

I touch the tattoo on his rib as I continue to kiss him. I have memorized everything about Tristan's body at this point. Every tattoo. Every muscle. And I am still in shock that he is completely mine. "You know what this means, right?"

"What's that?" He slides off my shirt and bra and he lightly licks my collarbone.

"You're going to have to change my initials on your rib to B.L." My core heats up as one of his hands plays with the button on my jeans and the other one grabs the back of my head possessively. All feminism goes out the window with this man. I have no problem with him being possessive over me. I am going to be his forever, after all.

He gives me a serious look. "Nah, I'm keeping it the way it is."

"What? Why?"

"The truth is, I lied when I told you the tattoo was for you. It really is for Bradley. He's my boy for life. Sorry to break it to you like this." He smiles that deviously playful smile of his.

I bite my lower lip and pull on his hair that is peeking out underneath his hat. I know he is just messing with me like he always does, so I tease him back. I lean down and nearly kiss him, but instead I whisper against his lips, "I hate you, Hot Shot."

He licks his lips and smiles at me, "And I love you, Cupcake. Always have. Always will."

AFTERWORD

Dear Reader,

I hope you fell for Tristan and Brooke's story as much as I did. I really pushed myself this time with creating characters who were so different from any characters I have written before; characters who were so far removed from who I am. Ironically enough, writing these characters unlocked a new version of myself and gave me the confidence to stand up for what I want and gave me permission to tap into a space where I was afraid to go before. I wanted Tristan and Brooke's chemistry to feel electric and the spice to be at the right level for the tension their relationship creates. Enemies-to-lovers has always been a trope that I've wanted to tackle and explore. It was so fun to navigate the delicate balance of Tristan and Brooke's banter and their constant oscillation between love and hate.

I knew I wanted to incorporate the whole notion of setting rules and the characters eventually breaking them. I figured the tropes of brother's best friend and secret relationship would be a great vessel to explore that side of Brooke and Tristan's relationship because there is a lot at stake for them if they break those boundaries they set for themselves.

I am also a big hockey fan and adore hockey romance novels in general. I love the competitive nature of hockey players and I wanted Tristan to embody everything that it means to be the face of a franchise and to be one of the best players in the league. I wanted his genuine love for the sport to shine through. This book is my love letter to hockey.

Brooke's struggle with living in her sibling's shadow was important for me to explore. Success manifests differently for everyone and it is hard when you don't feel validated in your accomplishments while others are receiving praise for theirs. We all want to feel seen and I hope Brooke's journey validates anyone who feels like they are stuck in the shadow of someone else. In the end, I wanted Brooke to find someone who loves every part of her and is willing to exceed any standard put in his path.

What did you think about it? I would love to hear!

It would mean so much to me if you take a couple minutes to leave a review on Amazon or Goodreads. You can also follow me on my socials and join my mailing list to find out about upcoming books and bonus content.

XO, Leslie

ACKNOWLEDGMENTS

I am the luckiest author in the world because I have the best readers, community and support team on the planet. My heart is so full with gratitude and love I have for each and every person who helped me make this book happen.

To Dallas Woodburn, my editor and book doula, thank you for working your magic and pushing me to be the best writer I can be. I am endlessly grateful for your input and care you put into my stories. Tristan and Brooke's story is infinitely better because of you! I adore you and cannot imagine having anyone else in my corner in the publishing industry.

Thank you to the incredible team at Breakthrough Books. A book doesn't just come together in one night. All the behind the scenes work to make this book what it is does not go unnoticed.

To my girl and PA, Andi. There are literally no words for how much you have changed my life for the better. My reach on social media, my growth as an author, and my life in general have been positively influenced by you. You are my woman in the corner, cheering me on, encouraging me to take the risks and to lean into the very things that I am most afraid of. Whenever I had doubts about what I was writing, you were there to tell me to go for it! So much of this book is dedicated to you. You are stuck with me forever, girl.

Thank you to my beta readers: Anahi, Michelle, Jenn, Mudge, and Charisse. I do not take for granted the time you spent reading my draft at its earlier stage. Without your invaluable insights and feedback, I wouldn't know if this book would be worth publishing.

You all pushed me and made my book the best it could be. Thank you to Edgar and Perla for consulting me on all things hockey and giving me feedback on the book's plot–it's because of you two that I was able to start writing this book in the first place.

To my friends and family, there aren't enough words to say to all of you that will fully express my gratitude for your support. You all hold me together in times where I felt I wanted to crumble and revert back to my old self. A self who was afraid of putting myself out there and exposing my words to this scary, critical world. You all have taught me that no matter what happens, you will always be there for me and support me unconditionally.

To my husband, Casey, who has given me the safe space and encouragement I need to be an author. There are pieces of our love story in every book I have published and I plan on continuing to revisit those moments because our love story is my favorite. You help make my dreams come true everyday and my life with you is the best happily ever after I could have ever imagined.

And finally, to you, my readers: You are the reason I keep writing. You are the reason I want to keep creating the magic that is present in every love story I write. I have you all in mind when I sit down at my computer and type words on a blank document. I already feel so connected to my characters, but it's because of you all, with your posts, shares, edits, reviews, and DMs, that my characters come to life. It is one of my greatest joys to be able to connect with you! I hope this book brought you the courage to take risks in your life–trust me, it's worth it. My biggest risk led me to you!

BOOK CLUB DISCUSSION QUESTIONS

1. What is the significance of the title? Did you find it meaningful? Why or why not?
2. What did you think of Tristan and Brooke at the beginning of the story? What about at the end?
3. Were there any quotes (or passages) that stood out to you? Why?
4. What did you like most about the book?
5. How did the book make you feel? What emotions did it evoke?
6. Who was your favorite character? Why?
7. What did you think about the female relationships in the novel? What was your favorite?
8. Who would you cast to play Tristan in a movie? Who would you cast to play Brooke in a movie?
9. Were you rooting for the couple to get together all along? Why or why not?
10. If you could talk to the author, what burning question would you want to ask?

IMMERSIVE READING KIT

SMELL: Cedar & Mint, Chocolate, Coconut

EAT/DRINK: Chocolate Cupcakes, Strawberry Cheesecake Ice Cream, Peach Moscato, Gin & Tonic, Old Fashioned, Spicy Ramen, Brownies, Pistachio Latte

WEAR: Pink Knotted Headband, Green Hockey Jersey

LISTEN:
The Sweetest Risk Playlist- Top 25 (in no particular order)

"Risk" by Gracie Abrams
"Bloom" by The Paper Kites
"Dress" by Taylor Swift
"Don't Worry Baby" by The Beach Boys
"...Ready for It?" by Taylor Swift
"Too Sweet" by Hozier
"Can I Be Him" by James Arthur
"I Should Hate You" by Gracie Abrams

"Sugar" by Maroon 5
"So It Goes…" by Taylor Swift
"Be More" by Stephen Sanchez
"Dive" by Ed Sheeran
"The Joker and the Queen" by Ed Sheeran (feat. Taylor Swift)
"How Sweet It Is (To Be Loved By You)" by Marvin Gaye
"Make You Mine" by PUBLIC
"Mercy" by Angelina Jordan
"imgonnagetyouback" by Taylor Swift
"Mr. Brightside" by The Killers
"Lovin On Me" by Jack Harlow
"I Like Me Better" by Lauv
"Daylight" by Taylor Swift
"Dangerous Woman" by Ariana Grande
"Lose Control" by Teddy Swims
"Never Be Like You" by Flume, kai
"Let It Happen" by Gracie Abrams

For the full playlist, search for "The Sweetest Risk Playlist" on Spotify

ABOUT THE AUTHOR

Leslie McElroy was raised in Santa Fe, New Mexico but currently resides in Dallas, Texas. She loves her family, cozying up with a good book and coffee, and watching sports. Leslie has always dreamed of becoming a writer since she was a teenager, but she finally wrote her first novel, *Stuck with Me*, after being inspired from reading other contemporary romance novels and knowing that she had a story to tell. She is also the author of the fake dating rom-com *The Expiration Date*. Leslie loves watching movies, listening to music, and is an introvert at heart. She is a mom of two boys and is married to her college sweetheart. Leslie hopes that through her writing, she can connect with people around the world and spread happiness with the characters and stories she creates.

Follow Me on Socials & Let's Be Friends
authorlesliemcelroy.com
Instagram: @authorlesliemcelroy

ALSO BY LESLIE MCELROY

The Expiration Date

Stuck With Me